BREAK AWAY

KAREN RENEE

ISBN: 9781957194363

Paperback ISBN: 978-1-957194-43-1

Cover Model: Alex Turner Smith

Photographer: Furious Fotog/Golden Czermak

Cover Design: Bee at Bitter Sage Designs

Editor: Barbara J. Bailey

To all the friends who took the leap and became more *than friends.*

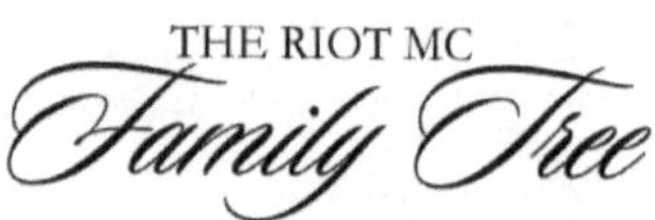

THE RIOT MC
Family Tree

PARENTS	CHILDREN
HENRY "VOLT" ADLER JACKIE ADLER	SIMONE BOBBY
CAL "CALLOUS" ROBERTSON MALLORY ROBERTSON	ALEXANDRA
HOMER "ROLL" ROLLAND TRIXIE ROLLAND	RAFFERTY JASMINE
CARY "VAMP" SULLIVAN LORRAINE SULLIVAN	GABRIELLA
GAGE "GAMBLE" GARRISON VICTORIA GARRISON	KILLIAN RYAN MICKAYLA

Let's Keep in Touch

Thank you for buying *Break Away*. The best way to keep up to date with my books is to **subscribe to my newsletter**.

If you don't hear from me regularly, please check your spam filter and set up your email to allow my messages through to you. This ensures you never miss a new book, a chance to win great prizes, or exclusive content.

PLAYLIST

LAST FARE by Little People
UNDER YOU by Foo Fighters
CUMBERSOME by Seven Mary Three
SHE SELLS SANCTUARY by The Cult
THROUGH GLASS by Stone Sour
SAILOR SONG by Gigi Perez
STARGAZING by Myles Smith
KING by Blue October
DREAMY SKIES by The Rolling Stones
DON'T START NO SHIT! by Rebirth Brass Band
BABY I LIKE IT by Slightly Stoopid
A FRAGILE THING by The Cure
MORE THAN FRIENDS by Jason Mraz (featuring Meghan Trainor)
INTERLOODLE by The Herbaliser

CHAPTER ONE

LEAN ON ME FOR ONCE

ALEXANDRA

FEELING NOTHING BUT DREAD, bone-wracking shakes, and an impatience to leave the hospital, I stared at the contacts on my cell phone.

Any other time, I'd call Mom without a second thought. This was different, though. It might bother her.

God knew, it bothered me.

I had to call Dad instead. Calling him should be a no-brainer, but his over-protectiveness would go into overdrive.

Deep down, I wanted to call Rafferty, but this felt like too much to ask of him. And he'd probably lose his mind. Or he wouldn't care at all. It could go either way with us.

Nope, calling him would be a bad idea.

After a deep breath, I focused on the screen. My hands weren't shaking *quite* as violently as they had been.

"Did you get a hold of anyone, miss?" a nurse asked, peeking around the curtain.

I held up my phone. "Doing that now."

She gave me a bland smile, nodded, and walked away.

I hit Dad's contact, then I put the phone to my ear.

"Hey, Lex, it's Blood. Your dad got a call for a last minute issue at a new construction home. He left his phone and he's out at the job site."

Great.

"Is everything good?" Blood asked.

"Not really," I muttered.

"What do you mean? Are you okay?"

"I'm fine. There was an accident, and I need a ride." I hesitated. "I'll call Mom and hope it doesn't trigger her."

Blood's tone turned steely. "Were you drinking?"

I tipped my head back. "No, I wasn't. I was a passenger. Ines was driving, but the other driver was drowsy, which they say is as bad as driving drunk."

"I'll send a prospect to get you."

"I'm in Georgia, Blood."

Without missing a beat, he said, "Then I'll send Rafferty. He's on his way back from our Memphis chapter and should be in Georgia right now."

I bit my lower lip. "No, no. Don't do that. I'll figure out something else."

"He isn't on his bike, sweetheart. We made him drive up there in a cage out of spite, because it's hard to beat riding the open road during the month of May. I'll text you when I find out where he is."

Should have called Mom after all.

"Okay. Thanks, Blood."

"I'm glad you're all right, sweet girl."

An ER doctor with striking gray eyes assessed the side of my head. "Wearing your seatbelt saved your life. I hope you know that."

I pressed my lips together and barely nodded, since he still had his hand at my neck. "Do you know if the others will be all right?"

He shook his head. "I'm not supposed to share that information, and it's too soon to tell right now. They should have been wearing their seatbelts."

I swallowed and wiggled my nose to fight off tears.

His hand left my neck and he stepped back a pace. "There's some bruising forming where the side airbag hit you. Take ibuprofen if it's sore, but otherwise, we'll get you discharged."

My eyes slid to the side and back to him. "Any idea when I'll stop shaking? Every time I think it's done, another wave comes over me."

Those gray eyes held compassion. "That's shock, and everyone's different. It should wear off in time. If it doesn't, come back to the emergency room."

I lifted my chin in a slow nod. "What about the police? I thought they had questions."

He tucked a pen into his shirt pocket and nodded. "Yes, they do. I'm not sure where the officer is, but don't leave without speaking to someone."

The EMTs at the scene had given me a blanket. I gathered it tighter around me and nodded. "It'll be a while before my ride gets here, so that won't be a problem."

A nurse whipped the curtain open soon after the doctor left. "I don't have your discharge paperwork yet, but we need the bed. Let me take you to the waiting room; we'll get your discharge papers to you shortly."

I followed her, wearing the blanket like a cape. I stopped mid-way to a row of chairs when the sliding glass doors opened and Rafferty stormed inside.

Under the best circumstances, I had to brace myself for being around him. It made no sense because we'd grown up together. I used to see him every day... then we went out of our way to avoid each other. Now, we continued to keep our distance. I stayed away because he'd become a man and every time I saw him, I swore he became *more* everything. More muscles, more height, more broody. He also had more facial hair, that I wasn't sure I preferred, but today, seeing his fuller, darker beard sent a warm tingle through me.

A chain attached to his wallet bobbed against his leg as he strode toward me. His jeans were so faded, I knew they would be soft to the touch. I closed my eyes and gave a tiny head-shake because this was no time to think about touching Rafferty's legs - no matter how much I wanted that.

Over the past few years, it seemed he'd put effort into avoiding me. My best guess was that he held a grudge, though, right now, that didn't seem to be the case. He scanned me from top to toe. The concern shining from his dark brown eyes made me yearn for things to be different between us. But that was a pipe dream.

"Lex, are you all right?" he asked.

I nodded.

"Is he your ride?" the nurse asked.

"Yes," I said.

"Wait for your paperwork before you leave, and Officer Peterson needs to have a word with you, too."

"Yes, ma'am," I said, as Rafferty drew even with us.

She gestured toward the chairs. "Have a seat."

I sat and pulled the scratchy blanket tighter around my neck.

Rafferty stared down at me. "You sure you're all right? You don't look too good."

The last few hours were catching up with me. I was hanging on by a frayed thread.

"I'm okay. I'm sorry I messed up your Sunday, and I'm sure you had—"

He squatted in front of me, planting his strong hands on my knees. "Stop. You didn't mess up anything, Lex. I just want to get you out of here."

I grimaced. "I think it's going to be a while. A police officer needs to speak with me, and I don't have my discharge papers. It'd be good to find out about Ines and the others."

He nodded. "It's fine, Lex. You want me to get you a coffee? Something to eat?"

Yeah, I should have called Mom, because him being this nice to me was killing me.

For the last few years, Rafferty and I put up with one another. If we were in the same space, I kept my distance like a moon orbiting a planet. He preferred it that way.

I didn't need coffee or food. I needed a hug, and a shoulder to cry on, but with our mangled past, I wouldn't get that from him.

"No, thanks," I whispered.

With a sigh, he stood, and then sat next to me.

He settled his arm on my shoulders, pulling me toward him.

"You don't have to—"

"Shut up, Lex. You're shaking like a fucking leaf, and freaking me out." His chest rose and he exhaled slow and steady. "Just lean on me for once, all right?"

After a beat, I rested my head on his shoulder. The frayed thread snapped and I let my tears stream quietly down my cheeks.

Rafferty's hand on my shoulder squeezed. "I'm sure Porter will be fine. Did you ask how he's doing?"

"They wouldn't tell me."

"Didn't you tell them you're his girlfriend?"

Strange how I knew from afar what was going on with him, but he obviously didn't know anything about my life.

I blew out a breath. "He broke things off a few months ago. The only reason he came along was because we bought the concert tickets back in January, and I guess he couldn't find anyone to buy his ticket."

Rafferty's fingers traced along my jawline and he tilted my face up. "I thought you were moving in with him."

I pressed my lips together and gave a short head shake. "Nope. Things didn't work out, and he's transferring to a college up north so he can help with the family business."

Raff's dark brown eyes stayed locked on me. I couldn't tell what was working behind them. Then he schooled his expression. "He's a moron."

"Wouldn't you put family first?" I asked.

"That's what I'm doing right now."

That felt like a bucket of ice water on our conversation. Rafferty and I were always on different pages. If I was family, then he clearly thought of me as a sister. I blinked and tried to pull away from him, but he held firm.

His eyes widened. "Lex, you're still shaking. Let me hold you."

Someone loudly cleared their throat and we looked in that direction. Porter stood near the nurses' station with his arm in a sling and a bandage on his forehead.

He trudged closer. "Should have known you'd call him. You talked about—"

I leaned away. Raff let me go, but kept his hand on my back. After the crazy morning, I forced myself to ask, "Are you all right, Porter?"

Porter's blue eyes darted from me, to Rafferty, and back to me. "Yeah. Ready to put this shitty day behind me. Was gonna offer you a ride, but it looks like you're covered."

"She is," Rafferty said, his hand clamping on my shoulder near my neck.

I turned to him, but he and Porter were having a stare-down.

What was that about?

I looked to Porter. He stopped staring at Rafferty and looked at me. "Be well, Lexi." His snide tone negated any semblance of actual well-wishes.

As I watched him walk to the exit, Rafferty gently pulled me back into his hold.

"Lexi," he said with a scoff.

I kept quiet.

"You let him call you that?"

I glanced down the opposite end of the corridor. "For a little while. I wanted to try something new."

"Alexandra Robertson," a nurse called.

I stood along with Rafferty and went to the counter.

She handed me my discharge papers and tilted her head to the side. "There's a small office to the right, here. Officer Peterson is waiting for you there. When you're done with him, you're free to go."

———

I stepped out of the small office with a pounding headache forming behind my eye. It was most likely because of the car crash, but my mounting frustration also might have been a culprit. Reading between the lines of Officer Peterson's questions, Porter and Brantley had blamed me for the accident.

Rafferty shoved his bulky body off the wall where he'd been leaning next to the doorway. "You're done?"

"Yeah, but I'd like to check on Ines."

His lips quirked to one side like he didn't want to speak. "Doubt you're going to be able to. She's in ICU."

"How do you know that?"

Another brother, and I probably wouldn't have been able to read him, but I knew most of Rafferty's tells. The way his eyes slid side to side, he really didn't want to tell me anything.

He dragged a hand down his face, his fingers pulling at his short beard. "This accident opened my eyes. I didn't know what to expect coming in here, and I heard a man on his phone say 'She's gone into ICU.' I thought he might be talking about you, but before I could turn to ask him, he said the name Ines. It isn't cool of me to say this, but I've never felt so relieved."

My chest seized up like a heavy weight sat on me. "Well, let's get up there. I can't leave her if she's in ICU."

His lips pressed into a hard line for a beat. "I knew you'd say that, so while you were in there with the cop, I asked a nurse about visiting. She said family only, and she was a real bitch about it."

I lifted my chin in a slow nod, then shrugged. "I don't care. I'm going to see if I can sweet talk someone into letting me see her."

Twenty minutes later, Rafferty and I exited the hospital into the thick, Southern Georgia humidity. The glare of the late-morning sun intensified my headache.

Rafferty grabbed my hand and intertwined our fingers.

My gaze darted from our hands to his profile. "Why are you holding my hand?"

He stayed focused on the parking lot. "To remind myself you're still here and in one piece."

"That's sweet, but as you can see, I'm fine."

Rafferty stopped us at the bumper of his beat-up Nissan Titan. My eyes darted to his gleaming silver motorcycle strapped down in the truck bed. I wondered if Blood knew he'd done that... then I thought better of it. Very little slipped past Blood.

Rafferty's words cut into my thoughts. "I'm not sweet and you know it."

I pulled my hand back.

He held firm.

"Then you can let go," I said.

Something shone in his eyes again - it wasn't concern this time - it was something I couldn't figure out. "Not until I get you in the truck."

My seatbelt locked with a snick. I glanced up at Rafferty when he angled into the driver's seat and closed his door. "Thanks for picking me up. I really appreciate it."

He stared at me and kept quiet for a long moment. Long enough to make me nervous. "Are you sure you're okay?" he asked finally.

"Yeah. They told me I'd be sore tomorrow, but I'm still concerned about Ines and Brantley."

"Is that her boyfriend?"

"Yeah."

"Why are you concerned about him?"

I glanced out the window. "I don't know, he..."

"He what?" Rafferty demanded, in a stern tone Dad would have admired.

I turned my face toward him. "Chill out, Raff. He seemed a little extra for this trip." I pressed my lips together and shrugged. "Maybe it's my imagination since I can't put my finger on exactly what bothered me."

Rafferty's brows shot up. "What do you mean, 'He seemed a little extra'?"

I rubbed my index and middle finger along my forehead. "I don't know, he convinced Ines to change her mind about things and do things she normally wouldn't do."

"What kind of things?"

I sighed. "Things that... it sounds crazy, but things that she'd have said no to just weeks ago. But I could be misreading the situation."

Rafferty shoved the key in the ignition, but didn't start the truck. "I'll take your word for it, but I always listen to my gut when it's trying to tell me something."

I nodded. "Yeah, that's true. It's the reason I asked the officer about Brantley's condition, and he said Brantley had been discharged and left already. That seems pretty callous - especially since Ines is in ICU."

"Maybe he got the same run-around that nurse gave you. He isn't family, there's not much point sticking around."

I narrowed an eye at him. "Do you really believe that? Would you leave if I were in ICU?"

His head tilted a bit. "No, but I wouldn't tell the whole truth either."

"Right," I whispered.

He nodded. "You ready to go? Or do you want to stick around here and see if a different nurse will be more lenient?"

I'd met Ines's parents outside ICU, and we'd exchanged numbers. They told me they'd call if there was news. The more I considered it, even with a shift change I didn't think I'd get in to see her anytime soon. I took a deep breath. The thought of getting back on the interstate made me uneasy, but I'd have to face that irrational fear regardless.

"Yeah, as ready as I'll ever be."

Chapter Two

We Aren't Family

Rafferty

The call from Blood earlier in the day shook me to my core. I'd been two hours from the outskirts of Macon, but the drive to that hospital in Valdosta felt like six hours of torture.

Now I had Lex in the passenger seat, her floral scent in my truck, and more silence. She'd switched off the radio as soon as I guided the truck back onto the Interstate.

"I'm sorry. I have a headache. I hope turning off the music is okay."

"Sure."

She didn't want music, that was fine, but something about this quelling silence unnerved me.

"Why are you so quiet?" I asked.

She inhaled, but I didn't hear an exhale. I struggled to keep my right hand on the steering wheel because the thought of touching her was the only thing keeping me together right now.

Finally, she exhaled. "I feel like this could have been avoided."

I hid my irritated and confused expression by checking my blindspot. "Don't do that second-guessing shit. You couldn't know there'd be a wreck."

From the corner of my eye, I saw her twist her face my way. "I made a scene about Porter before we left. He and Brantley blamed me for us running late."

Alexandra didn't usually cause a drama... and I knew because my mom and my sister, Jasmine, had a definite flair for being dramatic. The fact that Lex had grown up around them, too, meant she knew how to throw a drama even if it was uncharacteristic of her. "Why would you make a scene?"

"It's... a long story. But the whole trip, a little voice in my head said I should have stayed home."

I gripped the steering wheel tighter. "Stop it, Alexandra. Seriously, you can't go back."

"You're right."

Her defeated tone and her words bothered me. "What aren't you telling me?"

"Nothing, Raff."

She was lying. I let that go and recalled Porter staring at us in the waiting room. It felt creepy at the time, and I'd meant to ask Lex about that then, but the nurse had called her away.

"How did he know you would call me?"

She swung her face toward me. "What?"

"How did Porter know you would call me? That's what he said at the hospital."

She rubbed at her temple and I almost asked if she had a headache, but that would have changed the subject.

After another moment, she said, "I guess you could say because we're family."

My brows drew down and I glanced at her. "We aren't family."

"Eyes on the road, Raff."

I cocked a brow and stared at her for a second longer, then watched the interstate. "Elaborate, Lex. You told Porter we're family?"

Her voice held a hint of attitude. "No. *You* told me that."

"When?"

She let out a small sigh mingled with a scoff. "In the waiting room. I asked, 'Wouldn't you put family first?' And you said that was exactly what you were doing."

Nobody was in the right hand lane and an exit was coming up fast. I changed lanes and pulled off.

There was a single gas station, but it had shut down years ago, based on the incredibly low gas price listed and the boarded-up windows on the storefront.

I drove into the empty lot, put the truck in park, propped my left wrist on the steering wheel and stretched my right arm along the back of her seat. "I never said we were family."

Exasperation and confusion warred in her expression. She repeated our conversation at the hospital and I stopped her with a finger to her lips. Touching her was torture, but touching her lips went beyond torture. We'd kissed once when we were teenagers. In the last five years, every fucking time I saw her, I wanted to kiss her again... and then some. So I should have known not to touch those full, bow-shaped lips.

I powered past my urge to kiss her. "Can see where you interpreted my words that way, Lex, but we're not family. Coming to get you was me putting *you* first."

She cupped the side of her face, but that was to hide her fingers rubbing her temple again. "You're splitting hairs."

I shook my head. "I'm not. You've got a headache. Do you need some painkillers?"

She did a long blink and sighed. "They prescribed some, but I'll have to get them when I get back to Gainesville."

My brows shot up. "What are you talking about? You aren't going to Gainesville."

Her eyes flared with irritation. "What are *you* talking about? I have to get back to Gainesville. I've got classes this week."

I bit my lower lip. "I'm a prospect now, Lex. If I don't follow an order this simple, I'm gonna pay a steep price."

She shook her head and I admired that she didn't roll her eyes. "So what I want doesn't factor here?"

Part of me wanted to give her what she wanted, but I saw both sides of this fucked-up situation. "I'd do that for you Lex, but Blood said Cal and Aunt Mallory want to see you."

Her face darkened with what I imagined was guilt before she sighed. "Right. I shouldn't have called Dad."

That was the wrong conclusion. I tilted my head and softened my tone and my expression. "What are you going to do in Gainesville?"

She turned to me, her hazel eyes practically empty. "I'll gather some of my roommate's clothes, get my car, and drive back to the hospital so I can help Ines out."

I nodded once. "That's cool of you, but she's in ICU right now. It's not like she'll go home that fast. Her parents were there. I'm sure her family's going to take care of her."

She shook her head. "Okay, but why didn't her dad stop to talk to me after you came in?"

I had to resist touching her cheek. Instead, I leaned a little closer. "Lex, I wasn't there that long before they got your papers to you and told you to talk to the cop. Hell, I'm still pissed I didn't get to sit in there with you."

With a pointed look, she tilted her head. "He asked about the accident, Raff. It's not like he's going to pin it on me, even if... never mind that doesn't matter. I was in the backseat for heaven's sake."

Her last words had me biting back my smile. Every so often, Alexandra talked just like Aunt Mallory, and I dug that. She didn't care that other people gave her crap about the phrases she used, and I liked that too. Most of all though, I loved how close she was with her mom because something told me she'd be the same way with her own kid... or kids.

I shook my head and focused on her words. "You proved my point. Seeing as he only asked you about the accident, it should have made no difference to him for me to be by your side. The fact he wouldn't let anyone else in the room says something to me, and I don't like it. Somebody should have been with you. The only reason I brought up the cop was to point out that the questioning gave Ines's dad plenty of time to wander past me and go to a different waiting room or whatever."

Her expression softened and she nodded. "You're right." She suddenly shot me an annoyed look. "I still wish we were going back to my place. I told the nurse to fill my 'scripts in Gainesville."

I leveled a dry look at her. "Pretty sure somebody can fix that."

She nodded dejectedly. "Guess I'll call the hospital."

I grinned and pointed a finger at her. "Don't. I'll get my mom or Jasmine to call them. I should have asked this earlier, are you hungry? This looks like a lousy exit, but we can stop and get you something to eat if you want."

She shook her head. "No, we aren't that far from the state line and I'd rather get home." Her eyes went wide. "Crap. I need to call Dad... or Blood. I don't know if he talked to Dad or Mom or —"

I touched my finger to her lips again. "I told Blood that I'd update Cal, and you know he isn't going to tell your Mom shit until he knows you're okay."

She blew out a deep breath. "Okay, good. That's a slight relief. I'll—"

With my fingertip to the base of her chin, I tipped her face up half an inch. "Let me, Lex. You've been through the wringer today. Hell, if I'm not mistaken, you just stopped shaking ten minutes ago."

Her eyes locked with mine. "You're way too observant, Rafferty. No wonder Steel and the Devil Lancers wanted to recruit you."

In reality, I was only observant where Alexandra was concerned. If she wanted to think that was why the Devil Lancers had wanted me to join their motorcycle club, I wouldn't argue.

"Let's get you home."

Her hand grabbed mine. "Call Dad first, please. I don't want him to worry."

I dipped my chin and pulled out my phone.

Cal answered within the first ring. "Talk to me, Raff."

"She's fine, and we're almost to Florida. Should be at your place in two and a half hours."

He sighed. "Thank God. Did she give you shit about bringing her to Jacksonville?"

My eyes slid toward Alexandra. "She did, but she's on board now. Did that plan change?"

"No. I'll see you soon."

"Plug in your iPod," I muttered as I set the cruise control on the truck.

"I don't have it," Alexandra said.

If she hadn't replied so quickly, I might have believed her.

I glanced at her and back to the road. "You're lying, Robertson."

"I'm not."

I fought off a smile. Riling her up always gave me a perverse thrill. "You don't go on a road trip without your whole freaking music library with you, and you're the only woman I know who treats her iPod the way you do."

"I don't treat it in any way, Rafferty."

"What I mean is that you're the only one who still uses it. Everyone else our age has moved on to streaming services."

She failed to hide her groan. "Like I want to rely on a stinking algorithm to give me good driving music."

I chuckled. "Believe it or not, they've been known to work, Lex."

Her head twisted toward the passenger window. "Yeah, well, I don't have my iPod since Ines asked me not to bring it. Though that was her trying to keep Brantley happy."

My grin fell away. That wasn't cool of Ines, but I kept that opinion to myself.

We rode in silence for a good twenty minutes while I warred with myself. There was more to her story about Porter. I didn't want to press her, but I hated not knowing how big of a moron Porter really was.

Curiosity was more dangerous to me than the most addictive drugs.

"What's with Porter? Did he cheat?" I asked.

She scoffed. "No. Hell, if he'd done that, he'd be some other woman's problem."

Guess he was a little smarter than I thought.

She fell silent again.

I glanced at her. "What did he do then?"

She leaned her head back and stared at her visor. "Possibly two of the worst things he could do. He judged me after meeting Mom and Dad."

"Say that again?"

She glanced at me. "You know how it is. People judge you for being a biker. He didn't know Dad was a 'biker-biker' as he ineptly put it."

I waited for a Mini Cooper to pass us before veering into the left lane to pass a tractor trailer. "You're used to that, though."

Her rueful chuckle filled the cab. "Yeah, well, let's just say - while we were in the car today, he put a fresh spin on it."

Those words struck me strange. "What does that mean?"

"It means we aren't talking about this while you're driving."

I clenched my teeth. He'd clearly done something to her, and that pissed me off. If he hadn't, Lex wouldn't have any issues talking about it. Right?

We were fast approaching the interchange with I-75 and I-10. I let the conversation drop so I could concentrate on changing lanes and avoiding assholes who would cut me off because I-10 jumped out of nowhere on them.

———

Ninety minutes later, and I realized being in my truck with Lex was the *real* torture. She was right here, but so far away. Something beyond the car crash was wrong, and she wouldn't share.

Every few miles, I'd check to see if she'd fallen asleep. No such luck.

"Why were you in Memphis?" she asked.

The brothers had tons of bullshit they put prospects through, and like *Fight Club,* talking about it to non-members was frowned upon.

"Club business," I muttered.

Her chest jerked with her lone, bitter chuckle. "Should have known."

Truth was, until I got that call from Blood, I thought I was moving. It seemed to me that transferring as a prospect rather than as a patched member would be easier. Dad told me I was wrong, but everywhere I went in Jacksonville held reminders of Alexandra. We never really dated, but we had spent tons of time together running around the city. I couldn't take much more of it.

I blew out a sigh. "I plan to transfer up there."

"What? No."

I shot her a quick look because from the tone of her voice she sounded crushed. The disappointed look on her face matched her tone.

I shook my head and turned back to the windshield. "You look like I told you Santa isn't real."

She blew out a breath, drawing my attention and I saw her roll her eyes. "No, I'm just surprised. That's a big move."

I shrugged a shoulder. "Cross-town or across three states, a move is a move, Lex."

"Yeah. That's one way to look at it."

A rest area sign came into view. If we stopped maybe I could get the whole story out of her.

"You need to stretch your legs?" I asked.

"That'd be good."

Chapter Three

Not with Us

Alexandra

I tossed a bag of pistachios onto the dash, hauled myself up into Rafferty's truck, and buckled in while he did the same (minus the pistachios). After a moment, I realized he hadn't put the key in the ignition, let alone started the vehicle.

He leaned into his forearm on the center console. "I'm not driving and I won't drive until you tell me what Porter's deal is."

I stared into his dark brown eyes. "Porter doesn't have a deal."

His brows arched. "Bullshit. You said we couldn't discuss it while I drove. Truck's parked. Now spill."

He certainly was learning how to be an overbearing alpha while prospecting with the Riot MC.

I sighed. "Porter and I are over, Tee. Have been for over two months."

He cocked a brow at my use of a nickname I hadn't uttered in over five years. "Why would you cause a scene?"

I grabbed the pistachios. "It doesn't matter."

He snatched them from me.

"Hey!"

He stayed focused. "If it doesn't matter, then why aren't you talking about it? Plus, why would it make me angry?"

"I never said it would make you angry."

He chuckled, and it rumbled from his chest like the roll of thunder from a summer storm. "You didn't have to. Anything you can't say while I'm driving equals shit that's gonna distract me or piss me off."

I couldn't argue that, and it annoyed me. "Can we just go?"

"How did he hurt you?"

"You're making assumptions."

"No. You said you made a scene and that y'all were late because of it. You never do that shit, so Porter either pissed you off or he hurt you."

How I forgot certain things, I'd never know, but somehow I always forgot how well Rafferty knew me. It was equal parts annoying and endearing. Mainly annoying because I never knew what to do with that from him.

I took a deep breath. "It's over and done, Rafferty. I appreciate your friendly concern, but no joke - Porter is *not* worth your time or mine."

He pressed his lips together and stared past my shoulder, out the window. After a lengthy moment, his eyes met mine. "Did you tell your parents how he hurt you?"

Acid filled and churned in my stomach like a washing machine full of my secrets. I straightened. "They know I'm an adult, and haven't pried."

His left eye narrowed at me. "Hard to say what's worse: the fact you're a pain in my ass or how much I like feeling that pain."

My mouth fell open. "Oh my God. Did you really just say that?"

He closed his eyes and his lips slowly tipped up before he opened them again. "Tell me. Please," he whispered.

Something in his whisper made me crack. "You can't get mad and you can't tell Dad."

He lowered his chin as his eyes turned shrewd. "I'm not agreeing to that. One, because I'm already mad that he hurt you. Two, because whatever you're about to share... if it were Jasmine, Simone, Gabby, or any brothers' daughter - the brothers would pummel the shit outta me for keeping it from them. And I'd deserve that."

He was right, and that was the biggest reason I didn't want to tell him. Even though I knew it all came from a place of love, the overbearing, overprotective thing got old. I tossed my hands up. "Nobody can protect all of us all the time."

He reverted back to his gentle whisper. "I need you to tell me, so I can stop imagining shit. What spin did he put on assholes making assumptions about bikers?"

I didn't want to give Rafferty all of this, but I had to get it out there and be done with it. "He got physical with me in the car and wouldn't immediately stop when I told him to."

Rafferty's eyes danced side to side for a couple beats. "Did he rape you?"

I closed my eyes and sucked in a breath. "No. It didn't go that far, but it was the reason I insisted we stop off just before the accident."

Abruptly, Rafferty sat back in his seat, leaned his head against the headrest, and stared forward at the public bathrooms. "He didn't violate you in any way?"

"He didn't listen when I told him to stop," I murmured.

He turned his head toward me. "What does this have to do with Cal?"

I gave him a questioning look.

"You said he didn't know Cal was a real biker. What's that got to do with this?"

My stomach twisted. "People outside our world make assumptions about bikers, and those assumptions extend to the kids of bikers."

"I'm still lost, Lex. You two had broken things off. Why would he try something in a car with two other people?"

It seemed I'd have to tell Rafferty the last thing I wanted him to know about me.

Inadvertently, I'd saved my virginity.

Though I wouldn't call it saving, so much as an inability to give it up due to poor circumstances. It wasn't that I was religious or highly principled about it. Crazy as it sounded, I never intended for this to happen.

Yet, happen it did.

And after a certain amount of time, that led to all of my prior boyfriends tossing me aside.

By now, it had become far more of a problem. Almost any guy who met Dad got scared.

Understandable. Dad could be scary.

One ex-boyfriend said I was a tease. I wasn't, but after the way Rafferty shoved me aside, I'd shattered. I had a very difficult time trusting men, and an even harder time deciding if the timing was right. I'd dated a guy for two months, thought I was ready to take the next step with him, but he ended it because I hadn't put out yet.

Yeah. That left a bitter taste in my mouth.

I didn't want perfection. The first time had a reputation for hurting - and sucking, but not the good kind.

Then I moved to Gainesville, and I was too busy for much more than school, work, and sleep. Between semesters, if I went to Riot MC parties, every man there knew Dad... which made me as untouchable as Simone, the president's daughter.

It wasn't easy being the daughter of the Sergeant-at-Arms. Mom always said Dad had the friendliest eyes she'd ever seen, but to teenagers, Dad's eyes were deceptive because with his size and gruff, rumbly voice, he was straight-up scary.

Ines encouraged me to make time for the occasional party, which was how Porter and I met. He was only the fourth guy to meet Dad. Porter had sensed something was different about me, but after seeing Dad in his cut, on his maroon Harley... a confused look had crossed Porter's face. Rather than talk to me about his confusion, he kept quiet. I would learn a few hours later, he'd made assumptions. The *wrong* assumptions.

I swallowed as much of my pride as I could and looked out the passenger window. "We hadn't gone there, Tee. I had wanted to, but we both had roommates, and I'm a little..." I shook my head not wanting to overshare or admit to my inexperience. "Anyway, he made the assumption that a biker's daughter had to be easy and I'd been holding out on him for nothing."

Slowly, I turned my head to sneak a glance at him. Rafferty looked about as uncomfortable as I felt. The truck filled with the sound of his sharp inhale. "Why in the hell were you planning to move in with him?"

I shook my head. "That was all his plan. It so happened that my lease was expiring around the same time as his. He swung by to take me out one afternoon, and pulled a bait-and-switch. Rather than go bowling, we went apartment hunting. Nobody would have known if your sister hadn't called me and interrupted a leasing agent telling us about a one-bedroom luxury unit."

That earned me his side-eye. "A luxury apartment? Really, Lex?"

I held up a finger. "His idea, not mine. That was one of the first signs that he and I might not be totally compatible. He wasn't realistic about money. Then he judged me for being a biker's daughter, and we went our separate ways."

He stayed quiet.

I grabbed the bag of pistachios, opened it, poured a couple in my hand, and held them up to him.

"No, thanks. You never told Cal about this?"

I aimed a serious look at him. "He doesn't need to know." I tucked the bag of nuts into my purse. "It's over."

Nope. *Now* I had Rafferty's side-eye. "*He* oughta be 'over'."

My eyes went wide as I stared at him. "You don't mean that."

He arched both brows. "How many times did you tell him to stop when you were in the car today?"

"I didn't keep track."

"Once is all it takes, and you know it's true because we were both there when *my* mom gave us that hella awkward sex talk."

My lips trembled as I held back my laughter.

"Shit's not funny, Alexandra."

A strangled half-chuckle escaped when I spoke. "It actually is, if you remember half of what Aunt Trixie said to us and how she said it."

Rafferty shook his head.

Suddenly, he stared at me. Reading me like he always did. "Did he touch you?"

I *really* didn't want to share that with him. "My head hurts. Can we go now?"

It was like I didn't speak.

"He touched you. You told him to stop, and he didn't."

I kept quiet.

"Is that right?"

"Yes. Have you considered law school? I'm thinking you'd excel at cross examination, and you can fall back on that when you're too old for construction work."

"Stop being cute," he muttered, then refocused on me like something struck him.

"What?" I asked.

"Ines lives with you, so she had to know how Porter judged you, and she damn sure knew you two were over. Why in the hell would she have him in her car with you... also in that car?"

I twisted my hands up. "That was what the drama was about. I didn't know Porter was even going to the music festival until we went to pick up Brantley from his place early this morning. Porter was inside Brantley's apartment. Brantley opened the door to us, and Porter wandered out with him, which means those two had arranged it so he'd be there and they could spring it on us that Porter was coming along."

Rafferty stared at me. "Ines knew nothing about that shit?"

"No."

"But obviously, she still let him in the car."

I tipped my head to the side just a fraction. "Initially, she saw it my way. That the ambush wasn't cool and Porter needed to drive himself if he wasn't going to sell his ticket."

"That's logical," Rafferty muttered.

I nodded. "Yeah, but Brantley's very eco-conscious—"

"So are you. Hell, so is anyone who understands science," Rafferty muttered.

"Anyway, he pointed out how ridiculous it was for us to drive two cars to Atlanta, and even if Porter drove separately, he'd still be sitting right next to me in the stadium. And when I protested more, he pulled Ines away and he sweet-talked her into letting Porter ride along."

Rafferty locked eyes with me again. "I know you've been rooming with her for over a year now, so you obviously dig Ines. But, that's a bitch move."

My eyes slid to the side because to my way of thinking that wasn't the bitch move he thought it was.

"Now what aren't you telling me?"

I shook my head. "She's in critical condition, Tee. I don't want to speak ill of her right now, but to me that's nothing."

He gave my hand a squeeze. "Lex. You gotta tell me everything."

I swallowed. "So, since she wasn't seeing logic any more by making Porter drive separate, I told them to go without me. I'd stay home. She accused me of being a drama-queen, which hurt more than it should have because when I broke things off with Porter, Ines was there. He accused me of misinterpreting his words. Ines butted in and was the first to point out he was gaslighting me. Strange that she basically did the same thing to me when I didn't want to give into her boyfriend's plans." I sighed. "Sorry, I got off track, but Brantley and Porter piled right on with her that I was being too dramatic. Nobody appreciated me suggesting Porter take a Greyhound to Atlanta because it would have been too last-minute. There was still some time for me to try to sell my ticket online. I really should have done that. None of this shit would have happened."

He let go of my hand and slid his hand into my hair. "Dammit, Lex. You can't think like that. *She* should have had your back. That fuck-wit should have fuckin' known better and sold *his* ticket. Christ. I'm glad I didn't know this earlier. Moment I saw that guy today, I wanted to punch him in the fuckin' face. Now I wish I would have."

After the horrible events that morning, part of me wished he would have, too. Hearing his sincere tone, a pleasant warm sensation drifted through my belly. I ignored that.

"Anyway, to me *that* was the bitch move. I'd suggested as long as Brantley and Porter sat in the back, it might be fine. Brantley whined about how with his height he needed all the legroom he could get. That's another way he was being extra. She gave into him and made me feel bad about not wanting to be cooped up in a car with Porter for seven or eight hours."

"She did?"

My head wobbled. "Brantley had everything to do with that. Seems Ines shared with him what had happened. Brantley pointed out that we'd broken up. There wasn't any reason Porter was going to try to win me back."

"What a motherfucker."

"Yeah, and then came the guilt about how we were already running late before this and I was only making it worse with the drama... if we hit traffic we'd miss the opening act and Ines was excited about all of the performers scheduled for this afternoon and tonight - not just the headliner."

Rafferty's face was inches from mine. He parted his lips and shook his head twice. "And you wanted to stick around the hospital for her? After all that bullshit?"

My head tilted and he withdrew his hand from my hair. "One bad road trip doesn't mean I throw away our friendship."

He shot me a dry look. "You learn a lot about your friends on a road trip."

Those words immediately brought to mind one of the last times Rafferty and I had been in a car together.

I nodded. "You could say that."

He leaned back a little. "Seems to me, some road trips change us more than others."

I narrowed my eyes. "Are you trying to say something about my trip to Georgia?"

He shook his head. "No. I'm saying after the last road trip you and I went on, you became someone else afterward."

My chuckle mingled with a scoff. "That was back in high school, and Dad grounded me for weeks. Between skipping school, and talking Simone into taking us - at just sixteen - to Bike Week, it's hard to say what infuriated Dad most."

He nodded. "Yeah. You're right. That was a long time ago. Let's get you home."

———

The steady thrum of the truck speeding over the Buckman Bridge woke me up. I couldn't believe I'd fallen asleep, because I never slept in moving vehicles. I wiped my hand down my face. The way the sun reflected off the small swells in the river, I guessed it was a little after one in the afternoon. Glancing at the clock on the center console, I was close: one-twenty-five.

"Sorry you woke up," Rafferty murmured.

I yawned. "That's all right. Listen, I know you're following orders, but—"

"No 'buts,' Lex. Hell, we're fifteen minutes from your parents' house."

I glanced his way. "I was going to ask you to do me a favor. Assuming it doesn't interfere with club business."

His lips pressed together. "What's the favor? Aunt Mallory already picked up your meds according to the text I got a few minutes ago."

I nodded. "Great, and thank you for handling that. It's just that I really need to get back to Gainesville - tomorrow if possible. Finals are this coming week, and I can't afford to botch anything at this point in dental school. I don't have my car here, and it seems silly to send someone to go get it and come back when you or somebody could just take me tomorrow morning."

Even in profile, I saw that shrewd, calculating expression steal across his face. "Sure. I can do that for you."

I put a hand on his forearm. "You aren't going to hunt down Porter."

He almost smirked as he shook his head once. "Nope. Not gonna hunt down Porter."

"Or Brantley," I muttered.

"Can't promise you that. He forced you to be in the backseat because he's a jackass *and* he was in on Porter's bullshit stunt. Nah. He needs a wake-up call."

"Rafferty."

He stopped for a red light and turned his face to me. "Give me this, or I give your shit to Blood."

My face froze. To most people, they'd wonder why he wouldn't tell my dad, but most people hadn't met Blood. He was vindictive, ruthless, and lived to stir shit up. Only *after* he'd stirred the pot would he let Dad know what was going on.

"You suck," I muttered.

"You have no idea, Lex."

That sent a curl of lust through my torso straight to points south. But that would never happen.

Not with us.

Chapter Four

Free as a Bird

Rafferty

I STEERED MY TRUCK down San Jose Boulevard fighting a smile. Alexandra knew if I told Blood what happened to her all hell would break loose. Not that Cal wouldn't let all hell break loose, but as Vice President of the Jacksonville chapter for so many years, Blood was far more methodical in doling out vengeance.

It wasn't ideal to threaten her with telling Blood, because I wasn't sure I'd follow through on it, but it did the trick. I couldn't wait to get my hands on Brantley. He may not have hurt Lex directly, but to pull the shit he did, he needed a lesson. As I turned onto the street with Uncle Cal and Aunt Mallory's house, I wondered if teaching Brantley a lesson was the best use of my time.

For the first time in what felt like years, neither Lex nor I had anyone in our lives. She was in the midst of getting her degree in dentistry, but I'd known for quite a while... I didn't want anyone else but her.

Everyone thought I kept her at a distance because of the bullshit falling out we had in high school. I never said anything to correct that, but I kept her at arm's length so she could determine if what she said was actually what she wanted.

She'd been so damned adamant talking to my sister, thinking I wasn't around to overhear her. 'No MC life for her. No way would she become her mom and marry a biker.'

I'd known from the time I could put a full sentence together that I'd be just like Dad. Nothing *but* the MC life for me. And until I'd heard Alexandra's adamant declaration, I'd been pretty certain she'd be the person at my side.

Alexandra's voice pulled me from my thoughts. "What time will you be here in the morning? Monday morning rush hour sucks, but if we take San Jose south through Fruit Cove we'd be going against the flow of traffic."

Part of me wanted to spend the night at her parents' house, but that was overkill. The clubhouse was a fifteen minute drive, so there wasn't any need to stick close.

"Whatever time you want me to be here, I'll be here," I said, parking my truck in front of the privacy fence surrounding what I knew was a kick-ass pool, patio, and backyard.

The way she smiled at me right then...I wished I had a picture of it. Despite the swelling and bruising on her face, her eyes were lit with an expression like she thought I could move mountains for her. There was a tinge of something else there - it looked almost like regret. "God. I'm gonna owe you so much, Tee. Thanks again for coming to get me. I'd have been waiting forever—"

I put my finger to her lips again, this time wishing it were my lips instead. "You're more than welcome, Lex. Let's get you those painkillers."

"Where are you goin'?" Uncle Cal grumbled when I stepped toward the foyer.

He'd just given Lex one helluva bear hug, and now Aunt Mallory was swaying back and forth while hugging her.

With my eyes on Cal's, I tipped my head toward the front door. "Gonna give you all some privacy."

"Get your ass over here," he ordered, reaching out for a handshake.

I took his hand, but he yanked me forward and clapped me on the back hard enough I fought off a wheeze.

At my ear, he murmured, "Thanks for bringing her back safe. Don't know why you're runnin' off, but stick around if you can."

He let me go and I nodded.

Aunt Mallory had let go of Alexandra and she rushed to me. "Oh, Raff, I'm so glad you were able to get to her fast."

This felt really weird, how effusive she was with me. I'd never seen her like this... then I realized she knew more than any of us that the whole day could have been far more tragic.

I shook my head and gave her a light hug. "It was no problem, Aunt Mallory. Really."

She smiled up at me. "Well, you're staying for dinner right? That won't be for a few hours yet, but you can run the pool table on my husband. He needs a challenge."

Alexandra sidled up between her parents. "I'm sure Rafferty has somewhere else to be. There's probably a woman wondering where he's been."

I stared into her hazel eyes. "I don't."

Those eyes closed for a beat. "You don't?"

A small grin played at my lips. "Nope. Free as a bird, right now."

Cal glanced at Aunt Mallory. "I'm gonna get the marinade ready for the steaks."

She glanced at Alexandra. "I'm going to get some towels for your bathroom. I ran out of time earlier. A hot bath might be good for your headache, sweetie."

Alexandra watched her mom leave the room, then her eyes locked with mine. "Well, even though you're free as a bird, you aren't obligated to spend time with me."

I hated hearing her say that. I'd never feel obligated to spend time with her.

"Lex," I said.

"What?"

"You aren't an obligation. I'm here for you."

She rubbed her temple, caught herself, and dropped her hand to her side. "I'm fine. Hardly a scratch, because I was wearing my seat belt. Remember?"

"Yeah. Go get some rest."

Her eyes skated toward the staircase, then back to me. "You aren't going to tell Dad, right?"

"Right," I muttered. At least, not if I could help it.

She nodded and whispered, "Thanks."

"How's she really doing?" Cal asked and handed me a bottle of Yuengling.

I swallowed a sip. "Her head is killing her, probably more than she's letting on. It took her a long time to go to sleep in the truck, and even then that lasted maybe half an hour."

Cal tipped his head back, took a long pull on his beer, and swallowed. "Why do I get the feeling there's something else going on?"

"Her roommate is in ICU. She wanted to stick around for her, but there was a nurse who wouldn't let her visit. That seems to be bothering her, but on top of that she wants to get back to Gainesville tomorrow."

"That isn't happening," Aunt Mallory said, walking into the kitchen from behind me.

I took a deep breath. "I told her I would take her. She's got finals this week."

"Damn, you're right. She can't miss those," Aunt Mallory said.

The sound of Cal's beer hitting the counter got my attention. "Aren't you going back to Memphis tonight?"

"Zeus isn't sure he's interested in a prospect who hasn't ever lived in Memphis." I twisted my hand up. "That might be him busting my chops. He's the chapter president, so nobody's going to tell me if he is. Either way, I'm not in a rush to drive back if he doesn't want me there."

Aunt Mallory set a wine glass on the counter and pulled a bottle of white wine from the under the counter wine fridge. "You're probably going to say you're staying at the clubhouse, but you're welcome to the guest room so you can save yourself the gas and the hassle of crossing the Buckman."

I liked that idea, but I forced myself not to show it so Cal wouldn't pick up on my eagerness to stick close to Lex. "Thanks. I'll take you up on that."

After she finished pouring a glass, she let out a dejected sigh. "Oh. The guest bed doesn't have any sheets on it. I can run up and—"

I shook my head. "No need. I can make a bed, Aunt Mallory. Are the sheets in the linen closet?"

"Yeah."

"I'll go up there."

Cal pinned me with his gaze. "How about you finish your beer at least. Give Lex enough time to get out of the bathroom and then fall asleep."

"You got it."

Five minutes later, Cal insisted I follow him out to the pool. He grabbed a pole with a skimmer net on the end and dipped it in the water. "Mallory interrupted us. Now, what aren't you telling me?"

"Nothing definite. From what she said, she blames herself for the accident."

Cal stopped mid-skim and stared at me. "She wasn't driving."

"Yeah. There were some issues, and Lex... she thinks none of this would have happened if she'd... played the situation differently."

Cal pulled the skimmer out of the pool and flung the collected debris toward the backyard. "What situation?"

I crossed my arms on my chest. "There was some confusion since her ex-boyfriend was there unexpectedly." I swallowed, hating that I was lying to Cal by omission. "By the time that shit got sorted, they were running late."

"What did you tell her?"

"I told her she couldn't think that way. What's done is done and she isn't to blame."

Cal nodded and put the pole away. "Good. Is there anything else?"

I shook my head. "No."

Cal jerked his head toward the house. "Go make the bed for yourself. You look beat. I'll start grilling in a couple hours."

———

I'd taken off both of my boots and turned down the covers when I heard a faint cry from Alexandra's room, next to mine. After the day she'd had, I hurried to her room and checked on her.

The door was open just a crack. I eased it open further and stepped inside.

Her room was dark, but late afternoon sunlight provided enough light for me to see she was still asleep. Then she thrashed to her side facing me.

"No," she cried softly.

I edged closer and put a hand on her shoulder. "Alexandra. Wake up."

She jolted and her eyes opened wide. Her chest moved with her heavy breathing.

I squatted beside the bed. "You're all right. You must have been having a bad dream."

"Yeah," she breathed.

Something in her eyes wasn't right. Like whatever had her spooked was still right there with her. "You want me to lay down next to you?"

She sat up a little, grabbed her water bottle, and took a sip. "It was just a nightmare, Rafferty. You don't have to—"

I rose and propped a hip on the edge of the bed. "Nightmares are how our brains deal with pain, Lex. I asked you to lean on me for once. That means you aren't dealing with this shit on your own."

She glanced up at me. Her eyes were assessing me. "Why are you being so... sweet to me?"

I shook my head twice as my body shook with silent laughter. "I'm not being sweet, Lex."

"Could fool me," she muttered, putting the bottle back on the night-stand.

I blew out a harsh breath. "Any man biding his time to get in your pants is far from sweet."

Her head reared back. "You lie."

"About what? Every bit of that is true."

She tilted her head. "You don't want to get in my pants, Raff. I still remember how clear you made that during—"

"High school?"

She nodded.

"Lex, that was five years ago. We've changed, and I'd like to think we've both matured since then."

"Why now? Is it because of the car crash?"

My body went stiff for a long moment. I hated that she thought that, but I also understood why she did. "No, Alexandra. The accident woke me up, but I didn't know you kicked that asshole to the side."

She stared up at me. "He's not an asshole."

I leaned into my hand on the bed. "Did he make assumptions because of Cal?"

She didn't say anything.

"Did he touch you and not stop when you told him to?"

"Fine. He is an asshole," she said, in a slightly exasperated tone.

I loved that about her - how she could forgive. I also hated it because he didn't deserve her forgiveness.

"What was your nightmare about? Do you remember?"

Her eyes skated toward the wall. "The accident. It was like the other car hit us on purpose, but that's crazy."

That got my attention. "Why do you think that? I thought the other driver was drowsy?"

She nodded. "Yeah. That's why it's just a crazy nightmare."

I tucked her comforter around her shoulder. "You want me to go? It'll be another hour before Cal has food ready."

Her lips twisted to the side for a beat. "I don't want to send mixed signals, but it'd be nice if you laid down next to me."

I stalked to the other side of the bed and tugged my shirt over my head.

Alexandra took in a sharp breath. "Do you need a different shirt or something?"

I watched her eyes dance over my chest. "I don't sleep with a shirt on, bad enough I'll be wearing jeans."

"Right," she muttered, and rolled to her side away from me.

I climbed into bed and kept my distance. It killed, but I wouldn't take advantage.

"I didn't know you had so many tattoos," she said after a moment.

"Yeah," I whispered.

"They're in color," she remarked.

"Yep."

"Who did them?"

"Blake."

"Really?" she asked and shifted to her other side.

We went to high school with Blake. He'd been a tattoo artist for a long time, and with his talent, it boggled my mind why he didn't leave Jacksonville and make a killing out in a bigger city like Los Angeles.

"You sound surprised," I murmured.

She grinned. "Well, I just figured some of that ink happened in Augusta with the Devil Lancers."

If she only knew why I had so many tats with such vivid colors.

"Nope. Are you planning to chat or get some rest?" I asked.

She inched closer. "One more question."

I turned my head toward her. "Have at it."

"Will you tell me the story behind just one of them?"

Shit.

Dammit.

I got my act together and came up with an answer. "Another time, Lex. Every one of them has a long story behind it. You're in pain, so get some rest."

I woke up alone. Alexandra's floral perfume teased my nose. My stomach rumbled and I rolled out of bed. Lex had laid my shirt on the foot of her bed for me.

I tugged it on and went downstairs.

The microwave in the kitchen indicated the time was five-thirty-five. An unyielding silence permeated the space.

I turned to the sliding glass doors and saw Cal and Lex strolling up the pier back to the house. The house sat on an estuary that fed into Julington Creek. They must have gone down to the water. I craned my neck and saw Aunt Mallory watching their progress from a lounger near the pool.

Cal wrapped an arm around Alexandra's shoulders pulling her to him, then he kissed the top of her hair.

The door to a half-bath opened down the hall and Abby, Blood's wife, aimed a questioning look at me. "Why are you hiding out like a lurker?"

"Just woke up, that's all."

"Mm-hmm," she said skeptically. "Well, it's a good thing you did. Trixie was gonna come get you."

My brows furrowed. "Mom isn't here."

Abby slipped past me to open the door. "Yes, she is. You can't see her from here because of the bad angle, but she's sitting on the other side of Mallory."

I followed her out onto the patio and immediately heard the splat of a beanbag hitting a cornhole board. My gaze cut in that direction. Dad and Blood were standing opposite one another in the middle of a game.

"Startin' to wonder what happened to you, Raff," Dad said, lobbing a bright orange beanbag.

"You need our prospect to do a beer run, Cal?" Blood asked.

Cal shook his head, let Lex go, and wandered toward Blood. "No. When he's here he's not a prospect - at least not today."

Blood's eyes narrowed. "Why? Because I assigned him to chauffeur duty for your girl?"

Cal shook his head. "You know better, brother. Besides, you made me tap a fresh keg."

I nodded my silent thanks to Cal.

Five minutes later, I milled about the grill as Cal lowered the grill lid on some chicken and steaks.

Dad and Mom wandered up.

Mom said, "Your girl's home safe."

I almost nodded until she reached out to pat Cal's bicep.

Dad shot me an assessing look and tipped his head toward the house. "Abby said the salsa's running low and you knew where the extra tub was in the fridge, Raff."

"I can grab that," Cal said.

Dad shook his head. "Nah. You keep an eye on the steaks."

In the kitchen, I opened the fridge only for Dad to close it.

"I lied about that, Raff. Are you making a move on Alexandra?"

I faced him while tamping down my ire. It took a beat for me to get my thoughts together. "Mom's always called her 'my girl.' You're reading too much into this, Dad."

His brow slowly inched up. "Am I?"

God, I hated how well he could read me.

"You are, but what difference does it make?"

Dad stepped toe-to-toe with me, his face set like stone. "The difference it makes is that he trusts you like nobody else. You break that... it's a long road before you can repair it. *If* you can even repair it."

"Isn't it her choice? Or have I got to get Cal's permission first? It's not like you're going to treat Bobby, Ryan, or Killian that way if we were talking about Jasmine."

Dad's lip curled. "Don't muddy the water by bringing your sister into this. And you know it's Alexandra's choice, but it doesn't change how he'll see it if you sneak around. Like you took advantage of a situation."

I clenched my jaw and turned my glare toward the fridge. Finally, I met Dad's gaze, but he spoke first.

"I see you get me."

"No. You see that I'm pissed. It's only because of this fucked-up sitch that I found out she dropped that loser boyfriend months ago since nobody told me that."

"Why the hell would they? You've been actin' like a disinterested jackass the past four years."

The hiss of the glass door sliding open interrupted our stare-down. I leaned over and caught Mom glaring at me.

She bustled up to us. "What are you two arguing about? We can hear you outside."

That wasn't true. Mom hated being left out of a conversation between me and Dad, so I knew she'd been trying to eavesdrop.

Dad aimed a dry look at her. "If they can hear us, then you would know what we're arguing about."

"Don't get logical with me, mister. Besides, Cal figured out Abby didn't need more salsa right off the bat, so you two need to wrap this little soirée up real quick."

Normally Mom using the word 'soirée' would make me laugh. Right now, not so much.

I grabbed a tub of salsa, two bottles of Blue Moon (since that's what Alexandra drank), and moved to get out of the kitchen.

Mom snagged one of the bottles. "Your girl can't drink because of her medicine. And if this fucked-up day has extracted your head from your ass... I'm glad it only took you four-ish years to your father's ten. Just, do us all a favor."

I waited for her to say more.

She shot a coy grin at Dad, then pointed the bottle at me. "Don't fuck it up."

"Woman, this is not the same thing," Dad muttered.

She sipped the beer. "You're right... and yet, you're still wrong. Now I need some chips to chase this beer."

Chapter Five

Scary

Alexandra

By the time we'd finished dinner, my headache went from a pulsating pain to a semi-noticible throb. If it weren't for my pain, this would have felt like old times.

No. That wasn't entirely accurate.

It would have felt like old times if Rafferty and Uncle Roll hadn't been acting weird, with a side of Aunt Trixie bubbling with excitement. At first I'd wanted to blame her excitement on having one too many beers, but that wasn't it. I suspected I knew what it was, but that *couldn't* be right.

I went upstairs to the bathroom after everyone left. Even though I'd showered earlier, I needed to wash my face and brush my teeth.

It felt odd knowing Raff was staying the night in the house. At the same time, it was familiar, because when I was growing up Mom and Dad would let Rafferty and Jasmine sleep over at least once a month.

Rafferty's words from this afternoon kept repeating in my brain.

Any man biding his time to get in your pants is far from sweet.

He'd never been so forthright before, which made me doubt him. The look in his eyes, though - that was real... and totally serious.

We would never work. Even if I were living in town, Rafferty would get bored with me. I wasn't biker ol' lady material. Not by a long shot. I didn't party like they did. I drank every so often, but I'd never be like Aunt Trixie or the other ol' ladies who seemed to live for the next get-together.

When I was done with my night-time routine, I opened the bathroom door and found Rafferty milling about the hallway.

"About time you finished up. Thought you might have fallen in."

My lips quirked to the side. "I wasn't in there *that* long."

"Wasn't that short either."

"It's all yours now," I said, hurrying to my room.

I flipped on the light and froze. He'd made the bed earlier. That seemed like something new, because from what Jasmine told me, he was allergic to that particular chore. As quick as I could, I changed into a pair of spare pajamas I'd left here.

A few minutes later, Rafferty leaned on my doorjamb. "You good to sleep alone? Or are you gonna have fitful sleep?"

I shrugged. "It's hard for me to predict that."

"Is your medicine supposed to make you drowsy?"

My eyes slid toward the nightstand. The sticker running down the side of the bottle with the half-closed eye couldn't be missed. "Yeah. Seems that way."

"Then I'll be next door. Unless you're on a strict schedule, we'll leave whenever you wake up."

Part of me wanted him to climb into my bed, but a bigger part of me knew that wasn't the best move. I smiled and nodded at him. "Thanks, Rafferty. You're the best."

His eyes lowered into a slow blink before he shook his head. "I'm not the best by any stretch. See you in the morning."

That cleared things up. Those words that had been running through my mind in a loop faded away. If Raff wanted in my pants, then he wouldn't have let me bow out that easily. After all he'd said about Porter, it was clear he was learning the fine art of being an overprotective alpha. Undoubtedly that was why Dad was cool with him being here.

I quietly closed the door, pulled down my covers, and turned off the light before climbing into bed. My eyelids felt like two small weighted blankets, and I drifted to sleep in no time.

———

"How's your head?" Rafferty asked, stopping for a red light on University Avenue.

We had spent the last ninety minutes of the ride to Gainesville listening to alternative rock music. The lack of conversation was comforting and unnerving. Comforting because I liked that neither of us felt compelled to fill the silence. Unnerving because he obviously didn't mean what he said yesterday afternoon.

"My head's fine - as long as I don't touch the side of my face."

He sighed. "I'm sorry you're in pain."

I twisted a hand up. "I appreciate that. It's not that bad."

He reached out and gave my knee a squeeze. "Still. Bruises like that suck."

His words brought back memories of high school, when he'd get into fights and I'd bring him ice packs for the bruises on his face.

That was before he'd pushed me away and everything turned sour.

I kept quiet as he navigated the congestion around the campus.

"Do you still ride Simone's Vespa?"

My lips tipped up. "It's mine now, and yeah, I still ride it. Why?"

He pulled into a parking spot near my apartment building. "You need to stay off it for a while."

I aimed a closed lip smile at him. "Dad already made that clear." I grabbed my phone and wallet. "Thanks for the ride... again. You can come up for some coffee or something, but I don't want to keep you from anything."

He turned off the truck. "No worries, Lex. I'll walk you up."

As I led the way to the apartment, I realized some lucky woman would revel in Rafferty's steadfast over-protectiveness.

I put my key in the lock, and suddenly Rafferty moved in front of me. It happened so fast, I didn't even realize it until the door swung open.

"Who the fuck are you?" Rafferty demanded.

"That's Brantley," I said, peeking around Raff's shoulders before either of them started arguing.

Rafferty glanced over his shoulder at me. "Did you know he'd be here? Or that he had a key?"

"It's none of her business. Ines gave it to me," Brantley argued.

I pushed forward. "Cool it, Raff. I'm sure it's okay."

Brantley stared down at me. Once I pulled my key from the lock, he opened the door further.

Rafferty shot me a look, then pinned Brantley with his stare. "Her name's on the lease, yours isn't. It's absolutely her business."

I shook my head as I went inside. "Rafferty, forget about it. Are you here to get some things for Ines?" I asked, looking at Brantley.

"You can handle that," Brantley clipped out.

Rafferty shut the door, glaring at Brantley. "Say that again."

Brantley shrugged. "She's her roommate and she'll know what to pack better than I do. Only met Ines's parents once, and they didn't care much for me, so it works better if she does it."

I nodded to make my lie more believable. "That makes sense." I turned around to face Raff. "You said you wanted coffee. The Keurig should be ready to go if you want to make yourself a cup."

Rafferty stared at me for a moment, glared at Brantley for a beat, then shook his head. "I don't need any coffee, but I'm gonna hit the bathroom."

Once I heard the bathroom door close, I narrowed my eyes on Brantley. "I'll pack a bag for Ines, but aren't you going to see her?"

Him not going back to Georgia struck me strange because he'd been involved with Ines for over six months, and she'd told me how much she cared for him.

She usually had a thing for weight-lifters, but Brantley had the build of a long-distance runner. Thin, and a smidge over six feet tall; he was almost Rafferty's height. His dark eyes were almost hollow. He appeared to hide a lip curl before he spoke.

"No, you caused the accident, so you can take her 'some things.' Hell, I oughta sue you. My neck hurts like a mother."

His words felt like bullets aimed right at my chest - particularly since the police officer had shared that Porter said the same thing.

"I didn't have anything to do with the other driver hitting us, Brantley."

He put his hands on his narrow hips and leaned forward. "No, but *you're* the reason we stopped at that rest area - acting like Porter was attacking you or some shit. You're a goddamn tease, that's all. Wearing low cut shirts that are tight on your tits all the time. Self-centered, entitled bitches like you are the worst."

Anger roared through my body. "I'm not self-centered, entitled, or a tease."

Brantley narrowed his eyes on me. "You strung Porter along for months with the excuses. Hell, you wouldn't even go down on him. Typical tease."

Between the restless sleep and sheer anger coursing through me, I lost control of my mouth. "Not that it's your business, but I can't be a tease, when I'm a *virgin*, asshole."

The way his mouth dropped open, he believed me. That was little comfort since I hadn't shared that with anybody - not even Simone or Jasmine, my two closest friends.

While Brantley stood there staring at me, it registered too late that the bathroom door had opened during our argument.

"You got two seconds to leave the damned key and get the fuck out," Rafferty growled from behind me.

Brantley's gaze shifted to Rafferty. "I'll leave, but I'm keeping the key, asshole."

Rafferty stepped forward, but I put a hand on his forearm. "It's fine, Tee."

That earned me a fierce dose of side-eye. It was worth it since it gave Brantley time to hustle out of the apartment, and I didn't want to spend another minute around him.

The moment the knob clicked, Rafferty faced me and crossed his arms on his chest. "Woman, he can't have a key to your unit. There's no fuckin' telling what he might do."

I held up my hands. "Don't call me 'woman' since I know what that means in your world, and I'm *not* your woman. And just so you—"

My words were cut short when suddenly Rafferty grabbed my shoulders, guided me to the couch, and sat us both down. "Get this through your head, *woman*. You're as much mine as I am yours - it's been that way for years."

For a moment, I twisted my head to the side and stared up at the ceiling. "You've got to be kidding. *Now* you decide we're meant for each other or something? Even if I ignore what happened between us back in school, this will never work. I've got another two years of dental school, and you've got another eight or nine months of prospecting with the Riot."

Rafferty tilted his head back, closed his eyes, and took a deep breath. It gave me time to admire his thick dark hair, full beard, and the column of his throat leading to those strong, broad shoulders.

And the ink peeking out of the collar of his t-shirt.

Rafferty righted his head and leaned forward so an inch separated our noses. "Your locks have to be changed. Now that I've met him, I trust that asshole even less than you do."

He didn't address how we wouldn't work out, and I let that go, shooting him a coy smile. "Of course, I have to change the locks. Luckily, Dad insisted I keep a spare set of locks he had, so once I grab a screwdriver and get to work, I'm all set."

It wasn't until his hands slid up to my jaw that I realized Raff hadn't let go of my shoulders. Our eyes locked. As though his eyes had a direct line to my body, a tendril of warmth skated through my torso, slow and easy.

"God, I almost forgot how damn independent you are. Please tell me that you lied to him."

My brows drew together. "About what?"

His hold on my jaw loosened while his eyes gleamed with seriousness. "Alexandra. Did you lie to him just now?"

Understanding rolled through me which extinguished the earlier heat. I reared my head back, but his hold didn't falter. His expression shifted and I wanted to curl in on myself.

He wasn't supposed to know.

I despised that I'd slipped up and said anything, but I also hated that Brantley had been so horrible.

Some might say boys would be boys and they stuck together, but Brantley telling me that I was a tease was totally out of line. I had gone down on Porter, just not that often. Brantley didn't know anything about my relationship with Porter, so he had no way of knowing if I'd been a tease. Which highlighted why I should have kept myself in check, and *that* led to more self-loathing.

"You're a virgin," Rafferty whispered.

Why did him whispering affect me so much?

I tugged at his fingers resting along my jaw. He'd always been sneaky and somehow he kept me from pulling his hands away.

After a long blink, I exhaled, "Yes."

Finally, Rafferty's hands left my jaw, but he ran one along the top of my hair to cup the back of my head. "They both need a fucking ass-kicking."

I exhaled a chuckle. "How do you figure?"

He gave a short head shake. "I'd tell you to just trust me on this, but I know you won't. Porter's clearly a piece of shit since he let that jackass think you're a tease."

"What are you —"

He put his finger on my lips... and just like when he did it yesterday it gave me such a thrill that I wanted to nip at it. "If a man's friend says a woman's a tease... that man has obviously shared information with his friend."

I nodded and Rafferty's finger fell away.

Whew.

"Did Porter know?" he asked.

I swallowed down my shame. No use wallowing in my embarrassment. "It wasn't something I let anyone know. If Brantley hadn't made me so angry, I wouldn't have blurted it out."

He nodded. "Brantley's an even bigger asshole."

"Agreed."

"Is there a reason?" he asked.

"A reason he's an asshole?" I asked jokingly.

"Lex..." he murmured in a warning tone.

I wobbled my head. "Not really. The few guys who met Dad freaked out afterward."

Rafferty's eyebrows went up in acknowledgement as he gave a small nod. "I can see that."

"And for some stupid reason...the timing's been wrong with anyone else - assuming they kept my interest."

"Explains the cavalcade of boyfriends."

I spluttered. "A... caval..., did you just say 'cavalcade'? That's ridiculous!"

He shot me a shy smile. "Don't take offense. Porter was around for what? Five months? Maybe six. Who was the douchebag before that? Simone told me he made some ridiculous joke about you having lion hair? As I recall, you had five so-called boyfriends in the year and a half before you transferred to Gainesville. From what Cal said, none of them lasted more than three to four months with you. I'd call that a cavalcade even if I wasn't around for you to parade them in front of me."

"Dad can be scary."

He leaned closer. "Your dad isn't scary, Lex. You are."

I was scary? What was he thinking?

Chapter Six

You're Ruthless

Rafferty

She stared at me, looking gobsmacked. That expression shifted and I suspected she wanted to dismiss me out of hand, but those wheels were turning. I wanted to kiss her more than I ever had in my life.

Her brows lowered. "Then why aren't *you* scared?"

I grinned. "We grew up together. I know firsthand that you're all bark and little bite."

She turned her head away from me and muttered, "I should bite *you*."

"Have at it."

With her hair flying and wide eyes, she whipped her gaze back to mine. "You're trouble."

"The best kind though, Lex."

"I'm not scary," she muttered.

I laughed. "Right. Answer this: did you befriend that chick who cheated with Simone's ex-boyfriend? Just so you could find out which one of them made the first move?"

Her eyes slid to the side. "That doesn't matter. Simone's perfectly happy now."

She was trying to be funny, but I stuck to my guns. "Did you go out of your way to meet Tennyson?"

"Not *out* of my way," she muttered.

I raised my eyebrows at her. "Right. That's what makes you scary. What was it you once said to Jasmine? 'Lead with love, but master the throat punch?' You're ruthless and not only do you not take any shit, you won't let your friends take any shit either - not if you can help it."

She stood and wandered half-way down the hall to a small closet. "Speaking of not taking any shit, I've got a set of locks to switch out." She brought back an entry combo set and put it on the end table. "I don't want to keep you from anything, Raff."

I stood and grabbed the package from the end table. "I'm not leaving, Lex. It's great that you've got a set of locks at the ready, but after the vibe I picked up from him... I don't trust that asshole."

"He isn't coming back," she said, and just stopped herself from rolling her eyes at me.

"If you're right, then I'll eat those words, but at least you'll be around to make me do it. Because if you're wrong... then a new lock won't keep him from breaking in to hurt you."

She dipped her chin. "He cares about Ines, not me. Besides, hurting me would be a red flag to Ines."

That might be true, but I wasn't going to argue with her any longer. "Get the screwdriver and let's get this done."

I couldn't help but watch the sway of her ass as she went to the kitchen, opened a drawer, and plucked out a tool. As she came back to the living room, I cleared my throat and focused on the locks.

She drew even with me and tipped her head toward the door. "I appreciate you hanging around, but I can take care of this." She paused to shoot me a grin. "I'm not sure if you're aware, but my dad installs doors for a living."

I smiled. "Part of being a prospect means I work alongside your dad at least once a week, so yeah, I know about his business, and I can help you get this done faster."

She shook her head twice, went to the door, and began removing the screws.

I wasn't sure how I wanted to handle this. After her blow up with Brantley, I didn't want Lex to think I was suddenly interested in her because she still had her v-card. I also didn't want her to think I was coming on to her out of pity or worse, just to be her first. There was something instinctive, almost primal, inside me, though, that reveled in the notion that I would be her first - and possibly her only lover.

Unless she was still convinced the MC life wasn't for her, I would make it my mission to prove to her that I was the only man she needed.

"You gonna stand there staring at the locks all day, or you think you can bring me the doorknobs?" she asked.

"I'm coming, Robertson," I said, closing the distance between us in three strides.

I fitted the two pieces together after some jiggling and held them still. Alexandra scooted in close to tighten the screws. Her long dark hair brushed against my forearm.

"I didn't realize you had... you've almost got a full sleeve of tats on this arm."

"Yeah," I said, my voice husky.

Usually I could control myself around her.

She chuckled and stepped back. "That's cool, but will you even have room for the Riot MC tat?"

I twisted the knob to make sure it would hold, closed the door, and then I picked up the old locks. "There's room."

I needed to let her study. But I wanted to take her out to lunch.

"Are you okay?" she asked, moving in front of me.

"Yeah. I want you to think about something. Don't say anything now."

"Is this about Brantley?"

I took a deep breath. "No." She would likely think this had to do with him, but it didn't. "Yesterday... Lex, there was a moment I thought you were in ICU. I walked into that ER and you were being guided out..." I dragged a hand down my face. "The relief I felt was so damned overwhelming it was all I could do not to fall on my knees. Then you said you and Porter were done. I wanted to ask you to give me a shot right then, but it was the wrong time."

"Rafferty—"

I shook my head. "No, Lex. Just think about it. I'm gonna get out of your hair for a few hours so you can study."

She squinted one eye at me. "Why aren't you going back to Jacksonville?"

For a moment, I twisted my hands up. "For a couple reasons. One, I think Brantley will try to come back. Second, you'll think I'm selfish, but I wasn't joking yesterday. I've wanted to get in your pants for a long time, and after what happened earlier, I want to be your first."

Her eyes widened and she spluttered, "Tonight?"

I shook my head. "No, not if you aren't ready. But for now, you don't have a roommate to time shit around, worry about her overhearing us, or anything else - so just think about it, will you?"

She took in a deep breath. Then I noticed the deer-in-headlights look on her face. "All right. I'll think on it."

I nodded and stepped closer. "Good. It's been a few years for us, but do you mind if I kiss you before I leave?"

"You're not fooling around," she muttered under her breath.

I leaned toward her. "No, I *want* to be fooling around, but you need to study."

She grinned even as her warring thoughts played out on her beautiful face. "You're right. It's been a while. You can kiss me."

I didn't let myself think about it. I grabbed her left hand, pulled her to me, and put her hand on my back. I drove my right hand into her mass of thick dark waves, while I rested my left hand on her hip. She tipped her head up, those gorgeous hazel eyes full of curiosity. That curiosity told me we were on the same wavelength. We'd done this once before, but we were teenagers. So we both knew this would be different. And I couldn't wait to see how different it would be.

I lowered my lips to hers and groaned. This kiss felt like home and I didn't want to leave.

Her lips parted on a gasp. I swept my tongue inside. She tasted of orange cream lip balm with hints of the Kombucha she drank in my truck. Glimmers of our first kiss hit me as I recalled how timid we both had been.

Rather than letting one take from her, now, Alexandra was assertive and slid her tongue against mine until she could explore my mouth.

Instinctively, my hand at her hip slid around her waist, pulling her tight to my body.

Her free hand slid up along my beard and into the short hair along the side of my head. She must have risen up on tip-toes, because her lips pressed harder against mine and her breasts smashed against my chest.

Reluctantly, I broke the kiss and steadied my breathing. Her eyes stayed closed for a beat and when she opened them, it took her a moment to focus on me. "I didn't want to stop, Lex, but it would have gotten out of control fast if we didn't."

"Yeah," she whispered.

Her warm, lush body was still plastered to mine and her hand was still cupped around the side of my head. Then again, I hadn't moved my hands either.

"You think you can let me go, babe?"

Her eyes slid to the side and she lowered down on her feet. "Think that goes both ways, Raff. You've got a pretty strong grip on my waist right now."

That little bit of sass made me want to kiss her again, but I gave her hip a squeeze instead. "Smart-ass."

With her eyes locked on me, she stepped back. "I think what they say about bikes needs to be revised - even though it's true."

I wheezed out a laugh. "What are you talking about?"

She smirked. "That was just like riding a bike...but it was vastly different from back in high school."

Shoving my hands in my pockets, I chuckled. "Yeah, definitely a change. I'll be back at five-thirty with sushi unless you want something else."

She waved a hand in front of her stomach. "To-go sushi isn't ideal. A burrito would be better, thanks."

I traced the underside of her lower lip with my finger. "You got it, Robertson."

While I sat inside my idling truck, my cell rang before I could decide whether to call Cal, Blood, or Volt. The display showed my sister was on the line.

"Hey, Jasmine."

"Hey, Raff. Are you gonna be around for dinner tonight?"

"Not likely, why?"

"Mom's acting weird, and so is Dad."

That probably had to do with me, but I didn't want to tell Jasmine anything yet. For all I knew, Alexandra would stick to the idea that we had to go our separate ways because of her education or because I was prospecting. After that kiss, there was no way she'd mean a word of it, but I still didn't want to end up with egg on my face, especially not with my younger sister.

"Don't worry about it, Jazz. They act weird all the time. I'll be around tomorrow."

"I heard you picked up Alexandra. Is she all right?"

I clenched my teeth and forced myself not to think about the bruising on her face. "She was banged up, but she seemed much better on the drive back to her apartment this morning."

"Oh. I didn't know you drove her back."

"I did. Is there anything else? I gotta check in with the brothers, they don't give prospects a ton of free time," I semi-lied.

"No. If you talk to Alexandra before I do, tell her I'm glad she's okay."

"I'll do that, but you can text her."

"Yeah, I'll do that, too. Ride safe, Raff."

I ended the call and pulled up Cal's contact. Even if it earned me Blood's wrath since he was sponsoring me as a prospect, I owed it to Cal to talk to him first.

"Raff, everything okay?"

"It is now."

"What's that mean?" Cal asked, his tone steely.

I quickly told him about Brantley having a key to the apartment, but not being there to gather a bag for Ines.

"Then what the fuck was he there for?"

Shit.

"He never said, and frankly, I was more concerned that he give back the key and I forgot to ask."

"Did he give back the key?"

"No, so I helped Lex change the locks and the doorknob."

Cal scoffed. "She didn't need your help."

"Yeah, she mentioned that, too." I sighed. "I hate that I didn't tell you about my plan yesterday or this morning, but I've asked Alexandra to give me a shot."

The line went silent. Tension built along my shoulders.

"Cal? Are you there?"

He sighed. "Yeah. Not exactly surprised... Mallory saw you napping in Alexandra's bed."

I hesitated for a beat. "Sorry about that, she had a nightmare. Um, do we have problems?"

Cal kept quiet for another lengthy moment. "If you hurt her, I'm going to kick your ass until you wish you didn't have an ass for me to kick."

I fought a grin. "Understood. I don't have any intention of hurting her."

"Are you going to report in tomorrow morning?"

"That's another thing, though I don't know if I have to talk to Blood, but my gut says Brantley isn't done in that apartment. It sounds crazy, but Lex mentioned him making her uncomfortable before the accident. He damn sure makes *me* uncomfortable, now that I've met him. I want to stay here until midnight at least to be sure she's safe."

"You're damn lucky that I like you."

"Yes, sir," I muttered.

Cal went on as though he hadn't heard me. "Because I know that's an excuse to stick close to her and I don't want to think about what else you want to do to her."

He was right and wrong. I wanted to be close to her, but I wasn't about to force anything on her.

"That isn't likely, sir—"

"Don't start that 'sir' bullshit, and don't lie to me."

I paused.

"I'm not lying. Before I told her what I wanted, she made it clear she thought the timing was wrong and me being a prospect in Jacksonville wasn't great either."

"You don't agree?"

"It may not be great, but she's worth dealing with bad timing and long distance - though the distance isn't that long."

"He comes back, you call the cops. Got it?"

"Absolutely. Will this be a problem?"

"Not right now. I might change my mind later."

"I'll call Blood—"

"No, I'll let him know. Be sure to get your ass back to the clubhouse by four tomorrow afternoon."

I put my phone in the cupholder and reversed out of the parking lot. If Lex decided to take a chance on me, then I had a number of errands I needed to run because I fully intended to show her how good we could be together.

CHAPTER SEVEN

WORTH EVERYTHING

ALEXANDRA

I STRUGGLED TO CONCENTRATE on my microbiology notes. The moment Rafferty asked to kiss me, I knew it would dominate my thoughts for the rest of the afternoon...but did I refrain?

No.

Would I do it all over again?

Definitely.

Hands down that had to be the best kiss ever. It was leaps and bounds different from when we were teenagers.

Thank heavens, he ended it though. My hormones had taken over my brain and I was more than ready to blow off my test and hand Rafferty my v-card.

My phone chimed with a text from Jasmine.

> **In case my brother doesn't tell you, I'm glad you're okay. Sorry I didn't text sooner, I didn't hear about it until this morning.**

I was dying to call her, but considering this involved her brother, there was no way I could talk to Jasmine about my nerves. Rather than call her, I sent her a quick text to say thank you.

Next, I pulled up my text thread with Simone.

> **Do you have a minute to talk?**

Simone called me five minutes later. "What's up, Lex?"

I didn't know how to beat around the bush about things, so I spit it out. "Rafferty asked me to give him a shot."

Simone took a moment. "Okay, you're gonna have to back up because not that long ago - you know like Bike Week, back in March - the Atlantic Ocean wouldn't put enough distance between you two."

I sighed. Then I ran down everything that had happened from the accident, to Rafferty being the one to take me home, both of us learning we were available, to the nightmare I had.

"I imagine a crash like that was traumatic, but I get the feeling there's more to this."

My lips twisted to the side. "Porter made unwanted advances on me in the backseat. I resisted, he got aggressive, and after I insisted on it, Ines pulled into a rest area. Not long after we got back on the road the accident happened, and Brantley blamed me for it to my face today."

"What a shithead," Simone hissed.

A hint of a smile tugged at my lips. "Yeah, so anyway, should I go there with Rafferty?"

She laughed. "Do you even have to ask?"

"Well... yeah. I mean, if we mess this up, what then? It'll be too much to see him around with—"

"And there you go."

"What do you mean?" I asked.

"If you *don't* take the risk, it'll still be painful to see him at the clubhouse or around your dad. Hell, it'll probably be worse, because you'll never *know* what could have been. So, if you two are down with long distance, then yeah, you should give him his shot."

I took a deep breath. "Promise not to judge me?"

Her tone became affronted. "Honey, I would never."

"So, Brantley was here, Rafferty went to the bathroom, and Brantley said a bunch of nasty shit which made me angry and I blurted out that I'm a virgin."

"Okay," she drawled.

"I thought you wouldn't judge."

"I'm not judging, I just don't see how this ties in."

I nodded. "Sorry. Rafferty heard me, he says this isn't about my virginity, but he wants to be my first."

Simone made a low 'aww' sound. "I'm gonna have to brush my teeth after this, you two are too sweet!"

I couldn't hold back a short growl. "This isn't funny, Mony."

"I know. I'm sorry... but you gotta do what your heart tells you here. You care about him - that hasn't changed, no matter what either of you say. The first time sucks, but the way Rafferty is about you - there's no way he won't do everything he can to take care of you and make it more bearable."

Her words about 'the way Raffery is about me' were puzzling, but I wouldn't let myself contemplate that any further.

"Yeah," I whispered.

"Not to gloat or give you an earworm, but... it's about damn time."

"Oh, my God, stop it!" I said with a laugh.

"Nope. This makes my day."

I shook my head. "Please don't tell anyone about my status."

"Never - you know that."

I heard the cry of her baby, Felicity. "I'll let you go, you're a great friend and you've been a huge help, Simone. I miss you and can't wait to see your little girl again!"

"It was no problem, and I'll be back in Jacksonville in a few weeks...but you'll probably still be in Gainesville."

"I'll do my best to make it up there. Take care," I said, and ended the call.

With my phone in hand, I pulled up the contact for Ines's Mom. It went straight to voicemail. I left a message asking how Ines was doing, and asked her to text or call me when she had time.

My backpack sat next to an armchair in the living room. I unzipped it to grab my laptop and headed back to the kitchen table where my notes were. The conversation with Simone had helped me more than I'd thought it would, since I was able to focus on my studies.

A knock sounded at the door and I glanced up at the microwave, surprised to see three hours had passed. Rafferty had mentioned bringing back food, so it was too early for it to be him, but maybe he'd changed his mind.

I opened the doorbell app on my phone, saw footage of someone dropping off a package and leaving. Normally I would wait to grab the package, but the delivery reminded me of Friday evening when Ines told me she'd ordered her favorite perfume that was on sale and she didn't want it sitting out in the sun.

I opened the door. As I straightened from grabbing the box, Porter moved in front of me from the right (which was out of range for the doorbell camera), as though he'd been waiting against the wall.

"Don't freak out. I'm here to apologize," he said, stepping forward.

I held up the box. "Stop right there, Porter."

"Lexi, it's almost ninety degrees out here. I got limited time since I'm on my lunch break."

I wanted to tell him to stop calling me Lexi, but I shook my head instead. "No, you aren't coming inside. You apologized. Now leave."

"You don't even know what I'm sorry for."

I set the box on a nearby endtable. "It doesn't matter, Porter. You told the cops that I was responsible for the accident. That's going entirely too far."

His head tilted just a touch. "That's not what I said. Let me inside."

I shook my head and pushed the door to close it.

"Typical stubborn bitch move. You should have listened, Lexi," he said, then rushed toward me, grabbing my biceps and kicking the door closed behind him once he was inside.

I lunged backward, which freed my arms. My hope was that he'd move into the living room. If he did that, I could bolt out the door and run down the breezeway to the manager's unit.

Unfortunately, Porter trudged closer to me and I had to switch my plan.

A naïve part of me thought he just wanted to say sorry, but every instinctive alarm bell was going off in my head.

"Brantley tells me you're a virgin." He shook his head at himself. "How is that even possible? Your daddy's a biker. I can't imagine nobody's gone there with a hot piece of ass like you."

"Get out," I said, my tone steely as hell.

He chuckled. "Sweetie, you haven't even heard me out. I had to wait an hour for your 'friend' to leave."

"How do you know that?"

He smirked. "I have my ways."

I had slowly backed my way to the kitchen.

Rafferty's dad had told me I needed a gun - now I wished I had listened. The small of my back hit the kitchen counter.

Dad had taught me that if I found myself in a bad situation, I'd likely only have one shot to fight back. Everything had happened so fast, I wasn't sure what I could do to fight Porter.   Then it hit me. If there was anything I'd learned from the Riot Ol' Ladies, it was how to be dramatic.

I raised my voice loud enough so that the next door neighbors might hear me. "Get away from me, now! Stop!"

Confusion swam in his eyes. "What are you doing, Lexi?"

My gaze caught on the empty cake stand tucked away in the corner of the opposite counter. It reminded me of Ines and her marble rolling pin. When we first moved in together, she'd told me it was a weapon. I'd told her a rolling pin wouldn't mean shit to an intruder. Then she'd made me hold it.

"That's five pounds of dense weight I can wield at a motherfucker. Cave his head in, bust his lip, I don't give a fuck."

I'd never thought *I* would need to use it to save myself.

"I asked you a question," Porter said, cutting into my thoughts.

"I told you to leave," I shouted, as calmly as one could shout.

Advancing on me, he shook his head. "Hear me out. Please."

I edged left along the counter toward the area where Ines kept her rolling pin.

"Get out, Porter," I repeated.

He stopped advancing - *finally!*

"I never meant to tell the cop that you had anything to do with the crash."

I gripped the edge of the counter and leaned back. "Intention doesn't change what you did. Hell, Brantley said similar shit, it's almost like you two planned to accuse me."

He shook his head. "No, plenty of people would conclude that if we hadn't stopped we wouldn't have been in the wrong place at the wrong time."

Arguing about this wasn't worth it, even if stopping the car was the only way to stop Porter from being so damn handsy.

What had I ever seen in him?

"If that's why you're here, you can go now."

A sly expression entered his eyes as he gave a slow shake of his head. "Alexandra - now that I know your story, I want a second chance."

"No," I stated emphatically. "Now leave."

"I'll be gentle," he said.

Ines kept her rolling pin on a free-standing holder on the counter. Porter edged forward, I casually reached backward and grabbed the handle. I raised the kitchen tool between us.

"Get the fuck out, Porter."

His eyes darted to the pin and back to me. Then he laughed.

"A rolling pin, Lexi? What do you think you can do with that?"

I hefted it to the side for more momentum, swung, and caught Porter on the shoulder. He cried out in pain and grabbed his shoulder. Then suddenly he wasn't in front of me, and I realized Rafferty had grabbed him and slammed him against the opposite wall. He held him there with a hand to Porter's throat.

Porter's eyes burned with outrage, then shifted to retaliation. He threw a fist at Rafferty's stomach, but Rafferty twisted his hips, dodging the attempt.

"Let me go," Porter bit out.

Rafferty's lips curled into a sinister grin. "That's funny. You want me to let you go. Stop... touching you... like Lex asked you to stop touching her yesterday."

For a split-second, Porter's eyes darted to me. "Not the same thing."

"How many times did she tell you to stop? She never said when I asked. Had to be more than once."

Porter grabbed Rafferty's wrist. "Fuck you."

"No, Porter. You got a lesson to learn. Any woman says 'stop'—" Rafferty pulled him forward, then shoved him back against the wall, hard. "You *stop,* the first fuckin' time."

Porter seethed at Rafferty. "Why the fuck do you care? Or are you gagging to be her first?"

Oh my God!

Mortification consumed me. I forced it aside, set the rolling pin on the counter, and sidled up to Rafferty. "Let him go. He isn't worth it."

Rafferty's mahogany brown eyes glared at me. "No - but you're worth everything to me, and making sure this fuck-up doesn't treat another woman the same way is doing the right thing."

I felt a sweeping sensation in my belly at those words.

Porter let go of Rafferty's wrist and threw an uppercut at Rafferty's jaw.

Rafferty dodged that one, too. Obviously, he'd learned some new techniques.

"Step back, Lex," Rafferty said.

I took a step back and Rafferty let go of Porter with his right hand. Then he landed a vicious blow to Porter's ribs.

Porter let out a gush of air.

Rafferty moved closer and put his forearm to Porter's throat. "Hard to breathe yet, Porter?"

I bit my lip as I noticed my ex-boyfriend's complexion turning more and more pink. Porter narrowed his eyes at Rafferty.

"You gonna touch another woman after she tells you to stop? Just nod if we're clear?"

With his eyes still narrowed, Porter nodded.

"Good. Get the fuck out of here. Lex told you twice - that I heard - probably more. I won't hesitate to kick your ass if you stick around."

Rafferty dropped his arm and moved back so Porter couldn't see me.

After the door closed, Rafferty crossed the room and locked the door. He turned around, giving me a hard stare. "He ever shows up again, don't open the door to him."

I crossed my arms on my chest. "I didn't open the door to him, Raff. He didn't even knock. From the doorbell camera footage, Ines got a box delivered and I went to grab it. Then he appeared in the doorway, so he must have been lying in wait for that."

Raff narrowed his eyes at me. "He was just hanging out waiting for you to get a delivery?"

Then it hit me.

"No, he works part-time delivering packages. He routinely ran a route that included this complex. I'm speculating about this, but he probably had the ability to find out if me or Ines were getting an order. Hell, I'd have let the box sit on the doorstep until dinner if Ines hadn't made such a big deal on Friday morning about ordering perfume. You probably don't know this, but leaving a bottle of that stuff out in the heat ruins the fragrance."

Raff's lips set into a thin line, which brought my attention to his beard. He hadn't shaved at my parents' house, so his facial hair was much fuller. I wasn't sure if it was because he looked older with the beard or if it was the way his face set in anger, but it gave him a 'don't-fuck-with-me' vibe that I found irresistible.

"You have a final tomorrow, is that the only one?" he asked.

I shook my head. "I have one tomorrow, and two on Thursday."

He turned up his hand, swinging it out between us in question. "What about Wednesday?"

I shrugged. "I'll be studying, unless I need to assist one of the professors with something."

His brows drew together. "You're assisting professors?"

A tiny smile flitted across my face. "At this point, I'm doing whatever any professor asks of me, Raff. In a year or so, I'm gonna need help getting an internship and not long after that, I'll probably need references to land an actual job, so if a professor says jump, I ask how high?"

He stared at me for a long moment. "You're so driven, Lex."

I pressed my lips together. "So are you."

He looked past me and his eyes fixated on something. "A goddamn rolling pin. Ought to take a fuckin' rolling pin to his dick and flatten it out."

My eyes widened just before I laughed.

His head whipped toward me. On a scoff that might have held a trace of humor he demanded, "What the hell are you laughing at?"

"The visual you just painted. That's extreme."

He stalked closer to me. "If I hadn't shown up when I did, do you really think he'd have stopped? He laughed at you holding the rolling pin. Sure, you hit him with it, but you didn't aim for his temple."

My head reared back. "I didn't want to kill him."

His brows arched and he dipped his chin. "Then maybe *you* didn't listen to my mom when she gave us that talk. She's vicious as fuck, and she'd have told you to aim for the head. *Especially* with the way he snuck in here on you."

I didn't see the point in rehashing things. "Why did you ask about my schedule?"

He ran a hand through his hair. "I don't have to be anywhere until tomorrow afternoon. Beyond that, I'll have to reschedule some shit so I can get back here."

"Why would you need to come back?" I asked.

Seemed that wasn't the thing to ask, based on the anger suffusing Rafferty's features.

He took a deep breath and his body relaxed. "I asked you to think about giving me a chance. Also told you I'd bring you dinner, but something made me come back here sooner." His eyes shifted to the rolling pin on the counter behind me. "Thank God I did."

"Yes, I'm grateful that you did. Seriously. I'm not sure how to thank you for that."

"I wasn't finished. If you decide to give us a shot, then the last thing I want to do is spend the night only to leave tomorrow and not get back here until the weekend - if I'm lucky."

I dropped my head for a moment as I pressed my lips together. The idea of spending the night with Rafferty thrilled me. "As much as I hate to admit this, I need you to go back until the weekend because I won't get much done if you're around."

He grabbed my hand and pulled me closer. "Bullshit, Lex. You're the most disciplined person I've ever met. If you need to study, you'll tune out everything to make that happen. Are we gonna see where this goes with us?"

I bit my lip, took a deep breath, rested my hands on his broad chest, and decided to take the plunge. "Yeah, but I don't think you realize, I'm busy as fuck most of the time. Finals are pretty much the only time life slows down, and even then... that's so I can cram."

He wrapped an arm around my waist. "If we're both set to make this work, it will work, Robertson. Besides, the brothers are gonna run me ragged since I'm not gonna get my patch for another seven months at least—"

"You don't know that. It could happen sooner since you're a legacy."

He lowered his chin. "Yeah, but no matter how cool your Dad was with me on the phone about us—"

My eyes widened. "What? How—? Why does Dad know?"

"Seriously? He would lose his mind if I didn't tell him before we really started seeing each other."

I shrugged. "He loses his mind no matter who I date."

He gave a single nod. "Yeah, so I'm heading that off at the pass, but the other brothers...like Blood or Volt, or Razor are gonna give me a whole new ration of shit when they find out."

I tipped my head to the side and tried to hold back my smile at him mentioning the other brothers - especially Uncle Razor, since for some reason he had a soft spot for me. "I'll tell Razor to go easy on you."

His eyes widened. "Don't do that. Christ. That's a sure-fire way to get them to send me to Memphis."

That brought me back to reality. "I thought you were moving."

His lips tipped up. "And I thought *you* were in a serious relationship. That changes things, Lex."

I nodded slowly. "But you weren't moving because of me, were you?"

He wobbled his head. "You had a little something to do with it. Do you need to study more, or can I take you out to dinner?"

"We could DoorDash."

His fingers slid under my t-shirt at the small of my back. "No, we can do that some other time. If we order in, I'm not gonna be able to take my hands off you, and my gut says we need to get to know one another again."

I mulled that over. "You're right... and you're wrong. We may have kept our distance, Raff, but I think we both know plenty about each other. But, I'll do this your way." An idea hit me and I beamed up at him. "You suggested sushi? I'll take you to one of the best places in town."

He turned his head a touch. "Same place where Simone got sick last year?"

I shot him a cynical frown. "Simone got morning sickness, even though she didn't know she was pregnant yet. Get your story straight, sir."

He chuckled. "They got any food that's actually cooked?"

I tipped my head back and cried, "Oh my God, you really have been talking to Dad!"

The sound of his laughter was music to my ears, but it didn't last long before he put his lips to my throat and kissed a path to my jaw. Heat flooded my body and I righted my head. Before I could say anything else, Rafferty's lips found mine and he kissed me.

God, he could kiss.

I slid my hands up his chest to his shoulders and up along his neck. One hand went around to the back of his head and fisted his hair. On a groan, he pushed forward and arched me slightly over his arm.

I attempted to give as good as I got, but Rafferty had total control over this kiss. Seemed all he wanted me to do was hold on and enjoy the ride, which I did until he ended it.

His lips were a millimeter away from mine. "You're sure you want sushi?"

I swept my thumb along his throat. "I'm sure I want DoorDash is more like it."

He chuckled and straightened up taking me with him. "Nope. That's just a taste of what we're gonna do later. Put your shoes on while I put away the shit I bought at the store."

"What'd you buy at the store?" I asked, moving to the living room.

"Odds and ends," he muttered.

I glanced over my shoulder at him. "That sounds almost ominous."

"Hurry up, I'm hungry."

Chapter Eight

Riling You Up

Rafferty

The waitress set an appetizer sampler plater in the middle of the table, took our dinner orders, and hurried off toward the kitchen.

Alexandra sat across from me, sipping a French martini. She set it precisely on the round coaster in front of her, then glanced up at me. "Why did you ask me earlier if they had cooked food, if you were just going to order the rainbow roll?"

"Why do you think?" I asked, picking up my Stella Artois.

She gave a short head shake. "You just wanted to rile me up."

I grinned. "Riling you up is one of my favorite things to do."

"I've never understood that."

I sipped the beer, debating sharing this with her. "I'm pretty sure you do. Riling you up forced you to tip your head back... and how else was I going to get you to offer up that gorgeous neck of yours?"

Using a pair of chopsticks, she put a coconut shrimp and a crab rangoon on her plate. "Well, that explains today, but not all the other times you ever did it."

I loaded my plate with a spring roll and a chicken satay. "If you have finals this week, how long is your break before the next semester?"

She swallowed some food. "A week, but I'm scheduled to work at a pediatric dentist office in town...so I'm not entirely free to come back to Jacksonville. Best case, I'll have a four-day weekend before I start classes again, because this office doesn't offer Friday appointments."

I nodded. "Have you worked at the pediatric dentist office before?"

"Yeah. I've been shadowing Dr. Culverson off and on for the last nine months. Working there sealed my decision to specialize in that area."

The chicken satay had enough spice, it made my sinuses tingle. I swallowed it down and made a mental note to check out where this dentist's office was located before I left town tomorrow.

"What are you thinking about over there? I can practically see your diabolical wheels turning," Alexandra said.

"You're gonna tell me I'm going overboard, but the way your ex behaved at the apartment - I wouldn't put it past him to approach you coming out of a dentist's office at the end of the day."

She lifted her martini. "It's May, so the sun doesn't set until almost eight o'clock these days, Raff. He wouldn't do anything to me in the parking lot." She sipped her drink, then muttered, "I wouldn't let him."

"Don't get cocky, Lex. It's not like you've got a holster for that rolling pin."

She chuckled. "Very funny, smart guy."

"I'm serious. I don't know who's the bigger threat to you, him or Brantley."

"How about, neither," she suggested.

I stared at her. "Do you really believe that?"

Her lips pushed out in a small pout. She shrugged a shoulder. "I don't know. I'd meant to check Ines's room before you came back. It seems strange that Brantley had a key, went inside, but didn't leave with anything. You were so concerned with him having a key that I never got a chance to ask. I mean, what's that about?"

I twisted my head to the side just an inch. "Yeah. I wish I'd have asked him that, too, since Cal asked me the same thing."

Her expression fell. "You told him about Brantley, too?"

I faced her. "There was no reason not to, Lex. The more he knows, the better."

The way she pressed her lips together and lowered her brows, I had a hard time not telling her how cute she was, but I also understood her not wanting Cal to know. My sister, Jasmine, hated how much Dad demanded to know about her life, but it was all out of love.

"You're right, but I still don't like it."

Our server delivered our entrées to the table, interrupting us. I only ate sushi around Lex, Simone, or Gabriella which amounted to maybe three times a year tops. Somehow I always forgot how most sushi places gussied up the plates with flowers... whether or not they were edible, I had no clue. But I had a new appreciation for it as I watched Alexandra's face light up at her plate in front of her. It wasn't the food that made her face brighten, it was the tiny vase with a small, purple flower inside it.

Words my dad said to me years ago rushed back to me. 'Life is all about the little things, Raff. Always. Never forget that, because when you find the woman you want by your side, it'll be all those little things which matter to *her*, that will prove you matter, too.'

Alexandra's hazel eyes locked with mine. "Don't you love their presentation?"

I sipped my beer. "I love that you love it so much."

"Another round?" our server asked.

"Not for me. If she's having another, bring her a glass of water as well, please," I said.

Lex shot me a questioning look, then turned to our server. "I'll have a Thai iced tea, please."

After we dug into our food, Lex stared at me for a long moment. "Is there a reason you essentially didn't want me to have another martini?"

I swallowed a bite of rainbow roll. "We're going to take this at your pace, but I won't go there with you if you're drunk. I've never had that kind of martini, so I don't know how strong or weak it is, but I know I want you relatively sober later... in case things progress."

She turned her head to the side and laughed. "Progress. I'll never think of that word the same way again."

I reached across the table and grabbed her hand. "Lex. There's no pressure here. I'm trying to take care of you."

She closed her eyes, dipped her chin, and exhaled. When she met my gaze again, she was smiling. "Simone said you'd do that."

Turnabout was fair play most of the time, but I shot her some side-eye. "You told Simone?"

"Better than your sister, wouldn't you say?"

That made my stomach lurch. "Yeah. Jesus, we have too many mutuals, Lex."

She squeezed my hand. "You don't believe that."

"You're right. All of us being so tight-knit hasn't been a problem before—"

She shook her head. "It isn't now, either. It just feels different because we're changing things."

Reflexively, I asked, "Are we, though?"

Our server came back with Alexandra's iced tea, and we let go of each other's hand.

Alexandra picked up her chopsticks. "I don't want to sabotage anything right out of the gate, but it's something that worries me. What happens if we don't work out?"

That was a no-brainer.

"I move."

Her brows furrowed. "That's extreme."

"I said you had a little something to do with my willingness to move... but, it pretty much all had to do with you."

"That's crazy, Tee."

I shook my head. "Everywhere I go, there are reminders of you. Even when I was helping Steel and the Devil Lancers rebuild their clubhouse.

It's on the northside - a part of town that has nothing to do with you - and those assholes came back with shakes from the Dreamette."

She shot me a dry look. "And that sent you over the edge?"

I chuckled. "No, but it never stopped. I'd tell them to hit a place I knew you didn't like, which just reminded me of how strong your opinions are. I can't be in that town and not think of you... and it's fuckin' torture."

"That almost sounds obsessive."

"It feels that way, and I figure the only way out... is out. So, yeah, if for some fucked-up reason this doesn't work with us, I'll move."

Her gaze shifted to her plate, where she was swirling her chopsticks in a circular pattern. "That makes me sad."

I downed the rest of my beer and set the glass at the end of the table. "Alexandra, we're borrowing trouble here for no good reason."

Her hazel eyes met mine and the alarm there made me brace. "There is good reason, Raff. I care too much about you to mess this up."

I twisted my hand up on the table. "And there you go. We agree about that. We're more mature now... you more than me, I'm sure, but seeing as neither of us wants to fuck this up, then we aren't going to fuck it up. Seriously, we're worrying about something that hasn't happened yet, and if I have anything to say about it, it isn't going to happen."

"You can't predict the future."

"Yeah, I *can*. Cal said he'd kick my ass until I wished I didn't have an ass for him to kick if I hurt you. I have to imagine the other brothers will pile right on if I did something shitty to you."

She rolled her eyes. "Dad is so extra about me."

I leaned forward. "He should be."

A softness stole over her expression.

I smiled. "Are you done eating?"

She pointed her chopsticks at me. "You don't understand how much I love sushi, Raff. I don't leave anything behind."

Over an hour later, we arrived back at Alexandra's apartment complex. I'd talked her into taking me on a tour of the campus after we were done eating. It wasn't my first time in Gainesville, but I had two ulterior motives for taking such a long walk. It gave me an idea of where she would be most days, and it gave us both time to work off our nerves.

My instincts said Porter wouldn't try anything on campus with Lex. I'd forgotten how many students attended school year-round. It was cool to hear her talk about the classes she took in each of the different buildings.

I held her hand as we climbed the stairs to her floor. When we hit the last step, I paused.

"What's wrong?" she asked.

I looked at her and whispered, "Your door is open. Get your phone out, call 911."

She let go of my hand to grab her phone.

I nudged the door open with the toe of my boot.

"What are you doing, Raff?" she hissed.

"Call 911, babe."

She wandered to the other end of the breezeway. I peeked inside. The lights were off, but from the dim light shining into the unit, I saw papers were strewn everywhere.

Alexandra trudged back to me. "An officer is on the way."

I ran a hand through my hair. "Do you have a phone number for Brantley?"

She shook her head. "No. Why would he come back?"

"Why was he here unannounced earlier?"

"I'll try Ines's parents. Maybe her mom has a number for Brantley."

A police car pulled into the lot, parked, and a male officer came upstairs. "I'm Officer Hatcher. Have either of you been inside?"

I shook my head. "No. We found it open when we got back from dinner."

The officer entered the unit, leaving the door wide open behind him. I saw him wander into the kitchen, and then back to the living room and down the hall toward the bedrooms.

A sinking feeling filled my gut. Something was wrong. I fired off a quick text to Cal, Blood, and Volt, since a group chat with them was at the top of my text threads. I also put my phone on silent so it wouldn't interrupt anything.

The officer stood outside one of the bedrooms, and spoke into his shoulder walkie-talkie. He eyed me and Alexandra and that sinking feeling turned outright sour. I'd left my prospect cut in the truck, but it still felt like the cop was judging us.

I leaned toward Alexandra and lowered my voice. "Be careful when he asks questions; we might need a lawyer."

Concern shot through her eyes, then realization quickly replaced it.

She grabbed my hand. "Should have DoorDashed after all."

I heaved a silent chuckle. "Don't make me laugh right now, Robertson."

"Can't help it, Rolland," she said, nudging my bicep with her shoulder.

I'd missed this... missed *her*.

Officer Hatcher came to the front door. "Do you live here?" he asked me.

Alexandra moved forward half a step. "No, I do."

"May I see your I.D.?"

She pulled out her driver's license. The officer took a hard look at it and nodded. "You haven't been inside at all?"

Alexandra shook her head. "No."

The officer nodded. "Come see if anything has been taken. Is your roommate on her way here?"

Alexandra's lips twisted to the side. "She's in a hospital in Georgia. We were in a car accident Sunday morning, she's in ICU."

The officer nodded, and the flash of red and blue lights hitting the windows caught my attention. Through the blinds, I noticed another patrol car in the parking lot.

Alexandra hurried to her bedroom. I heard her rummaging through her drawers while Officer Hatcher spoke into his walkie-talkie again.

A moment later another officer came up holding a small kit. "Am I good to dust the door?"

Officer Hatcher nodded. "Yes, Officer Ramierez."

Alexandra wandered back into the room. "None of my jewelry is gone - do you want me to check the master bedroom, too?"

"Would you know if something is missing there?" Officer Hatcher asked.

Alexandra thought about it. "Not really."

"If she finds property was stolen, call me to report it," he said, handing her a business card. "You're a student?"

Alexandra nodded. "Dental program."

Officer Hatcher made a note of that. "This appears to be random—"

"Her ex-boyfriend was here earlier and wouldn't leave when she repeatedly asked him to. For that matter, her roommate's boyfriend was here this morning. She didn't know he had a key. He wouldn't give up the key, and we changed the locks because of that."

Officer Hatcher aimed a skeptical look at me. "Why do you suspect they would have done this?"

"I don't know, other than Porter being pissed that she wants nothing to do with him."

Officer Ramierez straightened from the front door. "Can you pull up your doorbell camera footage?"

Alexandra grabbed her phone and opened up the app. The screen was black. She rewound to after we left. Then fast-forwarded until someone's hand came up and the screen went dark. Officer Hatcher approached the doorbell and removed a lengthy piece of black electrical tape.

"Was anyone threatening you or Ms. Tallow?"

Alexandra shook her head. "Not that I know of. I can call her mom… I would assume Ines would tell her that sort of thing."

Officer Ramierez sidled up to Officer Hatcher. "Appears the door was wiped clean."

He nodded and looked at us. "I'll contact the two men who were here earlier today. Have your building management change your locks again. Don't hesitate to call if you find anything missing."

After the officers left, Alexandra muttered, "This sucks."

"Yeah."

"Should we hit Home Depot? They don't close for another hour."

I shook my head. "I'll do that in the morning."

She twisted her lips to the side. "Does this have something to do with the odds and ends you put away earlier?"

"No, I just want us to stay put for right now."

"Okay," she drawled. "Do you mind if I go through Ines's room? I may not know if something's missing, but I hate the idea of leaving it all ransacked. I'd ask you to help, but that feels wrong."

"That's cool. I'll pick up the papers and straighten your bedroom unless that's a problem."

She grinned. "That would be a big help. Thanks."

Fifteen minutes later, my phone dinged with a text from Cal asking for an update. I hated sending long texts, so I called him instead and quickly ran down what happened with Officer Hatcher.

"You really don't think it's random?" Cal asked.

"No. I mentioned that Alexandra's ex-boyfriend showed up and scared the shit out of her just before we went to dinner. Hatcher is going to question Porter and Brantley… not that I expect that to go well. Those two connived behind Ines and Lex's back before the concert. If either of them did this shit, I'm sure they got their shit together."

"That Porter asshole scared her?" Cal asked.

I grimaced for a beat. "Yeah. I got here just in time, and really let him know to leave her the fuck alone."

"I don't like the sound of this shit," Cal muttered.

"Yeah, but I'm not leaving her alone until tomorrow afternoon when I'm supposed to be—"

"No, you stay there until I tell you otherwise. I'll let Volt and Blood know what's going on. This isn't Riot business, but with two assholes messing with her, I want to know someone's watching out for her."

"Understood. I'll keep you posted."

After I'd straightened her room, I settled on the couch and turned on the television. Two minutes later, Alexandra came out to the living room. "I don't think Ines is missing anything from her room. Even her spare cash is there."

I nodded once. "Was it out in the open?"

She shook her head. "No, but that's beside the point. Both of our laptops are here... they're very portable, you'd think they'd take one of those at least."

I leaned forward. "That's why I pegged Brantley for this. He was here earlier. We probably interrupted—" I stopped myself. "Hey, can you pull the footage of when Brantley got here earlier? It would be great to know how long he was alone in here."

"That's a good idea," she said, grabbing her phone.

She found the spot where we arrived this morning. Then she went back another ten minutes, letting it play. After a minute of watching nothing happen, she shot me a questioning glance.

"Be patient, Lex."

Finally, Brantley appeared on the screen. He turned his head left and right, rang the bell, waited, and then pulled a set of picks from the pocket of his cargo shorts.

"Sonuvabitch," I whispered.

"What?" Alexandra asked.

"He doesn't have a key. Those are picks."

"How did I miss that? No wonder he wouldn't give up the key - he didn't have one!"

I tapped the screen to pause the footage. "Can you download that and send it to Officer Hatcher?"

She nodded.

My lips quirked in a half-grin. "Cool. Let it play some more."

We watched for almost two minutes before we saw ourselves arrive at the door.

"You don't have that set to play back at a faster speed, right?" I asked.

She shook her head. "No."

"He picked the lock this morning, it stands to reason he could have done it this evening."

Her head tilted to the side. "You're right, but why wouldn't he have covered the camera the first time?"

I shrugged a shoulder. "That early in the morning, he probably didn't think he would get caught and or he didn't intend to fuck things up. Hell, it might have been a test run."

She nodded. "I guess I can see that, but do we really expect the cops to do—"

"He broke in, Lex. At a minimum you should press charges for that."

Her eyes widened. "I know, but won't *we* be able to do more without the cops involved?"

"We?" I asked.

"Yeah."

"By 'we' do you actually mean the Riot?"

"Well..."

"You haven't wanted—"

"Rafferty, he was in my home and I don't get retribution?"

I put my hands on my hips. "He's not worth losing your place at school - and he's already got a grudge against you."

She shook her head. "What's he gonna do, Raff? I didn't cause that accident. The only way I lose my standing in the dental program is if I get arrested - and I'm the victim here."

"You're right, but he could still try to turn this around on you. I want to protect you from that, because he seems slippery as fuck."

"This is a lousy time for you to make sense. I want revenge."

I grinned. "And you think you aren't scary?"

She crossed her arms under her tits. "Vengeful isn't scary."

I laughed. "Not to a man like me. To those other losers you dated, you're scary as fuck."

She dropped her arms and took her phone to the charger. "Guess there's no point in changing the locks if he's just going to pick them."

I nodded. "I'm still gonna change them in the morning. You wanna veg on the sofa? I picked up mochi for dessert."

Her eyes lit up. "You did?"

"Yep. And you got a choice of champagne or ice wine."

"Ice wine - are you serious? That stuff's expensive."

I shrugged. "Feels like a special occasion. It's not every day we both get our heads out of our ass."

"You did not just say that."

I shoved my hands into my pockets. "Where's the lie, woman?"

Her eyes narrowed a touch. "You better take the mochi out. I like it a little soft so it doesn't hurt my teeth."

Chapter Nine

Taking Chances

Alexandra

THE BREAK-IN ASIDE, THIS had been a fantastic evening. Rafferty was right. We needed to get to know each other again - yet I felt so comfortable with him it was like getting my best friend back. I felt a warmth and relaxation I hadn't felt with anyone, ever.

The stress of straightening Ines's room wore on me earlier, and I'd been thinking it was too bad I didn't have any kind of ice cream in the freezer.

Leave it to Rafferty to remember my favorite dessert.

Then it hit me what his other motivation might have been for it.

No. No. He'd always been thoughtful and sweet.

'Any man biding his time to get in your pants is far from sweet.'

Gah!

Why couldn't I get those words out of my head?

"Your mochi needs five minutes at least, so which will it be, champagne or—"

"Champagne," I said.

Rafferty took the bottle out of the fridge while giving me a probing look. "Cool. Any reason in particular? If you think I can take that other bottle back for a refund, think again."

I wandered into the kitchen and grabbed two coupe glasses Grandma gave me when I moved out of Mom and Dad's house.

Once I set both glasses on the counter, I caught Rafferty's gaze. "I think you're right - that this is a special occasion. *Not* that either of us had our heads up our—"

He put his finger to my lips. "How many times did you high-tail it out of a room when I got there?"

This time, I gave into temptation and nipped at the pad of his index finger. "How many times did you ignore my presence in a room?"

"One hundred and forty-three," he said, taking his finger back and peeling the foil from the champagne bottle.

"What?" I almost yelled.

He smirked. "Give or take a few."

I laughed. "You are..."

"Just like you, Lex. Stubborn, loyal, and dependable."

"Here, I was thinking you're incorrigible. And stop listening to your mom about your Taurus astrology sign."

He chuckled. "*Our* astrology sign, since our birthdays are three days apart."

The pop of the champagne cork derailed any retort I had. "I love that sound," I muttered.

He poured into each glass. "Yeah, it's a good sound."

An awkward feeling threatened to overtake me, and with anyone else, it might have. Since this was Rafferty, I willed myself to ignore the awkwardness.

He handed me a glass and put his to his lips.

"Whoa. We aren't going to toast?"

He held his glass aloft. "To extracting our heads from our asses."

"Rafferty!" I cried.

He dipped his chin. "I'm a biker, Lex. Champagne toasts are for weddings and not much else. Unless you got a toast, I say we drink up."

I gave him my driest smile. "To taking chances... after all these years."

His smirk reappeared. "Always so eloquent." He touched his glass to mine. "To taking chances."

We sipped our drinks for a moment, then I wandered to the counter where he'd placed the mochi. I hadn't seen the box, and once I did, I whirled to face Rafferty. "S'mores? I didn't even know they made such a flavor!"

He kept his glass in front of his lips. "I didn't either, but I know you love s'mores, and I figured I couldn't go wrong. And if that doesn't work out, there's still strawberry in the freezer."

Words were on the tip of my tongue, but I had to hold them back. Telling him, 'Oh my God, I love you,' held a little extra punch at this point.

We ate our mochi bites, and I successfully kept myself from moaning. Once I knew where he found the S'mores flavor, I was going to that store and buying all the boxes. Budget schmudget and calories be damned.

"What are we watching tonight?" Rafferty asked.

"Something short. I have to be out the door by seven-fifty tomorrow morning."

His eyes darted to the time displayed on the oven. "It's not even eight-thirty, Lex. How many hours of sleep do you need?"

Maybe I'd misread him... dealing with a home invasion had a way of killing the mood.

"I'm getting up at six-thirty, so I can take a quick shower and cram a little more before heading out the door, which means I need to go to bed at eleven."

He downed the last of his champagne, set his glass on the counter, and closed the distance between us. "You have a TV in your bedroom. Are we vegging out there or on the couch?"

"My room," I murmured.

He nodded once. "More champagne or are you good?"

"Champagne is no good when it's flat, then it's just wine."

"Go cue up a show. I'll bring your glass."

Butterflies swarmed in my belly when I entered my room. Standing next to my bed, I took my shoes off. Then I realized I wasn't sure where the remote was. Rafferty had put my clothes back in the drawers, and stacked my books next to my desk and nightstand. Unlike at my parents' house, he hadn't made my bed. I moved to the other side of the room, thinking perhaps the remote had been tossed under the bed.

"What are you looking for?" Rafferty asked, putting two glasses on the night stand.

"The remote."

He lifted his chin. "Sorry, I put that under your pillow. I'd meant to put it on the nightstand and forgot when I got a call from Cal."

I put a knee on the bed and climbed in, grabbing the remote from beneath a pillow. "You told him about the break-in, too, I take it."

Rafferty sat on the edge of the bed and tugged off his boots. "Yep."

I turned on the television, navigated to Netflix, and froze.

"What are you thinking about, Alexandra?" Rafferty asked, settling next to me with his back to the headboard.

I glanced at him. "This is like... God, I'm such a stereotype."

"You lost me."

I cocked a brow at him. "Netflix... and chill?"

He closed his eyes and exhaled. Then he slouched in the bed, reached out and pulled me toward him. I went with the flow and stretched out alongside him.

"You're not a stereotype. Pull up YouTube instead and cue up a bunch of music videos. I don't fuckin' care. I'm going at your pace, and something makes me think you want to hold off for—"

The last thing I wanted was to hold off. Rather than let him finish his sentence, I let go of the remote, leaned up, and kissed him. His hands skated down my torso to my hips, and he lifted me on top of him. I spread my legs so I straddled him. He moved his hands from my hips to my ass. I loved feeling his fingers spread wide there. A variety of sensations coursed through my body, from sheer excitement, to heat in my breasts, to wetness in my pussy that did nothing to soothe the deep ache I felt there as well.

Rafferty pulled at my ass, which ground me against his erection. He broke the kiss and stared up at me. "Are you sure you're ready, Lex? I don't want you to do this because you feel rushed or obligated or—"

I moved my hips against him. "I'm very sure, Raff. It's gonna hurt, but as I understand it—"

He cut me off with a quick kiss. "Gonna do everything I can to make sure it doesn't hurt that bad, baby."

His words sent a chill racing down my body. Still, I smiled at him. "That's good to know."

"Do you want music playing? Or do you just want to make out some more?"

I lowered my lips to his.

"Both," I murmured just before I kissed him.

He chuckled, rolled us over, and grabbed the remote before he broke away from my kiss. "Time to see if your taste in music has changed," he muttered, and twisted at the waist so he could bring up one of my music playlists on YouTube.

The opening notes of "Sailor Song" filled the room. Rafferty tossed the remote on the other side of my queen bed, then he stole my attention when he pulled his t-shirt over his head.

I'd gone out of my way to ignore his bare chest yesterday, but now... I took in the entirety of his ink and muscles. "Great gracious, you're a walking work of art."

His eyes glittered. "For you."

My head tilted on the pillow. "What?"

"The majority of this ink is for you."

I blinked for a moment and shook my head. "That doesn't make sense."

A huge capital 'A' sat over his heart. He grabbed my hand and put it over the tattoo. "You wanted the story behind just one of my tattoos. That one's for you."

"No, Raff. That's a college football logo."

He dipped his chin, seriousness filling his eyes. "Look closer, woman. You've seen my dad's tat since it's on his bicep and he rarely wears sleeves. It's not the same."

I pulled my hand free of his hold, and traced the lines. He was right. It *was* different...but to an untrained eye, he could pass it off as a bad take on a popular logo.

My gaze met his. "But why?"

"You're the one who stole my heart a long fucking time ago."

This was getting way too deep... and venturing into superstitious territory for me.

As though he could read my thoughts, Rafferty said, "And Blake told me not to do it. Even said you'd be the first to point out it's bad luck."

"You did it anyway."

His brows shot up. "Yeah. Like I said, you're as much mine as I am yours."

"You're not allowed to be this sweet to me."

A sly grin curled his lips. "Trust me, I'm going to be anything but sweet in a few minutes. You gonna let me take your shirt off?"

I nodded, wishing I'd worn a fancier bra.

He leaned up so he stood on his knees, pulling me up to a sitting position. Then he sat on his calves and his eyes watched his hands lift the hem of my t-shirt. I lifted my arms and he pulled my shirt off.

His eyes roved from my face along my torso and back up to my eyes. "You are so fucking gorgeous, Alexandra."

I lifted my hands and had them half way to my bra clasp when Rafferty shook his head. "What? I thought I'd help you out."

He grabbed my hands and guided them to his shoulders. "No way, Lex. I'm taking your bra off. Can't fuckin' tell you how often I've thought about this very moment."

My chin dipped with my bashful look.

His hands went to my back and in seconds he unclasped my bra. "I'm serious, Robertson."

"Should we dim the lights? I wouldn't want to disappoint you."

"Nothing about you would ever disappoint me. You have to know that."

My hands dropped from his shoulders when he slid my bra off and tossed it aside. "So fuckin' perfect."

Before I could say anything, he leaned forward brushing his lips against mine. I fell to my back. He kept kissing me while he settled his weight on me. Feeling his warm chest against mine made me even wetter.

I moved my hands from his shoulders down his chest, under his arms, and past his rib cage in order to trace my fingers along his muscular back.

He slid a hand up to my breast. A tingle shot to my nipple as he methodically stroked his thumb there. My back arched and I broke the kiss.

"Oh God," I whispered.

With a dark chuckle, he kissed along my jaw, lightly engaged his teeth, dragging them down my neck. His tongue darted out when he hit the top of my chest and he went straight to my breast, and drew my other nipple into his mouth.

I was a virgin, but I'd made out with other boyfriends plenty. Enough to know that Rafferty had skills other men simply didn't have. The way he dragged my beaded nipple between his teeth made my hips buck and my legs squirm.

"Oh, yeah," he muttered.

In seconds, he had my shorts unbuttoned and his hands delved into my panties.

He paused and stared into my eyes. "Are you good with me taking your shorts off?"

"Yes," I half-moaned, half-whispered. "But you take your jeans off, too."

He shifted to the other side of me, and dragged my shorts and panties off at the same time.

I kicked them to the side. The sight of Rafferty undoing his belt held me captive.

He had a thin line of hair leading down his well-defined abdomen. As he lowered his jeans and boxer briefs, the line of hair became thicker. His cock bobbed free of his underwear and I licked my lips.

"Don't tease me, Lex," he said in a strained voice.

"I'm not, Tee."

He took a condom out of his wallet, dropped the condom on the bed, and then tossed his jeans on the floor. "You are because I'm gonna worship your body for a good long while before I let you have your way with me."

Those words heightened my excitement and anticipation.

Rafferty gave his cock a quick tug, leaned forward, and nudged my legs apart. He crawled between my legs and kissed my thigh. He kissed a path from my thigh to my pelvic bone. With his free hand, he used three fingers to stroke up and down my pussy. Heat surged through my body and the ache in my core throbbed.

"Rafferty," I whined.

"Love the way you say my name, woman. You sound so needy."

"Oh, my God, keep doing that," I cried when he stopped stroking me.

"You're soaked for me."

I tilted my hips, trying to brush my pussy against his fingers.

"Baby, patience."

I growled. "I've been fucking patient for years, Raff. I want you to—"

"You want me to what? Not gonna fuck you just yet. Let's see how ready you are."

He pushed a finger inside me.

"Oh," I sighed.

He began to pull away, and I squeezed against his finger.

"You like that?" he asked.

"Of course I do."

He hummed for a beat. "Gotta get you loose so I don't hurt you, Lex."

I tipped my head back on the pillow and touched my breast.

"Let go of that tit. It's mine now."

Oh shit. What was happening to me?

Growing up around the Riot MC, I bristled at hearing men get all alpha with their women. That possessive bossy tone from Rafferty, though? I fucking *loved* it. Hell, I wanted to poke the bear to get more of it. So, I grabbed my other breast, and shot him a devilish grin.

His lips set in a thin line. "It's like that, huh?"

He shifted to his belly, and then he dragged his tongue through my folds.

I inhaled sharply. My hands flew to his head.

"That's what I thought," he murmured against me.

"What?" I cried, loosening my hold.

"Don't you dare let go, Alexandra. I'm gonna drive you wild, which means I want your hands in my hair."

I couldn't wait to find out how he'd drive me wild. However...

"That's great, but I seriously want you."

His lips tipped up and his gaze softened on me. "Love that you want that, but if you knew how damn good you tasted, you'd understand why I have to make you come on my tongue."

With wide eyes, I stared at him.

"What's with the big eyes, woman?"

I gave my head a quick shake. "I've never heard you talk dirty before, and..."

"And what?"

How much to share? I loved it. He was better at it than any other man I'd ever dated?

"I'm a little surprised how much it turns me on."

He kissed the inside of my thigh. "Good. You tell me if you need me to stop, okay?"

As talented as he was... that wasn't happening.

"Okay," I fibbed.

He smirked as though he knew I was fibbing.

Then he put his mouth on me again, and it was divine.

No, beyond divine.

He wasn't just enthusiastic, he was intense. Driven. Reflexively, I tightened my grip on his hair, and he lapped at me faster. His hands gripped my ass tight, holding me to him.

I felt an overwhelming sensation building. Just as I thought I would come, he backed off and one of his hands left my ass.

I whimpered in protest, until that hand wandered up my body and he massaged my breast. He stared up my torso, focused on his hand at my breast. His thumb stroked over my nipple repeatedly. Then just when I thought I couldn't take any more, he sucked at my clit at the same time as he pinched and rolled my beaded nipple.

My hips bucked, I moaned, and realized I was riding his face. His hand still on my ass, tightened, and the zing of pain from that pressure built my impending orgasm even higher.

"Oh God, Raff. Don't stop, please."

I dug my heels into the bed and ground myself on Rafferty's face. The scrape of his beard added to the rioting sensations moving through me. I didn't want this to end, but I knew it would... and it would happen very soon.

He shifted up a little, and suddenly drove two fingers inside me. I gasped and felt my inner walls convulse against his fingers. Tiny dots floated along the periphery of my vision and my orgasm came over me.

I had no idea if a few seconds went by or a few minutes. To my surprise, Rafferty continued to lap at me. I moved my leg. He dragged his hand from my breast down to my thigh.

"What are you doing?" I asked.

He paused. "What's it look like?"

"I'm pretty sure you did the job... and did it quite well."

He chuckled. "Maybe I'm looking to be an overachiever."

With his tongue, he teased my clit.

"Rafferty," I drawled.

"Damn, I could get used to that," he said, grinning.

"Get used to what?" I whispered.

"The way you beg by just saying my name."

I shook my head. "C'mon. Quit teasing me."

He snatched up the condom, rose on his knees, and I watched him carefully sheath himself. "You better pay attention, Lex. The next time you're gonna do this."

"Is that so?"

He lowered his body to mine, his brown eyes probing. "Yeah. Are you ready?"

"Yes, Rafferty."

He kissed my jaw near my ear. "Are you sure?" he whispered.

"More than sure."

He reached down, dragged his cock through my wetness, lined himself up, and stayed still.

"Rafferty. What are you waiting for?"

"I don't want to hurt you, Lex. But—"

"It's going to hurt, I know. That's why I'm more than ready. I can handle the pain... and from what I understand, after this time, it won't be so bad."

"Right," he whispered.

Before I could respond, he kissed me. This kiss was so gentle, it was unlike anything else. He slid a hand into my hair and kept kissing me. I shifted my hips to give him a hint. His hips pressed in and I felt his cock drive an inch inside me. He pulled back and broke the kiss.

"Why are you—"

"It's killing me too, but slow is the best way to go, Lex. That way it shouldn't hurt so bad."

He moved forward again, this time going further.

"I can take it, Raff."

After a moment, he pushed forward again and I realized my mistake. I thought I'd taken a good look at his cock earlier, but I hadn't noticed how much girth he had.

"You're so fucking tight," he bit out.

He pulled back again and I exhaled.

His hand grasped my thigh, and he pulled my leg up. When he pushed in again, the angle was different, and his presence stretched me in ways no toy ever could.

"Oh God," I whispered.

"Almost there, babe," he whispered and pushed even further.

Even though it stung, I loved being with him like this. I loved that he was my first.

He moved again. "There, that's all of me."

"Right," I breathed.

"Are you good if I move?"

I nodded. "Yeah."

He moved in and out twice, his eyes intent on me, then he paused. "Hate to say this, but this is gonna be quick."

I pressed my lips together, fighting my snarky comment that quick would be good. Instead, I blurted, "Why?"

He gave me a sheepish grin. "Pretty sure your pussy is the tightest I've ever felt, and I'm liable to lose control here."

"Okay."

He planted his hands in the bed, and leaned up. His hips thrust slow and steady. I matched his rhythm until he picked up the pace and I wrapped my legs around him and held on for the ride.

As fast as things went, I sensed he'd held back in an effort to not hurt me. Once he finished, he gently lowered his body onto mine. The sound of our labored breathing filled the room. He grabbed my hand and kissed the side of my neck.

I ran my free hand down the ridges of his back.

He leaned up. "Not gonna ask if that was good for you because I'm pretty sure it wasn't."

I smiled. "You're right, but at the same time, it was better than I expected because you're incredibly thoughtful."

He slowly shook his head. "Not really. But, I gotta take care of the condom. I've never come that hard before, and I don't want this thing leaking."

"Yeah, I'm not ready to be a mom."

He gently withdrew and I watched him wander toward the door.

Wow.

I knew he filled out a pair of jeans, but the sight of him naked in my room was better than I *ever* imagined.

He came back to the bedroom, one-hundred-percent comfortable being naked in front of me. "Are you on birth control?"

I nodded once. "Yep."

In a fluid movement, he laid down beside me and slid his arm under my neck and tugged me closer. "You are?"

I rolled toward him. "Yes. Bad periods. We'll leave it at that."

With a slow nod, he gave my shoulders a squeeze. "Forgot about that. Does it help?"

"Immensely."

"Good."

"Stargazing" by Myles Smith started playing and we were silent for half the song.

Almost hesitantly, Rafferty said, "I have a physical in a couple weeks. I get tested, we can skip the condoms after the results come back clean."

"Okay," I murmured, not expecting him to bring that up.

"Honey, you'll probably like it better that way. I sure as hell will."

I could have slapped myself for being so slow on the uptake. "I see. That makes sense."

The song ended, and Rafferty hit the pause button, even though I hadn't seen him grab the remote. "Do you need to study some more? Is it time for you to go to sleep?"

My alarm clock sat on my dresser across the room, and I saw it was a little after nine. "No. I'll review my notes in the morning. We can put on whatever you want to watch."

"Music's good."

An awkward feeling bloomed in my chest.

Rafferty traced his finger along my jaw. "You're getting up in your head."

I put my hand on his defined chest as my lips tipped up. "Just a little."

"Don't," he said, running his fingers down my arm and putting his hand over mine at his chest. "Anyone else, I wouldn't be this honest because it'd be too soon, but if tonight weren't your first time, I'd be balls-deep in you again."

I didn't exactly squirm, more like I shifted against him. "What?"

"I'm saying when the soreness wears off, Lex, I want to fuck you in the many ways I've imagined over the years."

That sent a ripple of heat through my belly. "'Over the years'?"

"Yes, years. Don't act surprised."

"This isn't surprise, I'm flattered."

He slid his hand up my belly to my breast. "Yeah, well, I've spent more than my fair share of time imagining your tits. The real thing is far better."

I grinned. "I'm glad."

His eyelids lowered a touch. "Wanna fool around?"

"I don't want to be a tease."

I found myself flat on my back when he rolled into me. "Fuck that noise, Lex. You aren't a tease and never were. I just want to make out with you, and I'll stop when it gets to be too much."

"That sounds like a plan."

CHAPTER TEN

HERE UNTIL FURTHER NOTICE

RAFFERTY

THREE DAYS AGO, I never thought I'd wake up next to Alexandra. The satisfaction it gave me almost scared me, because I'd never felt like this. Like starting every day next to Alexandra was where I was meant to be.

Dim sunlight came through her blinds. I watched Alexandra sleeping. Her beauty stopped me every time I saw her, but her relaxed features, unguarded in her sleep... it stole my breath and made me wonder why she bothered to put up with me. She was so gorgeous, she could have anyone she wanted.

She rolled over and her hand landed on my bicep.

Her eyes opened wide and she gasped. "Oh crap! What time is it? I'm running late. Did my alarm go off?"

I held her hand to my arm to keep her from bolting from the bed. "Your alarm hasn't gone off yet. I woke up because of the sunlight."

"Oh," she said.

"Yeah. You aren't freaking out for any other reason are you?"

Her brows drew together. "No."

"Then do your thing and turn off your alarm."

She nodded and swung her legs to the side of the bed and sat on the edge. I didn't miss her sudden inhale.

"You sore?" I asked, feeling like a dumbass. *Of course* she was sore. I'd meant to tell her to take a bath after we were done last night, but I also didn't want her getting caught up in her thoughts.

"Yeah." She glanced over her shoulder at me. "Maybe I'm an idiot, but I figured it would go away by now."

I sat up. "Tomorrow you should be good."

Her head reared back. "Well, at least I should be able to... last longer this weekend."

I sat up, shifted her hair to one side, and kissed her bare shoulder. "Thought I told you, but I'm here until further notice."

"You are?"

"Yeah, at least until this break-in shit is resolved."

She twisted and leaned toward me. This new position made me appreciate her skimpy, fire-engine red pajama set for a new reason. Red was sure as hell her color, but the top didn't hug her figure and it gave me enough of a peek at her side-boob that my dick took notice.

"What are you talking about?" she asked.

I forced myself to focus on her hazel eyes, and I ran down my conversation with Cal.

She tipped her head back. "I swear it seems like I have less privacy here than I did back in Jacksonville."

I wrapped my arms around her, fell to my back, and pulled her on top of me. "This is for your safety, Alexandra. He loves you and wants to protect you."

A contrite expression stole over her face. "I know that. It isn't his concern that bothers me, it's the fact you had to tell him. Obviously, I should have called him, and I would have, but we—"

"Yeah, I'm not gonna make you go through that shit. Got news for you, Lex. I'm protective too, and I don't give a damn if that bothers you."

She bit her lower lip. "Can you let me tell him the next time something shitty happens?"

"No."

Surprise filled her eyes. "What do you mean, 'No'?"

"Exactly that. I tell Cal when something shitty happens to you this week, and it protects you. Keeps you from having to answer a bunch of questions and relive it. You want to talk to him about what happened, have at it... *after* you take your finals."

She tilted her head back again, and spoke to the ceiling. "Oh, my God, you're bossy!"

She had no idea how bossy I could be.

But her semi-outraged display turned me on, and with her tits in my face, I couldn't fight the urge. I pulled down her low-cut pajama top to expose one of her breasts and I sucked a nipple into my mouth.

"Oh shit," she moaned, her hands grabbing my neck. "Rafferty... I, we can't."

No, we really couldn't, but that wasn't going to stop me from having some fun. I kept at her tit and my free hand slid down to her sleep shorts and inside her panties.

"Raff! Seriously, we— Oh God, that feels good," she said when my finger circled her clit.

Her pussy was wet and getting wetter the more I played with her. I let go of her tit and kissed my way up her chest, her neck, along her jaw, and took her lips.

She kissed me back and I rolled us over. I had to stop soon or this was going to go too far, but tomorrow couldn't get here soon enough.

Her face twisted and she sighed... or maybe it was a quiet moan.

"Want me to make you come, baby?"

"Raff... I—"

Her alarm went off. More like, her radio went off at maximum volume. The college radio station news report was on, and that killed the mood.

"Shit," I muttered, and gently slid my hand away from her pussy.

She hurried to the alarm and turned it off. For a moment, I did some deep breathing to get my dick under control. Then I turned so I could sit with my back to the headboard.

Alexandra stood in front of her dresser holding some clothes in the crook of her left arm. She pointed her right finger at me. "You have to go back to Jax, Raff. I'm all frazzled now."

I grinned. "You come back to bed, and I'll unfrazzle you."

She tossed her free hand up in the air. "And then I won't have time to get to my notes."

"Baby, it'll be fine. Try me."

"You're evil."

I laughed. "Nah. I save evil for people who deserve it. I'll give you exactly what you need so you aren't distracted by how horny you are."

She mulled it over for all of four seconds. "Hurry up, Rafferty. I never knew this about myself, but being this wound-up makes me cranky."

"This will be fun," I muttered.

———

We stood at the front door, kissing. Alexandra's fingers skated out of my hair and down to my shoulders. I expected her to break the kiss, but she didn't. In fact, she went up on her toes and gave everything right back to me.

My blood rushed south, and I fought against pressing her up against the front door. I pulled back from her kiss and watched her eyes slowly open.

She gave me a shy smile. "Sorry. I got carried away."

"You never have to apologize for that, but we're cutting it close. You want me to give you a ride to class?"

She shook her head. "No, we'll end up making out in your truck or while standing next to your bike. This class is closer than my others, so I'm good to walk."

"You're sure?"

"Very," she said with a nod.

"All right. I'll see you when you get back."

Her brows furrowed. "What are you going to do while I'm gone?"

I smiled. "Gonna chat with your building manager. Then I'm hitting Home Depot. I may not switch out your locks again, but I want you to have another set just in case. After that...maybe I'll hit a grocery store so I can make you dinner."

She twisted her lips to the side. "I'm pretty sure there's a lie in there. That or else you've left something out. If you're going to be running that many errands though, let me give you my key so you can lock up."

She twisted her key off the ring and handed it to me.

I nodded. "Thanks. Not to rush you, but it's seven-fifty-one, Lex. You better get moving."

She gave me a quick peck on the lips. "Behave yourself. See you around noon."

Once the door closed, I grabbed our coffee cups off the breakfast bar and rinsed them in the sink. Lex had my number. I had left something out earlier, which was a lie by omission, but since I wasn't sure how to find Brantley, it might not have been a lie at all.

I planned to rummage through Ines's room to see if I could find anything that might point me toward Brantley's address. It was one helluva long shot, but it seemed like the only shot I had.

My phone rang, and I picked up from the counter, seeing Blood's name on display.

"Hey, Blood."

"Prospect. Cal says he wants you with Alexandra for a few days."

"Yes, sir."

"Did anything of hers get stolen in this break-in?"

"Not that she can tell. Her roommate isn't here, but she didn't think anything was taken from her room either."

"Right. When is she coming back to Jacksonville?"

I sighed. "This weekend, maybe. She wasn't planning on it at all... until yesterday."

From the shift in Blood's tone of voice, I could practically see the sinister smile on his face. "Yeah... I'm guessing that has something to do with you finally making your intentions clear with her."

"I don't know what you mean by 'finally,' but yeah, I have something to do with that."

"You fuck with her, Cal won't get a chance to teach you a lesson, because I'll kill you."

I took a deep breath, realizing why Lex found it overbearing when the brothers got so protective of her. "Yeah. If I do her wrong, I'll deserve that."

"Did you teach that asshole ex-boyfriend a lesson?"

My head wobbled as I thought about it. "I think so. He strikes me as the type who might have to learn the hard way... but he definitely understands that I'm not gonna take any shit from him."

"Good. You need bail money, be sure to call me, not Cal."

I nodded, a smile threatening. "Got it."

"Keep us posted. I may send another brother down there."

I had to bite back my knee-jerk reaction of asking him why. The brothers hated it when a prospect questioned them... to the point they did their damnedest to force a question out of us.

"If you insist," I muttered.

"Is there a problem?"

"No," I lied. I didn't need one of the brothers coming down here. That would be too much, and it would freak out Alexandra.

"Good. I hate going to Gainesville, but if it appears that you need help, we'll ride out."

We said our goodbyes, and I found Alexandra's charger. It was compatible with my phone, so I plugged it in to charge, and went to shower.

I had just rinsed the shampoo out of my hair when I thought I heard a noise through the spray pelting down on me. Then Alexandra's dense bar of fancy soap fell off the shower caddy and hit the top of my foot.

"Sonuvabitch," I hissed, picking up the sudsy brick.

The shower curtain whipped to the side and I straightened.

"Hey, baby..." Porter muttered, then stopped, realizing I wasn't Alexandra.

I clenched a fist around the bar of soap and punched him in the face.

He yelled and put his hands to his nose. Dripping wet, I dropped the soap in the tub, stepped out of the shower, and rushed him out of the small bathroom.

I shoved him against the wall in the hallway. "What the fuck are you doing here?"

"Get off me, you sick fuck," Porter yelled.

I had four inches and at least fifty pounds on this asshole. He hadn't learned how to defend himself any better since yesterday, so I put my forearm to his throat again. "How the fuck did you get in here?"

"Unlocked," he rasped out.

I narrowed an eye at him. Then I recalled that Alexandra gave me her key. She couldn't lock the door behind her, and I hadn't done it either since Blood called right after she left.

Shit.

Still... his willingness to just come inside didn't mean he *wasn't* the person who broke in last night.

"You just wander inside whenever the fuck you feel like it unannounced? You didn't even ring the doorbell."

"Knocked," he croaked when I let off his throat enough for him to speak.

My lips curled. "Why in the fuck would you knock when she's got a fuckin' Ring camera?"

"In case she was sleeping," he rasped.

None of this shit made sense. My gut said Porter was lying. I ran my tongue along my lower lip and realized I could use his help. "Where does Brantley live?"

I let up on his throat a little so he could answer. "I'm not telling you that?"

I exhaled through my nose. "You got two fuckin' choices, asshole. I call the cops and turn your ass over to them for trespassing at best and breaking and entering at worst—"

"I didn't break in!" he cried.

I replaced my forearm hold with my free hand at his throat. "You weren't invited inside, numbnuts. Seeing as we had a cop here last night because of a break-in, I'm sure they'll want to talk to you."

"I already answered their questions."

"Doesn't explain why you'd barge in here uninvited. Hell, maybe you decided to be a copycat. I don't give a shit. Your other choice is to tell me where to find Brantley."

"How should I know where he lives?"

I tightened my grip on his throat. "Don't lie, Porter. From what Lex tells me, you were at his place Sunday morning to ambush her."

"Ambush? I didn't do anything like that."

"Pick your poison. Cops or Brantley?"

His thin lips spread into a smile that made him look like a weasel. "Third option, I leave. You can't stop me, you're naked for God's sake."

I stepped closer to him and punched him in the stomach. "There's no fuckin' shame in my game. You leave, I'll come after you. So which is it? Cops or Brantley?"

"Brantley," he wheezed. I let go of his throat, and he took in a big gulp of air. "He's across campus from here at the complex behind Vicious Vinyl. Unit one-oh-two."

That helped, but I figured I had to have Porter with me. Without him there, Brantley would ignore me outright. Not to mention, Porter could just as easily be blowing smoke about the address.

"You're going with me. You gonna try to run while I get dressed, or do I need to knock your ass out first?"

Anger glittered in his blue eyes. "I could charge you with assault."

"You broke in while I was in the shower, moron. I'm standing my ground."

He went silent for a beat. "Whatever. I'll stay."

I kept the bathroom door open in case Porter went back on his word, turned off the shower, and put my clothes on. When I came out of the bathroom, I saw Porter hadn't moved from the wall. Maybe I had scared him after all.

I darted into Alexandra's room, grabbed my boots, went to the living room, and sat on the arm of the couch to tug them on.

Porter raised a brow. "You don't waste time."

"This needs to be taken care of."

His expression shifted. "I meant with Lexi. Your boots are in her room, you obviously didn't sleep on the couch."

I straightened from the couch. "Last night, someone ransacked the whole place, dipshit. Not a chance I was going to leave her side after that."

"So now you care."

I should have let it go because we didn't have time for this, but I couldn't help myself. "What are you talking about?"

"You broke her heart. Tossed her away without a second thought. Strange that you suddenly care now."

Part of me thought he was lying, and yet... That would explain her distance over the past five years. It was water under the bridge now. A little voice in the back of my head said I had to talk to her about it anyway.

There was a gleam in Porter's eyes that gave me a hint he was goading me - wanting to know what was going on with me and Lex. I wouldn't give into his bait.

"Let's get this done."

I followed Porter along the sidewalk to a first-floor corner unit at a small apartment complex that looked like it was built over thirty years ago.

Surprisingly, there wasn't a peephole on the door, so I didn't bother to hide when Porter knocked.

The door opened and Brantley took a look at Porter, only to ask, "What the fuck do you want? It's not even ten yet."

Brantley looked like he'd just woke up. I figured I had the element of surprise on my side and I went inside the unit. Luckily, Porter followed me.

"What the fuck? Who are—" He trailed off and glared at Porter. "Why the fuck did you bring this dickhead?"

Porter opened his mouth to answer, but I beat him to it. "He didn't have a choice, since he broke into Alexandra's apartment."

"That was you?" Brantley asked.

Porter shook his head. "I didn't break in; the door was unlocked this morning."

Brantley's hair was cropped close around the sides of his head, but he had enough hair on top of his head that he'd put it in a ponytail. He continued to hold the door open. "Get out."

"Did the cops talk to you last night?" I asked.

"That's none of your business. Get out."

I had a theory that Brantley had bigger problems than being accused of breaking and entering. Bluffing wasn't typically my strong suit, but neither of these dipshits knew that.

"The drugs you left at the apartment are gone."

Porter's head reared back and his eyes filled with surprise.

Except for the smallest jerk of his head, Brantley appeared unfazed. But he'd twitched just enough that I knew I'd caught him off-guard.

"I don't know what you're talking about."

"Did you come back for the drugs, or did your source break in for it?"

"I'm calling the cops," Porter said.

"Do that," Brantley said.

I hadn't moved fully into the room, and only a foot and a half separated me from Porter. He had his phone in his right hand and his finger poised to dial with his left.

I swung a stiff arm down on his forearms. He dropped his phone.

Brantley charged toward me. I expected as much, and used a sweeping kick to knock his legs out from under him.

Porter lunged for his cell. I pulled him back by his shirt collar and shoved him to a nearby couch.

Quickly, I shut the front door and locked it. From behind me, Brantley swung an arm around my neck, attempting to put me in a headlock. Years of self defense came back to me. I bent forward, turned us around, and flipped him over my back and onto the floor.

Porter stared at me in wide-eyed confusion - like he didn't know if he should be in awe of me or just couldn't believe what he saw.

I rested my hands on my hips. "I'll take on both of you if I have to, but I'm not leaving until I get answers."

During Porter's hesitancy, I picked up his cell and put it in my back pocket.

Brantley leaned up on his elbows, glaring at Porter. "Fuck, man. Get him!" he wheezed, trying to get his breath back.

Porter stepped forward and bounced side-to-side on his feet like a boxer.

What did Lex ever see in him?

He noticed I was distracted and sucker-punched me in the mouth.

"Shit! That hurt," he hissed, waving his hand and stretching out his fingers.

"Idiot," I muttered, landing a solid right hook at the side of his head.

He staggered and fell back on the couch.

"You killed him!" Brantley shouted.

I felt my lip swelling. I bent over, gripped Brantley's small ponytail and yanked him up from the floor. He yelled, which made me wonder if his neighbors were going to call the cops.

I shoved him up against the wall. "What the fuck did you hide in the apartment?"

"Fuck you."

I stared at him. "No, you're the one who's fucked here. If the cops don't get you, your supplier will."

His brown eyes widened, and I swore I saw a glimmer of fear there. "You're whacked."

"Am I? Why were you in the apartment? We showed five minutes after you got there. Either you couldn't find something or you planted something. Which is it?"

"You don't know shit," he hissed.

One of my brows jumped. "What you don't know is that I'm a prospect with an outlaw motorcycle club. I wanna earn my patch, I gotta kill someone." I glanced around. "Quiet apartment like this, you threatening my woman yesterday… The universe might be saying something," I lied.

My bluff went better than I thought, from the terror flooding Brantley's face. *And* his pants.

I couldn't hide my lip curl. "You're disgusting. Answer my fuckin' question before I make you shit your pants, too."

After a long moment, he said, "Fine. I hid half a kilo of coke in her bathroom."

My vision went red and I took a deep breath. "Whose bathroom? Ines or Alexandra's?"

"Ines. I didn't go in that, erm, her room."

"Good call not insulting her in front of me. We interrupted you, so you had to break in last night after we left?"

"No. Jesus. Told that fuckin' cop I didn't do it like seven times last night."

I shook my head. "When did you hide it?"

"Last Thursday. That's when I put it in Ines's bathroom."

This asshole was trying my last ounce of patience. "Where in her bathroom?"

Brantley rolled his eyes. "Her vent. They have the kind that are in the floor."

I gave that some thought. "Yesterday morning, did you get your fuckin' coke out of the apartment?"

"It wasn't there. I'd ask Ines about it, if your bitch hadn't gotten us in that damn—"

I punched him in the gut. "It's not Lex's fault that someone drifted into the damned lane. You got me?"

He nodded and struggled to get his breath back.

"Is there any chance Ines moved it? Did she know you're into coke? Hell, are you dealing to her?"

My mind was moving faster as I considered various possibilities on how this could blow back on Alexandra. I hadn't asked her much about Ines because I was so pissed about how Ines had treated her on Sunday.

Shit.

Brantley blew out a breath. "She might have moved it. I'm not dealing to her...but she sometimes likes a hit before finals."

I clenched my jaw. "So, she knew that you're into drugs?"

"She knew I could score for her. I'm not a dealer."

I shoved him against the wall again. "You hid a fuckin' half-kilo in her goddamned apartment, asshole! Any cop in their right mind is going to call that intent to distribute."

"Not my problem," he muttered.

It wasn't until I heard Brantley gargle that I realized I was squeezing his throat for all I was worth. I let go and stepped closer. "It *is* your fuckin' problem. If *you* didn't break into the unit, then who the hell did? Your supplier would be my guess, seeing as a half a kilo of coke is worth thousands."

"Could be Tobias. He has the other half."

I closed my eyes not believing what I heard. "You're telling me you split a kilo of coke with someone... and the supplier doesn't know it? Did you steal the fuckin' drugs?"

"They have plenty of—"

The stench of his urine was getting to me, but I stepped closer to him anyway. "You fucking moron! Tell the fuckin' cops."

"Snitch? No fuckin' way, asshole!"

I saw red again, and struggled to keep calm. "Does Tobias know Ines? Know where she lives?"

He made a strange sound in his throat and I couldn't tell if it was a garbled laugh or a groan. "Know he's stupid like Porter and has a thing for your bit—"

I punched him in the gut. "Does he know where they live?"

"Yeah."

"What's his last name?"

"Smith."

I pulled my fist back. "Are you lying?"

"No, really. That's his last name."

Slowly, I lowered my fist. "Who did you steal from?"

"It doesn't matter. They're small time."

I fought rolling my eyes. "Who's the dealer?"

"The dealer is out of Orlando. I only know him as Carlos."

I narrowed my eyes. "You're bullshitting me."

"I'm not."

"An Orlando dealer isn't going to spend their time in Gainesville. They'll outsource it to street gangs so they know the product sells." I slammed him against the wall again. "Who the fuck wants that coke?"

"The Twenty-Sixers, they're new. Just started dealing six months ago, but they get their supply from Orlando."

I nodded once. "Two more things. How often did you *score* for Ines?"

He shot me a half-snarl before he answered. "Only twice, three times if you count the gram she wanted for the concert. Had to fuckin' get rid of that before the cops or the EMTs found it on me."

Now I understood him blaming Lex. He wasn't mad about the accident, he was pissed he had to ditch the drugs.

"Where the hell do I find Tobias?"

"I'm not a snitch, not to you or the cops."

If he hadn't pissed his pants, I'd have kneed him in the groin. Instead, I punched him in the gut again. "Where do I find Tobias?"

Brantley wheezed out a breath. "Eden Park - it's a complex near State Road 24. I don't know what building he's in..." I glared at him and he spoke faster. "But, he always parks close to his unit and he drives a lime green SUV. I think it's a Porsche or some shit. He had it custom wrapped."

I debated what to do next. Odds were good he'd warn Tobias that I was looking for him; then again, that might draw Tobias out. Either way, I couldn't worry about that. I needed to check if that cocaine was anywhere in Alexandra's apartment. I'd hunt down Tobias later tonight.

"You two must have intended to sell the coke. Where's your buddy planning to off-load it? Clubs or some place near campus?"

"Fuck if I know. We didn't plan to take the brick, it just fuckin' happened, and then he offered to split it. Who can't use an extra seven or eight grand?"

I hated drugs. It cost the lives of too many people, including my maternal grandmother. Hearing Brantley minimize it to money angered me anew. Rather than just walk away, I punched him in the eye.

When I got to the door, he called out. "Hey! What about Porter?"

His question reminded me I had Porter's phone in my back pocket. I tossed it on the couch next to Porter's body.

Turning back to Brantley, I shrugged. "You take his ass home. Or he can get a fuckin' Uber."

Chapter Eleven

Carried Away

Alexandra

After I finished my final, I stood at the corner across from my apartment complex and reached for the carabiner clip holding my keys. Before I unclipped them, it hit me that Rafferty had my apartment key, so I dug my phone out of the side pocket.

Normally, I'd text but I called him instead.

"Hey," he answered.

"Hi. I'm across the street but wanted to make sure you're home. If not, I can head over—"

"I'm here. I'll unlock the door."

"Cool. See you soon."

The signal changed and I hurried to the other side of the street. Giddiness welled up inside me, like he was my first crush.

Then again, he *was*.

At the door, Rafferty opened it before I could. My smile faltered when I took in his face. His beard almost hid it, but I'd been studying oral health for a while. I'd developed a bizarre habit of looking at everyone's lips, mouths, and jawlines a little more closely.

"How did you get hit in the mouth?" I asked.

Rafferty turned his head a touch, grabbed my hand and pulled me inside. "You're way too observant, Lex."

"True. What happened? That looks like it hurts."

His tongue darted out and touched the area where his lip was swollen. "I paid Brantley a visit at his place. Porter was there and got in a lucky sucker punch."

I shook my head in confusion. "There's no such thing as a lucky sucker punch, Raff. How did you get to Brantley's? I don't know his address, Ines doesn't have a physical address book, and I barely recall which streets she took to get to his place on Sunday morning since the sun hadn't risen."

He shot me a grin that I hadn't seen since we were teenagers, and now, that panty-melting grin had been perfected. "Will you forget about it, if I say it's nothing to worry about?"

"No."

"I didn't think so. Give me your backpack, and sit down."

I slipped my arms free of my backpack and set it next to the wall. He watched me settle on the sofa with my foot under my tush.

"Are you tender?"

I was, but it was easing up. "I'm fine. How on earth did you find Brantley and Porter?"

He sat down next to me. "I forgot to lock the door after you left. Porter came inside while I was showering—"

"He did?"

He gave a rueful chuckle. "Yeah, even whipped open the shower curtain since he thought you were behind it."

My eyes went wide. "You're shitting me!"

"No."

He shared about the rest of his morning.

I sank back into the couch. "Half a kilo of cocaine? Are you... And Ines uses, too?"

He dragged a hand down his face. "According to Brantley. I don't know if I believe him, though."

My eyes closed and I attempted to process everything he shared. I opened my eyes and focused on him. "Did you try looking for the drugs when you came back?"

"I did a cursory search. I wanted to wait for you to get back before I started rifling through drawers or her closet shelves."

I nodded. "Do you think Tobias has the drugs?"

He pressed his lips together then stopped with a hiss. "I think it could go either way at this point."

"You should get some ice on that lip, Raff."

"I'll be fine. I've suffered much worse."

I leaned forward. "Where's the card for Officer Hatcher? We should call him."

"Are you shitting me?" he asked in an almost mocking tone.

I twisted my hands up. "I'm sure they have a drug-sniffing K-9 that might be able to help us."

"Sure, until the coke shows up in your bedroom."

That brought me up short. I twisted my lips to the side. "Well, I guess we should search her room more—"

"No," he interrupted.

"What do you mean, 'no'?"

He grabbed my hand and tugged me toward him. "No, first you need to give me a kiss. Then, we can go through her room. But I think we need to go through *your* room, too. Seeing as there's three people in the mix here, your room or bathroom might make for the best hiding spot."

I lifted my hands up. "Or even the kitchen or living room."

Rafferty shook his head. "Not the living room. I searched earlier, even turned the furniture over and unzipped the cushions to check inside. No drugs. The kitchen is a last resort. Too much happens there. Somebody drops by, they could open the wrong cabinet or something... I don't know. It just seems like it wouldn't be a decent spot. But if we don't find anything, we'll check there last."

"Okay," I whispered.

Every time I thought I had pinpointed the exact shade of Rafferty's brown eyes, I found reasons to doubt myself. Today his eyes had a shine like chocolate chips that had just melted. Tomorrow they would look totally different.

"What are you waiting for, Robertson?" he asked.

I shifted, leaned up, slid my hands along the side of his neck, and ever-so-gently brushed my lips against his.

He wrapped his arms around my waist. "What the hell are you doing, Lex? Kiss me like you mean it."

"I'm not going to hurt your lip, Raff."

His chin lowered as he gave me a pointed look. "A split lip is the least of my worries. Kiss your man."

I stopped myself from widening my eyes, but my whole body froze. *Your man.* That was fast... then again, we'd known each other our whole lives, so no, it wasn't fast at all, really.

"Lex," Rafferty said, breaking into my spiraling thoughts.

"Fine," I whispered, and planted my lips on his.

He didn't give me the chance to deepen the kiss. In seconds, he took full control, his tongue dipping between my lips and dancing with mine. My hand glided up his neck and through his hair at the back of his head.

I hadn't been kissed like this... Well, not since this morning.

I shook my head and Rafferty broke away. "What?"

"Nothing. I, erm, we're getting carried away."

He rested his forehead against mine. "No, babe. That's not carried away."

Out of nowhere, he pushed forward and I fell to my back, pulling my foot out from under me at the last minute. I had his weight on me, and I realized how much I loved it. All that bulk and power. His lips met mine, and he kissed me again. He ratcheted this kiss up quite a bit compared to the other two.

Clearly he was proving a point.

God, he was stubborn.

Then again, we had that in common.

He slid a hand along my jaw and held my head still while his other hand trailed a path down my side to my hips. I shifted that leg, but he kept his hand where it was.

He kept kissing me and our breathing became labored. Part of me wanted to stop him, but far more of me enjoyed what he was doing.

Gently, he broke the kiss. He lifted his head just an inch. "*That's* getting carried away."

"Yeah," I breathed.

My stomach growled.

He sat up. "You haven't eaten lunch?"

"Not yet. Have you?"

He pulled his phone from his back pocket. "Nope. We'll Doordash something, that way we can start searching Ines's room. What do you feel like?"

I sat up and shrugged. "I don't care. I picked dinner last night, you decide. Anything except seafood."

He arched his brow. "But you love seafood."

I nodded. "Yeah, but I'm not in the mood for that today."

"Do you still hate barbecue?"

My lips tipped up. "I don't exactly hate it. There's a 4Rivers here."

"Done. Cookie or red velvet cupcake?"

I hesitated too long.

"Fuck it, I'll order both. You want to get started in Ines's bedroom? We can break when the food gets here."

I stood. "Sure, but what's the hurry?"

He glanced up at me from his phone. "The hurry is so that we have more time to fool around - even if I'm not going to fuck you tonight."

"Why?"

"I don't intend to hurt you, and I'm pretty sure you lied earlier about being sore, so giving you a little extra time is a good idea."

"Fine. Make sure you get the sweet barbeque sauce and not the mustard or vinegar based stuff."

He shot me a dry look. "Lex, it's me you're talking to. You think I don't remember that about you, think again."

———

While Rafferty ordered our food, I pulled out all six dresser drawers in Ines's room and put them on her bed. I squatted down and looked at the inside of her dresser frame in case she (or Brantley) had taped the drugs to the sides of the dresser. No such luck.

Rafferty came into the room and looked impressed. "That's smart - taking out the drawers. Can your bathroom drawers be removed?"

"I don't think so."

He nodded. "I can go through these if you want to go through her bathroom cabinet - or vice versa. From how bitchy Jasmine gets when I move her make-up and shit, I figure it'd be better for you to do that."

My lips pursed as I tried not to chuckle. "Your sister is far from bitchy, Raff."

He pulled out a stack of folded t-shirts from one of the drawers. "Have you messed with her foundation and eyeliners and shit?"

I shook my head. "Of course not. I know better."

"Hardy-har, don't forget to check the toilet. Or I can handle that if you want."

By the time I'd finished in the bathroom, our food had been delivered. We ate, and then got back to checking Ines's room. I helped Raff move her mattress to the hallway so we could check the underside of the box frames.

"Why do you think it'd be in the box frames?"

He looked at me. "Now that I'm a prospect, let's just say I've learned a whole lot more from the brothers, and Roman mentioned some things to me. Like hiding something under a mattress is good, but hiding it dead center is better, and more difficult."

I narrowed my eyes. "But Roman's in Biloxi."

Rafferty nodded. "Yeah, and not long after I started as a prospect, the brothers rode out to Biloxi. Har convinced Volt to leave me there for two weeks. 'Put me through my paces', as he put it."

I grimaced. "Sorry to hear that."

He shook his head. "Don't be. It was worth it. Gave me some clarity about the kind of work I want to do, and it helped me rule out moving there."

"What kind of work do you want to do?"

"I've worked a lot of different construction jobs, Lex. Brute has his own general contracting business...I had thoughts of doing something similar. Just not in Mississippi."

We pulled the box springs off the metal frame and checked the bottoms. No drugs.

I sighed. "What's next? Are you going to check the back of the headboard?"

He blinked and shook his head. "I hadn't thought of that." He eyed the furniture like it might bite him. "That looks like solid wood, it's gonna be heavy as a mother. I'll pull the headboard back an inch or two and you take a look."

I stood to the side while he squatted to get a grip on the bottom of the headboard. His biceps bulged as he dragged the piece of furniture away from the wall. Arms weren't typically my thing... or I hadn't thought they were until now because seeing Rafferty in full flex?

Yes, please.

I checked the narrow gap and spotted a small bundle taped to the back of the headboard. "Shit."

Rafferty straightened. "It's there?"

"Yeah," I breathed out.

He went to the other side of the bed frame, took a look, and ran a hand through his hair.

"What's wrong? Aren't we going to take it down?"

He stared at me for a beat. "You aren't going to like this, but I need to call Blood."

"Why?"

"Because we could go to the cops with this...which could backfire. Who's to say we didn't plant this? Or I could take it to the dealer Brantley and Tobias ripped off - let that asshole deal with those two."

"You sound like you left something out."

He shrugged a shoulder. "Or, I'm thinking I could use this to talk to Tobias and figure out if he really was the one who tossed the place yesterday."

"At this point, I'm thinking it doesn't matter."

His eyes widened. "Your safety matters, Lex. If the person looking for this doesn't know it's been found, they'll probably come back. And they'll think you know exactly where it is."

My eyes slid to the other side of the room. I felt betrayed - though until I actually spoke to Ines, I needed to give her the benefit of the doubt. 'Innocent until proven guilty' and all that. Plus, Brantley had a self-centered streak and I could see him lying about where he put the drugs.

I locked eyes with Rafferty. "Not that you - or Blood - care, but I say take it to the dealer. They're pretty vicious when people steal from them."

Rafferty pressed his lips together and lowered his chin. "You still don't think you're fucking ruthless?"

My eyes went wide. "This is different. If that cop caught sight of that yesterday, you and I'd have spent the night in jail, most likely."

He shook his head. "Like the club wouldn't send a lawyer for us. Plus, this is circumstantial."

"Whatever. Let's get the mattress back in place. Then you can call Blood while I make the bed."

At quarter to three, I collapsed on the sofa next to Rafferty. "What did Blood have to say? Or are you going to tell me it's club business even though it's one-hundred-percent my business since I live here."

He shifted on the couch and I noticed he'd taken off his boots. He arranged us so we were stretched out and snuggled on the couch. "No. I'll always do my damnedest to share everything with you, Lex. Only reason I wouldn't is if it would incriminate you or put you in danger."

"Will it incriminate me to know what's going on?"

His lips quirked into a sideways smile. "He's sending a couple brothers out."

"Why?"

"We're going to confront Tobias tonight."

I could just imagine that kind of confrontation. "You know, honey attracts more flies than sledgehammers."

He closed his eyes and sighed. "Brantley said this asshole has a thing for you."

My brows furrowed. "Whatever. I'm just saying, he might explain if I ask him."

"You're not part of this," he said, his tone brooking no argument.

"You think Brantley or Porter haven't warned him about you already? Porter was in your truck, so he's sure to tell him what make and model you drive. Once he knows that, why would Tobias open the door to you?"

The smile on his lips redefined 'devious.' "I'll be on my Triumph, Lex."

"That seems like overkill," I muttered.

"More like it kills me being in a cage around here. I loved having you on the back of my bike last night."

That *was* fun... and I probably loved it far more than he did.

"Obviously, you enjoyed it, too. I have one question though. Why did you say you would never be part of the MC?"

"I didn't say never."

He leaned up on an elbow. "Lex, you did. It was a long time ago when you were so adamant, but Jazz asked if you still meant it last summer."

I narrowed my eyes recalling the night I said that. "You weren't even there. How do you know what I said? Jasmine wouldn't tell you."

An almost bashful expression crossed his face. "I was right outside the room."

I narrowed my eyes. "No. You were out with Steel. I specifically asked where you were when I got there."

He shot me a sheepish smile. "Steel sent me home early because I hadn't committed to prospecting with the Devil Lancers versus the Riot. I saw your car in the drive and made sure I was quiet when I went inside." He paused and when I said nothing he continued. "So... Why'd you say it?"

If we were going to work, I had to be up front. "Because I hate the domineering over-protectiveness and the fact that most brothers leave their women in the dark."

"Sounds like bullshit," he muttered.

I shot him a look. "When anyone else gets too protective, it feels like control." I hesitated a beat. "The few times you did it in high school, it didn't feel like that."

He stared at me. "What did it feel like?"

"It felt... natural." Deep down, I suspected that nobody else would be able to pull that off.

"Still think there's B.S. in there, but do you still feel that way about the MC? Because I'm not leaving the club and you're the woman I want at my side."

The past two days felt surreal. Everything about us was fast, but not fast at all. It was intense, but easy at the same time. All because we had so much history.

"What are you thinking, Lex?"

"That I love you even if it's way too soon to say that, and— Oof!"

Rafferty planted me under his body. "*Not* too soon, Alexandra. I love you, too."

"No kidding, since you basically just said you want me to be your old lady."

His eyes flared. "Yeah, but you didn't answer my question. Are you still determined not to be part of the Riot after you graduate?"

I debated it for a moment. "Not determined exactly, but I don't want to be the club's dentist either."

"Your dad would never—"

"Vamp and Razor already mentioned it."

"They were kidding. Seriously, Razor would never put you in that position."

I shrugged. "That's true. Now that I know where things stand with us, I'm *not* determined to break free of the MC life."

"Good," he said, lowering his lips to mine.

We were getting lost in this kiss when my phone rang.

I twisted my lips free. "I better get that. It might be Ines or her mom."

Raff blew out a sigh and let me up. "Yeah."

My phone sat on the dinette table. The number listed on the screen had the name of the hospital listed above the phone number. My stomach suddenly felt like a pit. "Hello?"

"Alexandra, this is Dolores Tallow, Ines's aunt."

"Hi. How is Ines?"

Her breath hitched before she spoke again. "There's no easy way to say this, Alexandra. Ines passed away just after two o'clock this afternoon."

I sank into a chair. My vision blurred with tears, and I rested my head in my hand. "No, you can't be serious. What happened?"

She sighed. "Her heart gave out. Might have been a blood clot from one of the surgeries."

I fought back a sob. "I'm so sorry she's gone. This is devastating. Do you need me to call Brantley and let him know?"

Even though I didn't know Dolores at all, her voice sounded weary. "Thank you, it's kind of you to offer, but I just got off the phone with him."

"Okay. That's good that you were able to talk to him. Is there anything else you need me to do?"

"Not right now. I'm sure we'll be in touch once we've made arrangements."

My voice hitched. "All right. Um, I had to change the locks here, so if you need a key, I can put one in the mail."

Her voice dropped to a whisper. "Yes, an officer contacted my brother, Barry, about the break-in. He'll let you know when they're coming, or the building super can let them in."

"Right. God, I don't know what to say. You all have my deepest sympathy."

"Ines spoke very highly of you, Alexandra. You're just as sweet and caring as she said."

A fresh wave of tears rolled down my cheeks. "If you need anything, don't hesitate to call me."

"It's appreciated," she said, and ended the call.

I pulled the phone from my ear, and Rafferty dragged a chair up next to me and sat down. He pulled me toward him and gave me a hug. "I'm sorry, Lex. I know you wanted to be there for her."

"Yeah," I whispered.

Rafferty held me while I sobbed. Death always sucked, but losing Ines like this felt like a two-ton wallop to my heart. I pulled myself together after a couple minutes, but I had no doubt my eyes were puffy and pink.

The doorbell rang and I pulled away from him. With my phone in my hand, I hit the icon for the doorbell camera.

"Seriously?" I hissed, when I saw Brantley standing at the door.

Rafferty glanced down at my phone. His sinister grin made another appearance. "Let me, babe."

I squeezed his leg before he stood. "Raff...don't be mean. He's a jackass, but I think he cared about Ines."

He arched a brow. "Got that, but you know the deal. If he doesn't want any shit, he shouldn't start any shit."

That almost made me smile since it brought back memories of my parents' back yard. Mom loved playing 'Don't Start No Shit, Won't Be No Shit,' and we loved it growing up because it gave us an excuse to curse. I gave him the tiniest grin and nodded.

Rafferty opened the door. "What do you need?"

"I left some things here. I want to get them."

The way Rafferty's body straightened even as he twisted his head, I suspected his temper was brimming to the surface. "Lex just found out Ines passed away. From what I heard on her end of the conversation, they called you before her. And you think it's a good idea to barge in here for 'some things' you left behind, have I got that right?"

"Don't be an asshole. I'm not gonna take long and—"

"You're the asshole here. Come back tomorrow."

I stood and crept close to Rafferty's side. "It's okay. Really."

For a lengthy moment Rafferty stared at me, then he turned back to Brantley. "Fine. But I'm watching your every move, asshole. If you're here to look for your lost drugs, that isn't happening."

Brantley's lip curled and he shook his head. "Whatever."

Raff opened the door wider and Brantley went straight back to Ines's room.

"Stay here," Rafferty whispered to me.

I wanted to follow after them, but decided only one of us needed to hover.

A couple minutes passed in silence.

Then I heard a muffled conversation between Brantley and Rafferty.

Finally, Rafferty said, "I don't know what you're talking about."

Brantley raised his voice, but he wasn't quite yelling. "You obviously went through her shit. She never kept her t-shirts neat like this."

"What the hell are you looking for? Alexandra can help you."

"Why did you mess with her shit?" Brantley asked, his tone fully agitated.

I hurried to the doorway. "Whoever broke in tossed her stuff everywhere, Brant. I had to do something, and folding her clothes seemed like the right thing to do. What are you looking for? One of your t-shirts or something?"

A muscle ticked along Brantley's jaw and I saw this was taking a toll on him - even if he was doing his damnedest to hide it. After a moment, he spoke in a low voice. "Gave her one of my sweatshirts. She always looked so damned adorable in it... And I want it back, so I can remember her in it."

Tears ran down my cheeks and I nodded. "I think I put that in her closet organizer. Is it a baseball sweatshirt?"

"Yeah," he said, his voice rough with emotion.

Ines had a thing for baseball. She'd grown up outside Ft. Lauderdale, and her dad took her to Marlins games as often as he could afford tickets. I recalled folding two baseball sweatshirts - one for the Marlins and another for the Red Sox.

I brought the two sweatshirts out of her closet. Brantley nodded at me, grabbed the Red Sox sweatshirt, and moved to the bathroom. He came out with a small see-through travel kit that held a razor, toothbrush, and deodorant.

Without a word, he strode out of the room.

Rafferty's eyes widened in annoyance and he followed. "You sure that's it? What about the coke you hid?"

Brantley turned around. "What about it? I looked for it, and it was gone. The fuckin' dealer doesn't know I took it, and I don't have it, so I'm done with it. If Tobias has it, I don't fuckin' care."

Rafferty opened his mouth to say something else, but Brantley turned and left.

Rafferty locked the door, and came back to where I stood in the middle of the living room. "I almost think he cared about her."

I sighed. "He did care about her, Raff. That's more emotion from him than I've ever seen. I... I really think he loved her."

Rafferty slid his arms around me. I wrapped my arms around his waist and rested my cheek against his chest.

"What do you want to do now, Lex?"

I tipped my head up. "What do you mean?"

"People deal with death in different ways. Wanna get drunk? If we were close to the beach, I'd take you there so you can scream at the ocean."

"Why would I do that?"

He shrugged. "Hell if I know. Jasmine says she does that sometimes."

I chuckled. "Your sister has far more angst and rage than I do."

He stroked his hand up and down my back. "Yeah, she's also close to three years younger than you...which probably plays a part. So, get drunk? Go for a run?"

I planted my forehead against his hard chest. "Raff. Who am I gonna go running with now?" A sob bubbled out of me. "Who's gonna drag me to the gym?"

He tightened his hold on me, giving me a bear hug. "God damn it."

"Why do you sound mad?"

He blew out a breath that might have held some humor to it. "When men get hurt, we funnel it into anger. I hate that you're hurting."

"But that doesn't mean you're hurt," I murmured.

"No, but it kills that I can't say *I* will be the one to run with you or that *I* will get your ass to the gym when you don't feel like it. And it isn't because I don't want to do that, because I *absolutely* want to do that - it's because we'll be in different cities - at least for a little while."

"Yeah," I whispered.

"So, after Beast and I take care of some things tonight, you want to go get drunk? Might be able to talk Beast into being our designated driver. Or do you want to hang here and tie one on?"

With a wan smile, I shook my head. "I can't get drunk tonight. I have my last two finals on Thursday, and I plan to study in the morning. It's a bitch to study with a hangover."

He brushed his lips against my forehead. "Got it. Do you need to call anyone? Mutual friends? If you want to go to the gym, I'll take you."

I shook my head. "No, on the gym, but I should call our friends. They deserve to know."

Chapter Twelve

Bluffed

Rafferty

ALEXANDRA CALLED SEVERAL FRIENDS to let them know that Ines had passed away. Hearing Lex's side of the conversations hurt, and I wished like hell I could make the calls for her, but I couldn't. Every effort I made to soothe her felt ineffective, but something was better than nothing.

As I sat there with my arm around Alexandra's shoulders, trying to comfort her, I'd lost track of how much time had passed since I spoke to Blood. Someone knocked at the door, and I cursed.

"Who do you think that could be?" she asked.

I let her go. "I'm about to find out."

I opened the door to Beast and Tundra. Rather than open it any wider, I stepped out into the breezeway, pulling the door closed behind me. "Hey. You two must have sped the whole way."

Beast cocked a brow. "No. The two of us were out in Middleburg when Blood called. We hit the lights just right. Is there a reason you aren't letting us inside?"

I lowered my voice. "Her friend didn't make it. We just found out a little over an hour ago. She's been calling their friends to let them know."

"Fuck," Beast muttered.

"She lived here, too, right?" Tundra asked.

I nodded. "Yeah. Let's go inside."

Beast earned his road name because he was too handsome - though he was very strong and well muscled, like a beast. He'd patched in with the Biloxi brothers, but transferred to Jacksonville later. He had two kids with his old lady - both boys. I had a feeling he'd always wanted a daughter because he had a soft spot for all the daughters of his Riot brothers.

"Alexandra, you holding up all right?" he asked, grabbing her hands.

She pressed her lips together and nodded. "One thing at a time, right?"

He hugged her. "I'm sorry, sweetheart."

"Me, too, Beast."

He let her go, and Tundra moved in to give her a bear hug. "You call us anytime if you need anything, you got it?"

"Yes, sir."

Tundra shot a look at Beast. "Sir." He tipped his head toward me. "Has *he* ever called us 'sir'?"

Beast grinned for a moment and shook his head. "Let it go, man. Not today."

Alexandra sat down on the sofa. From the look she aimed at Beast and Tundra, I suspected I wouldn't like what she said next.

"So, Raff basically shot this idea down already, but—"

"Then the answer's yes," Beast said, grinning.

She smiled and shook her head. "I wouldn't be so sure about that. The guy you're going to see... I'm an acquaintance of his and I think—"

"Nope," Tundra said.

Beast shook his head and held up a hand for a second. "No, let's hear her out."

Her lips tipped up, but she didn't fully smile. "I think you might have better luck if I ask him what's going on."

The room went silent for a few seconds.

"Did you expect her to say something else?" Tundra asked, looking at Beast.

"Not really, but I had hoped for a surprise." Beast sat on the opposite end of the sofa and faced Alexandra. "Your idea isn't a bad one, except for one problem."

"What's that?"

Beast leaned forward. "The moment drugs enter the picture, everything changes, sweetheart. Everything."

"How so?"

Tundra sat in the arm chair. "Lies, to start with. Dealers will lie and cheat to get more money. Users will lie about whether they need a score or just had a hit. Considering that this guy's just an acquaintance, I'm not sure you'd realize when he's lying to you."

Alexandra nodded. "Fine, but why not go to the dealers themselves, and throw Tobias under the bus?"

Beast looked alarmed. "I thought you knew this person? Why would you want to do that to him?"

"I figure they'd be more vindictive than even you three seeing as nobody likes thieves... And it might keep you all out of trouble."

Beast chuckled. "We live for trouble, Alexandra, and your boy has to prove that he's down for causing trouble when the situation calls for it, too."

She twisted her lips to hide her frown. "I was afraid you'd say that."

Tundra cracked his neck. "Know you've got lots of tests this week, but have you got any beer in this place?"

I chuckled. "There's some Blue Moon, if that works for you."

A couple hours later, the four of us sat around Alexandra's small dinner table eating pizza and a salad.

Tundra polished off his beer and set the bottle down with a hollow thunk. "I don't understand how you found out about the drugs in the first place. Most people wouldn't own up to that shit."

I swallowed the last bite of my pizza. "Yeah, I took a calculated risk and bluffed with Brantley."

That got Beast's attention from his swift head twist and his furrowed brow. "You bluffed. How exactly did you do that?"

Alexandra held her beer bottle in front of her lips. I noticed the bruising at the side of her head was starting to fade.

"I've been wondering the same thing," she muttered.

I twisted my hands up. "We were thrown off to find Brantley here Monday morning. He left without taking anything - we never found out what he needed. After I checked the doorbell camera footage, it was clear he didn't have the time to take anything. Which meant he probably left something... Or he'd been looking for something, and we'd interrupted him."

Tundra shook his head. "That's a hell of an assumption."

I gave a single nod. "Yes, but without Ines here, why be in the apartment at all?"

"That's fair."

"Right. That evening, my gut said Brantley was behind the break-in, since we'd been gone long enough he had plenty of time to toss the place. But I recognized that was an even bigger assumption."

Beast stroked the stubble along his jaw. "Why bluff about something like that?"

My eyes slid to Alexandra for a beat and back to Beast. "Because of Porter. Something told me I could play the two of them against one another, and that's what happened."

"I'm impressed," Tundra muttered.

"Yeah," Beast said.

Alexandra shook her head with a small smile on her face. "He's always been a bluffer, he used to do it all the time."

Tundra shared a look with Beast. "Seems like that could be his road name."

Beast cocked a brow. "He's gotta get done prospecting first, Tun."

Alexandra stood and grabbed Tundra's empty beer bottle. "Are you going to corner Tobias before or after the sun sets?

"Don't worry about it," I said.

She dropped the bottles into a recycle bin, shoved the paper plates into the garbage, and came back to the dining nook. "It's not that simple, Raff."

"It is, Alexandra. The less you know the better, right now," Beast said.

She pressed her lips together into an angry pout. "That's the last thing I want to hear."

"Tough," Tundra said.

"Don't you have studying to do?" Beast asked.

"Always, but seeing as Brantley insinuated that Ines was using drugs and that's as crazy as the day is long, I think I can put off studying until tomorrow. I want to know what's up with Tobias and him stealing a kilo of cocaine."

"Did Ines have a part-time job? Or any kind of internship?" Tundra asked.

Alexandra gave it some thought. "Not this semester. Last fall, she delivered auto parts for a distributor - but only part-time, mainly on weekends."

Tundra cocked a brow. "You mean when they needed a timing belt or some other part that they didn't have already, she would deliver it that day... or did she deliver it later?"

She sat down in a chair at the table. "I think that day, but I don't know because I never really asked that."

Keeping my mouth shut proved to be a massive struggle. I sensed that Tundra had a theory. My gut said Ines was more involved than we realized, and maybe Brantley had lied to me about her wanting to score a hit. In fact, part of me suspected he'd reversed the roles. If Ines were selling drugs... I couldn't mention that in front of Lex. But from the way Brantley behaved, he definitely seemed the type to score a hit off Ines.

"How long did she have the job? Last semester only... or did she have the job for a year?" Beast asked.

That didn't help my wayward thoughts, and seeing as Alexandra was damned intelligent, it keyed up her suspicions, too.

"Why do you ask?"

Beast held up his hands for a moment. "I don't have a reason, I'm just curious. If it's too difficult to talk about your friend right now—"

"No, it's just that I get the feeling you and Tundra are assuming the worst of her."

Beast slowly shook his head. "Not at all, honey. Seriously, I'm not assuming anything. Just trying to get a feel for the situation."

I watched Alexandra. The way her chest deflated, she'd exhaled, and her expression softened on Beast. "Fine. The past few days have been so crazy. She worked the auto parts job for a little over a year, but not more than a year and a half, because that would have been more than three semesters."

Tundra pushed his chair back from the table, but didn't stand. "I don't want to sound callous, but you two split the rent right down the middle, yeah?"

Alexandra aimed a pointed look at him. "Yes. And before you ask, no, she didn't have any extra money all of a sudden. She didn't have expensive clothes or anything out of the blue, either."

I dragged my chair up next to hers and draped my arm over her shoulders. "Honey, they aren't accusing her of anything, they just want to rule things out. Did she change since being with Brantley?"

Instantly she said, "No."

We stared at her.

Her shoulders rose with her deep breath, as she pulled herself together. "I mean, not any more than most people. She spent time with him and that meant we didn't hang out as much... She definitely skipped early morning workouts, but it's not like you can blame that on drugs." Her cheeks turned a little pink. "People spend lots of time together when a relationship is new."

Anyone could see this took a toll on her. After today's news it was unlikely she'd be objective.

I gave her shoulders a squeeze. "Don't get worked up over this."

She pulled away. "How can I *not* get worked up over this? I've lived with her for almost a year and a half. She didn't sell drugs."

Tundra sat forward. "Nobody said anything about selling. She could have been a go-between."

Beast nodded. "And she'd be the first person they'd suspect if they were low on supply or cash."

Lex twisted her lips to the side and gave Beast a pointed look. "You're right, but why wouldn't they have found the drugs like we did?"

I shook my head. "It took both of us to move that mattress. I could have done it alone, but it takes time. Hiding drugs in the box springs or the mattress itself is doable. That headboard is solid fuckin' oak. They'd never expect her to stash it there."

Alexandra looked at me. "Then how did she do it? It's why I think someone may have set her up."

"No, sweetheart," Tundra said.

Beast sat back in his seat. "Actually, let's play that out. Who would do that and what would they gain?"

My temper flared to life. I widened my eyes at Beast. "She just lost her friend. She's in no headspace for this kind of speculation." I glanced at Lex and back to Beast. "That's why we need to find this Tobias asshole and fuck him up if he doesn't give us answers."

Alexandra turned wide eyes to me. "You can't go..." She stopped on a sigh and looked away.

"Lex," I called.

She held up a hand. "I get it. This is what you do. It's what Dad would do."

"Then why does it bother you?" I asked.

"Because I know most of these people. I never knew anyone that Dad roughed up."

"When did you get soft?" Tundra asked.

Beast shook his head. "I don't think she's soft. It's different when the problems have something to do with you. And she probably doesn't want our prospect to get roughed up in the process either, though why she cares about him, I'll never know."

Tundra chuckled. "Yeah, she needs to get over that."

Alexandra glanced out the living room window. The sun had finally set. She looked back to Beast. "Are you going to trust me to stay here alone while you three bust heads?"

Beast smiled and winked at her. "Yeah. So you better not make me regret it."

At eight-fifty, I led Beast and Tundra into the Eden Park apartment complex and parked my bike near the community clubhouse. I hadn't had time to do any reconnaissance before they arrived.

Tundra swung off his bike. "This guy doesn't live at the pool, prospect."

I nodded. "That's the thing. Brantley didn't give me a unit or a building number. Just said I'm looking for a lime green SUV - probably a high-end model - and he parks close to his building."

"Fuck," Tundra muttered.

Beast started to speak, but stopped and turned toward the approaching sound of thumping bass. An older model Porsche Cayenne pulled into the lot and as it rolled under the street lamps, I saw it was lime green.

"Speak of the devil," Beast said.

I grinned. "It's better to be lucky than good sometimes."

Beast nodded. "Don't get cocky. Let's leave the bikes, it isn't ideal, but we'll draw instant attention otherwise."

We took off at a jog in the same direction as the SUV. At a breezeway between two buildings, Tundra gave a hand signal that he was going to split away from me and Beast. For some reason, Beast picked up the pace and we rounded the corner.

Bass notes filled the air, reverberating against my body. Tobias had parked but hadn't left his vehicle.

"I don't miss apartment living. I fuckin' hated assholes who sat like that making everyone listen to their music," Beast muttered.

I didn't point out that our bikes did the same thing when we had our radios on during a ride and we came to a stop.

From the other side of the building, Tundra wandered out toward the SUV.

"What's he doing?" I whispered.

"Don't worry," Beast said.

Tundra strode across the parking lot, holding his keys out like he owned a car parked beyond the SUV. Then he doubled back the way he came as though he'd forgotten something.

Moments later, Beast's cell chimed with a notification. He pulled his phone from his hip, glanced at the screen, and tucked it away. "He's alone. Let's make an approach. You get in the passenger seat. I'm sliding in the back. Have your gun out."

The music stopped, the engine shut down, and a tall lanky man with curly brown hair got out of the SUV. Before closing the car door, he blew out a huge plume of smoke.

Beast stood still. "Change in plan. We'll rush him inside his place."

We watched Tobias walk through the parking lot, casual and oblivious. We stalked down the sidewalk the moment he reached his door.

By the time he had opened the door, Tundra was at his side. "Hey, man. I'm your new neighbor. You know where I can get some weed?"

Tobias pulled an Airpod from his ear. "What did you say?"

From behind, Beast clapped him on his shoulder while shoving him forward. "Let's go inside."

"What the fuck?" Tobias yelled, while trying to shake Beast off.

"Don't struggle or I'll have to shoot you," Beast muttered.

"That would harsh your mellow, man," Tundra said, following them into the apartment and aiming his gun at Tobias.

"Who the hell are you assholes?"

I stepped inside the apartment, closed the door, and then moved in front of Tobias. "Do the Twenty-Sixers know you lifted a kilo of their product?"

The way he stared at me, he was scared. "I don't know what you're talking about."

I inched closer to him. "That's not what Brantley said."

He paused too long. "Who the hell is that?"

Out of nowhere, I punched him in his solar plexus. He wheezed out and his face went bright pink.

"Jesus, man. We need him to talk, not force him into a fuckin' asthma attack or some shit," Tundra said.

"Did you bust into Brantley's girlfriend's apartment last night?"

"Fuck you," he hissed.

"Funny thing, Brantley said the same shit before he spilled about your involvement." I grabbed a fist full of his curls. "Did you break into her apartment? Yes or no."

"No. Someone stole my half of the kilo," he clipped out, his voice an octave higher.

Beast moved in and I took his cue to get out of the way. "When did that happen?"

"Fuck off."

Beast grabbed Tobias by the throat and shoved him up against the wall, his gun pressed below Tobias's ear. "Recognize what you're up against, dumbass. You stole product worth thousands. Then you *lost* that product, and your fuckin' buddy is runnin' his mouth that *you* were the one who stole the fuckin' drugs. You're worth more to us as a bounty to the Sixers than the missing drugs."

Tobias paled. "A... bounty?"

"Yeah. So where the fuck were you last night? I'm gonna know if you're lying because you're shit at it."

"I, I don't know," he spluttered.

"You don't know where you were last night?" I asked.

Beast pressed closer to Tobias. "One of you bring the truck, we'll take this useless asshole to the Sixers right now."

"No! No, I'll talk. Don't take me there, they'll kill me."

Tundra leaned his shoulder against the wall near Tobias. "Why would they kill you?"

"I fucked one of their sisters."

"She help you get to their stash?"

"Ye...ah, no. What are you—ulk," Tobias bent forward when Beast punched him in the mouth with the hand he'd had at his throat.

Beast tucked his gun into the waistband of his jeans. "Answer my fuckin' question, asshole. Did you break into an apartment last night?"

Tobias glared at Beast. "Yeah, and I couldn't find anything. Even tossed her hot roommate's shit because that's exactly what Ines would do. She's fuckin' diabolical when she needs to be sneaky."

I sidled up to Tobias. "What does Ines have to do with this?"

He glared at me. "Nothin'... any more."

News of Ines passing was making the rounds, especially since Alexandra had called several different people. Tobias might have spoken to Brantley already or heard about it from a mutual friend with Brantley. Or, perhaps Alexandra's gut feeling that the accident could have been avoided was more than just a feeling.

"Answer my fuckin' question, or we're handing you over to the Twenty-Sixers. What did Ines have to do with the coke?" Beast asked.

"She sold two of the kilos we stole."

Shit.

Beast spoke through clenched teeth. "How many fuckin' kilos did you steal from them?"

"Two that Ines knew about. Brantley and I took a third kilo and split it," Tobias said.

"And you expect us to believe that your half got stolen?" I asked.

Beast shook his head. "Who'd she sell it to?"

Tobias's brown eyes went wide. "Fuck if I know. I just know I got my cut of the money, and it's the most money I've ever made in such a short time."

"And you couldn't upgrade your fuckin' wheels?" Tundra asked.

Tobias turned his head toward Tundra. "A Cayenne is a sweet ride."

"That model has to be ten years old and ugly as fuck."

Tobias rolled his eyes. "Yeah, Ines pitched a fuckin' shit fit when I said I was buying a brand new Porsche. Insisted we couldn't be too flashy. That's how people got caught. She sent me a listing for the used Porsche I'm driving."

Fuckin' hell.

How could Lex miss the signs? But then, if Ines knew not to be flashy and she was as diabolical and sneaky as Tobias said, maybe there weren't any signs for Lex to miss.

"Yeah, lime fuckin' green is real subtle," Tundra muttered.

Tobias aimed a lopsided grin at Tundra, but his eyes held irritation. "Did that to spite the bitch. I hate when women shove their opinions down my throat. The only person more opinionated is her damn roommate, but I'd still love to force her to suck my cock."

My fists clenched and I shifted my weight to line up a punch, when Beast made a low noise and I forced myself to calm down and keep my shit tight. If we didn't hand this asshole over to the street gang, I was damn sure gonna come back for him - the brothers could kiss my ass. A threat like that against Alexandra was unacceptable.

"You're choking me," Tobias gurgled.

I saw Beast's hand relax and it seemed I wasn't the only one who wasn't down with Tobias wanting to force himself on Lex.

Beast let go. "Does the gang know who stole from them?"

"I don't know. I'm not part of that crew. Brantley and I got an invite one night and made the most of it."

"I don't trust this asshole," Tundra said.

Beast cocked his brow. "Neither do I. Call Suarez." He turned to me. "You got the number for the cop who showed at the apartment?"

I nodded.

Beast continued, "If Suarez doesn't have the time—"

Tobias squirmed. "Wait, wait, Suarez? Do you mean—"

Beast turned a devious grin to Tobias. "Anton Suarez. He leads the Twenty-sixers. If I turn you over to him, he'll owe me a favor."

Tobias narrowed his eyes. "You're lying."

Beast glanced at the door and back to Tobias. "You want to call my bluff, that's fine. Damned little of what you've shared is believable. Suarez would love to have a shot at you and Brantley."

Fear filled his eyes to the point, I thought Tobias might cry. "No, no! I swear I told you the truth. I broke in last night, tossed the place. The only thing I didn't do was move her bed frame because it's so fuckin' big. Hell, I couldn't even find where she had the money from our cash sales."

"Weren't they *all* cash sales?" Tundra asked.

Tobias looked annoyed and almost rolled his eyes. "No. Students don't carry cash. Most of the sales were through Bitcoin."

"Then how did you get paid?" I asked.

A hint of sadness came over Tobias. "Ines routed the crypto currency to us every two weeks. More of her 'we can't be flashy' decrees. As if anyone would pay attention to my crypto account."

I gave a single nod. "And since she has nothing to do with this any more - you and Brantley are screwed."

Earlier, I'd been wrong. I thought it was ditching the drugs that had Brantley so pissed, but it was more likely that *and* the fact he had no way of getting his next paycheck if Ines was in ICU.

Beast grabbed Tobias by the lapels of his polo shirt. "Do yourself a favor. Get out of the fuckin' drug business, you're not cut out for it. I hear you're back to selling, you're dead."

"Fuck that, I'm calling the cops. You're both wearing patches for your biker gang and I memorized your names."

Tundra pulled his phone from the inside pocket of his cut. He held it up in front of us. "I only went back about sixty seconds...but you were recorded the entire time." He hit a play button and our conversation replayed from the point where Tobias yelled that he was telling the truth about breaking into the apartment.

Tobias went pale.

Tundra grinned. "You call the cops, I got a tech guy who can send this to the local cops, the FBI, and the DEA. After that whole Silk Road case, they're keyed up to take down more assholes who use crypto to sell drugs... amongst other shit."

Beast glared at Tobias. "You calling the cops?"

"No," Tobias muttered under his breath.

"Good."

Tundra turned for the door. I followed him for three paces.

Beast didn't move. "Last thing. Do you force women to take your cock?"

Confusion swept over Tobias. "Um—"

Beast leaned forward. "It's a yes or no question, dumb ass. Have you forced yourself on a woman?"

"No doesn't always mean—"

Beast slammed his fist into Tobias's gut, then he followed that punch with a mighty left uppercut. Powerful enough I heard teeth clacking. Then he kneed Tobias in the groin. "*Never* force yourself on a woman, you fucking coward."

Tundra opened the door and the three of us walked back to our bikes.

"What time is it?" Beast asked.

"Nine-thirty," I said.

"Let's get back to Alexandra's. She needs to know how big an asshole that bastard is, and we need to break it to her about her roommate."

I nodded. "Yeah. One thing, though, he could have lied about Ines to take pressure off himself and Brantley."

Beast widened his eyes. "That dickhead isn't smart enough to be that conniving. Let's ride."

CHAPTER THIRTEEN

NINE DAYS

ALEXANDRA

ON THE DINETTE TABLE in front of me sat a glass of Crown Royal Apple, the only liquor I had in the apartment. I glanced up from the glass and locked eyes with Beast, who sat opposite me with his own glass. "Tobias has to be lying."

Beast poured himself another finger of flavored whiskey. "About which part? Your friend's involvement or his intention to force himself on you?"

Ugh.

"Both, but definitely about Ines. She's... I mean, she was a political science graduate student. Why would she help them sell drugs? For that matter, what would she even know about selling anything?"

Tundra shifted in his chair next to me. "We aren't sure if he's telling the truth either, Alexandra. But you need to be aware of your surroundings. Your friend passed away. If anyone thinks there's cash or drugs here, they're going to turn this place upside down."

I nodded. "They did that already."

He dipped his chin. "I mean even *worse* than what you reported to the cops. Hell, they might even break in and wait for you to come back from class."

That was a distinct possibility. I pressed my lips together as I thought about it. "Where's Raff?"

Beast sipped his whiskey and put it down. "He's around. Don't forget, he's a prospect."

"I know. We've talked about that."

He cocked a brow. "Then you don't have to worry about where he is."

I dipped my chin. "He knows where Brantley lives, that's my concern."

A minuscule smile on his face, Beast shook his head twice and focused on me. "Tundra and I have to hit the road. I didn't expect this to take as long as it did. Do you have any idea where Ines might hide cash? Did she hit the bank quite a bit?"

I scoffed. "No. I still can't believe we found cocaine behind her bed. She hated running errands, so as far as I know, she rarely went to the bank."

Tundra shared a look with Beast. "That jackass said her bed was the only place he didn't look because it was heavy." He looked at me. "Does that bed have a footboard?"

"No, just the headboard."

He frowned. "Do you mind if I take a look at it?"

I tossed my hands out. "Have at it. I just don't want to move the mattress again."

We went into her bedroom. The faint scent of her perfume brought back memories of hitting the clubs last September before Brantley or Porter had entered the picture. I pushed the memories aside, determined not to cry in front of anyone.

Tundra moved a nightstand to the side and squeezed in so he could look at the wooden headboard. It was dark stained, almost mission-style construction. At each end, the leg of the headboard went higher with a round, decorative wooden piece at the top. Tundra reached up and twisted the decorative piece. His face went a touch pink, then after a dull squeak, the piece moved.

He pulled the wood free. "Hollow on the inside."

"Grab a flashlight," Beast said, looking at me.

I held my hand out. "Your phone has one, we can use that."

He pointed a finger at me, pulled out his phone, the flash lit up, and he handed it to Tundra.

Tundra took it, went up on his toes, and peered down at the hollow opening. "Looks like it's empty. You wanna take a look, Beast?"

Beast took his phone back and checked the headboard leg. "Yeah, that's empty. My hunch is the other one is too, but let's check it anyway. Hand me that piece, I'll put it back while you loosen the other side."

Unlike the first one, Tundra barely touched the decorative wooden piece on the opposite side. It moved immediately.

"That's weird," I muttered.

Tundra pulled the piece free and his head went back an inch. "Oh, that's not good." He pulled out a rolled-up wad of bills, and a little baggie of drugs that looked like small rocks. He tossed the bills over to Beast and threw the baggie onto the bed.

I wasn't wise to the drug world, but I knew a bag like that had to be serious.

"That's meth, Lex. You're sure your roommate wasn't into chemistry?" Tundra asked.

"Definitely not. I really think this is a set-up."

Beast wobbled his head. "You might be right. This isn't a lot of money. It'd be nice to know how much Bitcoin they were bringing in."

"You regret being so harsh with that jackass an hour ago?" Tundra asked.

Beast jerked with a quiet chuckle. "Never. But..." Beast looked at me. "You said Rafferty knows where the other guy lives... Brantley?"

I nodded. "Do you think he's going to tell you how much he was earning?"

Beast grinned. "He might... with some encouragement."

Tundra put the bed post back together. "What about your bed? Does it have a similar setup with these decorative posts that are hollow enough to hide something like tightly rolled wads of cash?"

"She does," Rafferty said from the doorway. "And she's got a footboard, so if they're hollow it makes for twice as many hiding spots."

I whipped my head toward the sound of his voice. He leaned against the doorjamb like he hadn't missed the last hour of conversation. His hair, which normally fell across his forehead, had a muss to it as though he'd run his hand through it repeatedly. A sheen of sweat dotted his hairline and glistened along his neck.

Sweaty Rafferty... yum. Who knew I'd dig that?

"Why are you sweating?" I blurted.

Rafferty shot me a look, while Beast and Tundra ignored my question altogether.

"Let's check that," Tundra said, moving to the door.

Five minutes later, we stood in my room, Beast and Tundra had removed the top of the decorative headboard pieces and they frowned.

"Fuck! I thought for sure this would pan out," Tundra said.

Rafferty twisted a piece of the footboard. "You haven't checked down here, yet."

I grabbed the top piece on the opposite side. It twisted easily and I removed it. A roll of cash was wedged inside. I plucked it out and blinked. Another roll sat beneath it.

"Oh, hell," I muttered under my breath.

Beast sidled up to me. "Get that one, too. I'm gonna guess the whole leg is filled with cash."

"There's more here, too," Rafferty said.

I glanced over at him. "Are you shitting me?"

He shot me a sympathetic look. "Wish that I were."

Tundra crossed his arms on his burly chest. "You thinkin' what I am, Beast?"

I shook my head. "Don't say it. Obviously somebody's trying to set me up, but I don't think it was Ines."

Raff threw another wad of cash onto my bed. "Lex, this is a shit load of money. It might only take us the next five or ten minutes to get it all out of the footboard, but who else had access to your room?"

Logically that made sense, but I refused to believe the worst of a woman I had come to love like a sister.

I shook my head. "You saw Brantley pick the lock on the doorbell camera footage. He could have had access easily. Hell, he and Ines hung out here routinely. He watched me come and go plenty - he'd deny it, but he had the opportunity to figure out my schedule."

Beast had taken the rubber bands off the rolls of cash. "I don't like this shit. Alexandra, dig the rest of those rolls out."

I did as told, adding at least five more rolls to the pile. It might have been six, but Rafferty kept adding along with me and my mental count was muddled.

Beast set a pile of bills to the side and glanced up at us with a grimace. "I've gone through five rolls, all of them held fifteen hundred each. That doesn't guarantee the other rolls are the same, but... we're at seven thousand five hundred dollars. If those other rolls are the same, it'll be almost fifteen grand in cash."

Tundra's head bobbed in three short nods. "That checks out with what that asshole told us tonight. If Ines sold two kilos and they split the third, two kilos would amount to about fifteen grand assuming a kilo goes for seven to eight grand. We have no idea what the purity is or whether they had a clientele that cared about that."

Rafferty sighed. "But why hide it in Alexandra's room? No matter who put the money here, they wouldn't be able to easily access it when she's in her room. I can see where Ines might expect people to come after her, but hiding it here doesn't make sense."

My mind had been fixated on that problem, too. I had a theory, but they'd probably shoot it down. Nothing ventured, nothing gained. "Brantley blamed me for the accident. Not just behind my back, but to

the cop. If he knew the money was stashed in my room, maybe he thought
—"

"Alexandra, we can't work with if's and maybe's here," Tundra said.

Rafferty came to my side. "No, I see what she's saying. He has access
when he's here with Ines, he has lock-picking capabilities evidenced by the
doorbell camera, and after the break-in... Maybe he expected the cops to
find the drugs and the money - which would implicate Lex."

Beast closed his eyes as though seeking patience. "He doesn't gain anything from her being arrested. Cash is king, Rafferty. Why leave the money
behind? He could have implicated Alexandra by leaving drugs behind and
taken all this cash for himself."

I sighed, feeling like the weight of the world was on my shoulders. The
more I listened to Tundra and Beast, the more I saw their logic. How could
Ines do this to me? How could I report it to the cops? They would never
believe me, and something told me Brantley and Tobias would find a way
for me to take the blame.

Beast glanced at me, then tipped his head toward the door. "Grab
a shopping bag, sweetheart. I'm not sitting around here counting this
money. We're gonna take it. I'll count it at a hotel—"

"Hotel?" Tundra asked.

Beast frowned and nodded. "Yeah. We aren't gonna make it back home
tonight. After I call Janie, I'm gonna check in with Volt. Tomorrow, we're
confronting this Brantley asshole."

"Awesome," Rafferty whispered.

"What about the drugs? I don't want either of you getting caught with
it," I said.

Beast reached out and squeezed my shoulder. "Raff already gave me the
coke. I'll take that baggie of meth, and handle it."

"Handle it?" I asked.

"The less you know, the safer you are," Tundra said.

"Right."

———

After a quick shower, I came out of my bathroom wearing my teal leopard-print sleep tank and shorts. I had my hair twisted up on top of my head since I didn't feel like running the blow-dryer. My body froze when I entered my room.

Rafferty lay shirtless in my bed with the covers bunched around his waist and a paperback in his hand. He truly was a living, breathing work of art. All that colorful ink beckoned to me.

"Stop staring and get over here, woman," he said, tossing the book on the nightstand.

As I approached the bed, I noticed his hair was still mussed from his earlier shower. "You could have used the blow-dryer."

He whipped the covers lower on my side of the bed for me. "And miss the way you stare at my wet hair? Not a chance."

I rolled my eyes. "When did you get so cocky?"

He patted the bed next to him. "When did you get so timid?"

I climbed into the bed. "Not timid, more like, bashful."

He slid his arm behind the small of my back and tugged me closer. "I want you to think about something."

I put my hand on his bare shoulder, my chest resting against his. "We did this yesterday, and I agreed."

He smirked. "No, this is something different. I should probably give you a day before bringing this up, but most places are understanding when there's been a death in the family."

My lips drew together and I resisted arguing with him. Ines wasn't family, but at the same time, she was part of my extended family.

Rafferty watched me war with my thoughts. "You know she's your family. Hell, we both know a thing or two about finding family for yourself. You tell that dentist that you need next week off, you can come back to Jacksonville."

I opened my mouth to inhale and he cupped my cheek. "I'm asking you to think about it."

Twisting my head, I quickly kissed his palm. "Yeah, and I will, but I have questions."

He suddenly pushed forward so I was flat on my back. His eyes burned with intensity and surprise. Then he lowered his lips to mine and kissed me, long and lingering. I got into the kiss and let my hands rove his body.

He grabbed my hand before it went down to his ass and he broke the kiss. "What are your questions?"

That kiss had distracted me and I gave my head a short shake. "What's the point of going back to Jacksonville? I mean, how is a week that much different than a four-day weekend?"

He let go of my hand. Ever-so-slowly, he dragged his fingers up along my arm to my neck, and slid his hand into the hair at the side of my head. "My gut says certain people don't know who you are right now, but that will change once word gets out that Ines is dead. You got a chance to get out of town, and I think you should take it. I might be paranoid, or maybe I'm selfish, but having you in my bed for nine days will beat the fuck out of just four."

I couldn't remember the last time I'd had nine days away from school or work. The closest might have been the four-day weekend I spent with Simone at Bike Week, but that was well over a year ago. And I'd cut my time in Daytona short because I knew Rafferty was hanging with the brothers. Nine days off sounded like heaven.

His words replayed in my mind and I shot him some side eye. "Wait. *Your* bed? You said you were planning to move, so where are you even staying? Do you have a room at the clubhouse?"

He stared at me for a beat. "Would it be a problem if my bed were at the clubhouse?"

My eyes skated to the side and back to him. "Yeah, if Dad's around... Gah! Or worse, *your* mom and dad."

He wheezed out a laugh and lowered his head to my pillow. His body shook with his mirth and I took the opportunity to run my hands up and down his back.

He raised up on his forearms. "I hadn't thought about that, and you're right, that's fucked up. My lease is month to month, and I haven't indicated I'm moving, so I still have a place close to the clubhouse. Though I want us to spend the night at the clubhouse when we know neither of our parentals will be there."

"Why?" I blurted, and instantly regretted it.

He cocked a brow. "It's who I am. At some point, when you're my old lady, we're gonna spend the night there, and they'll likely be there, too."

It was on the tip of my tongue to say that we'd just be spending the night there and we wouldn't have to have sex while our parents were under the same roof, but I knew better. No way would Raff go for that, and now that we'd had sex... I wouldn't want that either.

I nodded. "You're right. I'll check my bank account in the morning and give it some thought."

He squinted an eye at me. "What's your bank account got to do with it?"

My eyes widened. "Money's tight, Raff. It might only be a week's worth of work, but it pays well and offers me more experience than any of my classes do right now."

He stared at the headboard for a beat. "Have to confirm with Beast, but something tells me that you just earned an extra fifteen-hundred dollars minimum tonight. One of those rolls of cash going MIA is—"

I put my finger to his lips. "Don't say that. I can't take that money, even if it's foolish for me to wave it away. Sure, they might not miss it if they end up with fourteen grand or whatever amount Beast said, but I don't want to spit in the eye of the snake."

His finger traced along my hairline and down to my jaw. "I'm just saying, depending on how this plays out, you might not have to be so strapped for cash this summer."

My free hand still rested on his back. I slid it down expecting to find his underwear, but encountered his bare ass instead. With wide eyes, I glanced up at him. "How did I miss that you're naked?"

He dragged a hand up and under my sleep tank. "Don't know, but I'm damned happy you figured it out. Are you sure you aren't still tender? I know you fibbed earlier when you got home from your exam."

"That was a good seven hours ago, so, no. I'm not tender or sore."

He glanced at my clock on the nightstand. "When do you have to be up in the morning?"

I grinned. "I thought I told you. Tomorrow, I'm going to study in the morning."

"How early in the morning?"

I smirked. "Not that early. Nine or nine-thirty would work, which means we have time right now. Actually, I might spend some time studying your body and these tattoos."

His gorgeous brown eyes blazed and his hips bucked, which allowed his erection to graze my pussy. "I'm an open book, Robertson."

I shifted my hips up, seeking that contact again. "Then I better get started."

He shook his head. "As much as I'd like that, tonight, I want to watch you take me."

Even though I knew what he meant, there were nuances to his words and I asked, "Take you?"

He smirked again, and this one was devilish. "Yeah. I want to watch you bounce on my dick, and if you can handle it, I'm gonna fuck you again reverse cowgirl afterward."

All of that excited me, but I was a realist. I widened my eyes at him. "I'm still pretty new to this."

He grinned. "Yeah, and that makes it even better, baby."

I returned his grin. "Just pointing out, there's no reason we can't do what we both want."

"You're right," he whispered.

He dropped his lips to mine while his other hand went inside my sleep tank. I gasped when both of his thumbs slid across my nipples. His tongue pushed inside my mouth and no matter how I tried to keep up with his kiss, he controlled it. He took what he wanted from this kiss and I liked what he took.

I dragged one of my hands up his back and slid my fingers into his semi-damp hair. My legs spread, his hips dropped down, and I moaned at the sensation.

I loved this - even if we were just making out - there was a nearness to it, a comfort that sent a thrill down my spine.

Out of nowhere, Rafferty rolled to his back and I pulled back with a smile. "That was fun."

His eyes heated. "It's gonna *be* fun when you get naked and settle your wet pussy on my cock, Lex."

I reached for the hem of my tank, but he shoved it up forcing me to raise my arms. He sat up to tug it off me. Then his mouth was on my nipple.

My head tipped back while my hands clutched him to me. "God, yes."

He chuckled and let me go with his mouth. His hands shoved into my sleep shorts and panties. "Gonna have to help me out here, baby."

I was so turned on, any awkwardness I might have felt fell by the wayside and I lifted up a leg so I could help him get my clothes off.

Once I was naked, Rafferty slid his fingers between my legs. I moved instinctively.

"Fuck, Lex. You're so wet for me, I don't know if I want to feast on your sweet, wet pussy, or if I want to fuck you, or play with you some more just to see how goddamn wet I can make you."

I swallowed down a moan because I wanted all three of those options.

Rafferty chuckled and I stared down at him. He'd bulked up in the past few years. Up close like this, I noticed how well-rounded and muscular his shoulders had become. His shoulder featured a tattoo of what looked like a female leopard... or it might have been a cheetah.

I leaned down and used my tongue to trace the outline of the animal.

Rafferty's voice came out thick and raspy when he spoke. "Found the leopard."

"It's a great tattoo," I murmured.

"First piece I ever had inked."

I glanced up at him. "Really?"

"Yeah."

The warmth in his eyes...it was like it had something to do with me.

"When did you have it done?"

"The fuckin' day after everything went wrong."

"You weren't even eighteen! Hell, Blake wasn't licensed then."

"That didn't stop either of us. He filled in the color later on after he got licensed."

"Geez, Blake is a damned artistic genius."

"He is, but that's you. You're the leopard on my shoulder."

That took me aback. "Why am I a leopard? I'm not the one who ran that day in high school."

His eyes went unfocused like he was remembering that day...or maybe it was the day he got the tat. "No. Even though I was pissed, I wanted something that represented you. Blake said you were like a leopard."

"That doesn't make sense," I murmured.

He slid a hand into my hair. "Sure it does. At the time, you were a little shorter than you are now; leopards are the smallest of the so-called big cat family. Blake also pointed out that leopards are daring. That rang true to that afternoon, and I asked if he had a sketch. He did, and here we are."

I nipped at his shoulder. "I wasn't daring that day."

He tilted my head, and I looked into his eyes. "You were. That stunt could have backfired, but it's done, Lex. We've moved on, and I'd much rather focus on right here and right now. You agree?"

I smiled and brushed my lips against his. "Yeah."

Chapter Fourteen

A Club Problem

Rafferty

Sunlight filtered through the blinds, and I woke before Alexandra again. On the one hand, it made me miss my bedroom with the blackout curtains I'd installed. On the other hand, it gave me time to wake her up the best way I knew how - with my mouth between her legs.

When I had her good and primed, I knifed off the bed, much to her dismay. I scooped her up in my arms and finished what we started in the shower.

Since her schedule was somewhat flexible, we got on my Triumph and I took her to Metro Diner for breakfast.

"I really should be at home studying, Raff," she said, sipping her coffee.

I nodded. "And you need a good meal to start your day right. I know you love any form of eggs Benedict, and Metro has some of the best - so that's what you'll get."

"Thanks for taking care of me," she said.

"It's not a problem, Lex. Besides, how else was I gonna tear you away from your notes to get you on the back of my bike?"

A sexy grin twisted her lips. "Yeah, your bike far and away beats being on the Vespa."

I chuckled. "That isn't sayin' much, Robertson."

She set her coffee cup down. "We should have invited Tundra and Beast."

I shook my head. "No, we shouldn't have. They're probably just getting up. And this would cost me twice as much since they'd force me to buy them breakfast."

———

Alexandra and I had just dismounted from my bike when Beast and Tundra rode into the apartment complex parking lot. We waited on the sidewalk for them.

Beast tipped his head toward the building. "Let's head up to her unit."

Once we were all inside, Beast motioned for us to settle at the dinette table.

"This shit's fucked up, Alexandra," Beast said.

She gave a short nod. "You're telling me."

His lips quirked in concession. "Yeah, all the money tallied up to fifteen thousand three-hundred dollars."

Alexandra's mouth dropped open, and she went pale. "That's a shit-load of cash."

Tundra sighed. "Yeah, and it stands to reason that someone's gonna be looking for it. Soon."

Beast locked eyes with Alexandra. "How soon are you done with your finals?"

"Tomorrow," she breathed.

Beast nodded. "Good. Volt and I spoke this morning. He's sharing this news with Cal within the hour. No doubt, Cal will want you away from here until this shit gets settled."

"That was already the plan," I murmured.

Tundra leaned forward. "When's she coming back? The longer she can stay away, the better."

I looked at Tundra. "She'll be gone nine days. And unless the brothers have a problem with it, I'm staying at least two days with her when she comes back."

Beast pushed back from the table, but didn't stand. "That's good. We're taking the cash and the drugs back to Jacksonville with us. Any other decisions will be made during church."

Alexandra's brows drew together. "Why church? This isn't a club problem."

Beast's gaze cut to me and back to her. "You got two brothers and a prospect here. It became a club problem when they decided to set you up."

She shook her head. "But for all we know, Ines could have done that thinking it would keep the money hidden."

"Doesn't matter, we're keeping you safe," Tundra said.

From the pointed look she aimed at Tundra, I braced for what Alexandra said next.

"What about cornering Brantley?"

Tundra smiled like he enjoyed her spunky attitude. "That's club business now."

Beast stood before Alexandra could retort. "You got studying to do. Tundra and I have to hit the road, so give us hugs and we'll let you do your thing."

She moved to him and gave him a hug.

Tundra said, "The prospect has some shit to do for us before we go. Lock the door after us."

I waited until I heard the lock click behind us before I followed Beast and Tundra downstairs.

They stopped at their bikes.

In a low voice, I asked, "Are we going to talk to Brantley?"

Beast gave the slightest of nods. "I didn't want her to know that. If I hadn't had whiskey last night I'd have kept that to myself."

I nodded. "You want me to lead the way?"

Tundra grinned. "Bikes are noisy. We need you to drive us over there."

We loaded into my truck and headed over to Brantley's.

"Don't park too close to his unit," Beast said as I turned off University.

I smiled. "Not a problem."

Five minutes later, I found a street-side space half a block from Brantley's building.

Beast shrugged out of his cut, folded it, angled out of the truck, and placed his cut on the seat. I glanced to Tundra, but he didn't follow suit.

"I'm thinking Tobias told this asshole everything. Only one of us has to convince him to open the door. That'll be easier if I don't look like a biker," Beast explained.

I nodded. "He won't be thrilled to see me again. He's in unit one-oh-two."

Beast knocked on the door, and to my surprise, Brantley opened it.

"Whatever you're selling, I'm not interested, man."

Beast shot him a gleaming white smile. "Even if it's that half-a-kilo you've been lookin' for?"

Brantley kept quiet.

Beast tipped his head toward the apartment. "I think you're gonna want to talk to me. Or I can just send the Sixers your way."

Brantley opened the door further. Beast waited a beat while Tundra and I joined him.

The moment he caught sight of me, Brantley's eyes widened. "He's not comin' in here."

Beast had a foot over the threshold. "He's with me, so yeah, he *is* comin' in here. You tell us the fuckin' truth and keep your cool, you won't have to worry about him hurting you."

Brantley shot me a dirty look and Tundra and I went inside the unit.

On the far side of the room, there was a hallway. Beast walked to the mouth of the hallway and turned around. "You got anybody else here with you?"

"No," Brantley said.

"We gonna believe him?" Tundra asked, standing at the walkway into the kitchen.

If I stayed where I was at the door, we had Brantley blocked from any exit.

Beast shook his head. "That's a good point. Check that out for me, Tun."

Brantley stepped forward. "He can't go back there."

Beast shot me a look and I pushed Brantley up against the wall.

He glared at me, then yelled over my shoulder, "There's nobody else here, why would I lie about that?"

Tundra lumbered down the hall.

Beast smiled at Brantley, but it held no humor. "I don't know, but my rule of thumb is never trust anyone who's into drugs. Whether they sell or use."

Tundra returned to the room and stationed himself in front of the kitchen. "Nobody else, here, man."

I let go of Brantley and moved back to the front door.

"Who was the brains behind your drug sales? You or Ines?" Beast asked.

Brantley gave a short head shake, his lank hair grazing his shoulders. "What do you care? I thought you found the drugs?"

"Humor me, asshole. Who was in charge? You or Ines?"

"Ines," Brantley hissed.

"How much of your sales were through Bitcoin?"

Brantley narrowed his eyes at Beast. "I didn't keep track."

Beast pulled in a breath. "A rough guess will work here. Half? More than that?"

"Yeah, definitely half, probably closer to three-quarters."

"How'd you meet Ines?" Beast asked.

"I'm not telling you that."

"Why not?"

Brantley's chest rose as he took a deep breath. "She just passed on, man. I don't feel like reliving that."

"Did you meet her because of drugs?" Tundra asked.

He shook his head. "No. We went to the same gym. I was leaving and some asshole was giving her a hard time."

Beast arched a brow. "What kind of asshole?"

Brantley twisted his hands up. "An asshole, it's not like there's different kinds."

Tundra grunted. "Yeah, there are. Was it an asshole like us? Someone like the Sixers? Or a run of the mill asshole who spotted her leaving the gym, liked what they saw, and thought she owed them the time of day or some shit?"

Realization crept over Brantley's expression. "Probably like the last. This guy looked like a mechanic, but it was dim in the parking lot."

Beast crossed his arms. "Did you ask her if she knew him?"

Brantley closed his eyes and shook his head. "I don't remember. The only thing I remember is that I didn't think I'd be able to get him to leave."

Tundra shook his head. "So when he finally left, did you bother to ask Ines what he wanted?"

For a long moment, Brantley stared at the floor. "I'm pretty sure she told me he wanted money."

Beast's eyes brows went up. "But he didn't ask *you* for money?"

"No," Brantley said slowly.

Tundra nodded once. "You ever see him again?"

Brantley shook his head.

"She ever mention having a run-in like that again?" Beast asked.

Another head shake.

Beast shoved his hands in his pockets. "Your buddy Tobias mentioned getting paid every two weeks. How'd you convert your crypto to actual cash? Not that many places let you pay with that shit."

Brantley rolled his eyes. "It isn't shit, and there's ATMs that let you access your crypto currency. You make a withdrawal like anyone else."

The room went silent.

I stared at Brantley. Something in his posture told me he was keeping something from us. "You want to tell us what you're hiding," I prompted.

He turned his head to me. I could practically see him arguing with himself. "Ines told me she wasn't taking that card with her. Said she'd left it in her underwear drawer. When I went looking for the drugs, I searched for that card too, so I could get Tobias and myself paid for the month."

"And the card wasn't there?" I asked.

"No."

"Maybe she forgot to take it out of her wallet," Tundra suggested.

"Yeah, my woman does that all the time," Beast said.

"Ines wasn't like that."

"They were running late coming to get you, that's what Lex told me," I said.

Brantley shook his head. "She wouldn't have forgotten."

I pressed my lips together.

"What are you thinking, prospect?" Beast asked.

I shrugged a shoulder. "He could ask her parents. Maybe it's still in her wallet, and at this point, they've probably received her purse and other effects from the hospital or the police. Assuming the purse wasn't thrown out of the car during the accident."

"Oh yeah, they're gonna tell me if her ATM card is in her wallet. Hell, they probably won't even talk to me."

Beast rolled his eyes. "No joke, you and your buddy aren't cut out for drug dealing. Be more creative. Tell them that you and Ines opened an account together. She said she'd left the card in her dresser, you can't find it. You don't want someone to make a withdrawal."

Brantley nodded. "That might work."

Beast and Brantley went into a stare down. Finally Beast said, "Your cell phone. Call them now. I'm not counting on your ass to call me later or some shit to tell me what they said."

"Why do you care about this?" Brantley asked.

Beast widened his eyes. "Because I care about Alexandra and it looks more and more like someone's trying to put her in the middle of this shit."

A cell phone sat on the coffee table. I picked it up and took it to Brantley.

We listened to him awkwardly explain about the bank card.

There was a long pause. Then his eyes went wide. "It's there? In her wallet?"

Pause.

Brantley shook his head. "No, no. I'm just relieved it's still there." His words came out in such a rush, it made his relief believable. "Would you mind sending it to me? Or can I pick it up at her funeral?"

My head tipped back at his stupidity since that question blew a hole through the lie.

"Oh, yeah. I can try going to the bank, but I haven't wanted to tell them Ines is dead yet. They might want a, um, form like a..."

"Death certificate," Beast whispered.

Brantley nodded. "Death certificate, and I just—"

He stopped short. His eyes closed and he swallowed. "Yeah. That'd be good. I appreciate it, Mr. Tallow. I'll text you my address, and I'm sorry to bother you."

Pause.

"Right. I'll send you half the money that's there. No problem."

Beast and I shared a look that said, there wasn't a chance of that happening.

Brantley ended the call and sighed.

Tundra edged away from the kitchen. "Now that we know the ATM card is good, how are you gonna get the money? Do you know her PIN?"

He shook his head. "No, but I figured I could guess it."

Beast shook his head. "Okay, I'm pretty sure we're done here."

"What about the drugs? You said you found them. I need to sell it so I can pay my rent, man."

A mischievous glimmer hit Tundra's eyes. "Work with your boy Toby, sell that other half of the kilo."

"It got stolen," Brantley clipped out.

Tundra threw his hands out and shook his head. "What can you do? There's no honor among thieves or drug dealers. Another reason not to do drugs, man."

At Tundra's words, Beast stopped. He glanced at Brantley. "You know, I didn't pressure your buddy last night about the stolen coke...but I find it strange that you hid cocaine in your girlfriend's apartment, and then your buddy suddenly can't find half of the stolen kilo."

"What's your point?" Brantley asked.

"Maybe good ol' Toby's just lying about the product being stolen. Like he said, there's no honor among thieves. Just a thought."

I drove us back to Alexandra's, and cut the engine. "Before we go up there, do you think Ines was stashing the cash in Alexandra's room and just hadn't told her?"

Beast ran his hand down the side of his face. "Maybe. That would be the best case scenario, but my gut says someone wants to set her up for a fall."

I shook my head. "But why? It doesn't make sense."

Beast shot me a questioning look. "Doesn't it though? Her father's the sergeant-at-arms of an MC. We're legit now, but there was a time when we weren't and Cal was part of that. Alexandra's friends might not know that, but if they thought someone was onto them, who better to take the fall than a biker's daughter?"

I mulled it over. Porter's actions and reaction to meeting Cal came to mind, but I kept that to myself. He wasn't part of this... at least, not until I'd forced him to take me to Brantley's.

"Right. You two headed back?"

Beast nodded and opened his door. "Yeah. You're coming back tonight, right?"

"Tomorrow night."

"Good. You need to be at the clubhouse first thing in the morning."

Tundra leaned forward. "Beast, we need to grab lunch. Why don't we take Alexandra to lunch before we go."

Beast mulled it over. "That works. We'll go to McAllister's since they aren't in Jacksonville anymore."

Chapter Fifteen

At My Mercy

Alexandra

I STOOD NEXT TO the front door staring at Beast, Tundra, and Rafferty. "I'd love to go to lunch with you all, but I have a study group at two o'clock."

"You still need to study?" Tundra asked.

I sighed as guilt crept in. "I suppose at this point if I don't know the material by now..."

"Be straight with us, Lex," Rafferty said.

He always knew when I was trying not to be an inconvenience. The truth was that even if I spent the next two hours with the group, the material wasn't likely to penetrate because I still couldn't believe Ines was gone.

Beast grinned. "She's always been a smartie. If she says she's got this, I believe her."

I gave Beast a head shake. "I need to get on campus by one-fifty. I don't want to force you all to eat fast and—"

Beast shoved his sunglasses up on his head, his blue eyes full of confusion. "You aren't forcing us to do anything, Allie-Alexandra."

I blushed at him using the nickname he gave me when I was a kid. "Okay, where are we headed?"

"McAllister's," Tundra said.

We piled into Rafferty's Titan, Beast and Tundra insisting that I sit up front.

"Are you good on rent for the next few months? Or are you going to start looking for another roommate?" Tundra asked.

I stared out the window, my mind flooding with memories of Ines and me after move-in day. We'd been neighbors at our last complex and bonded before Simone moved. Which was good because when our old complex raised the rent, we both needed a roommate and we'd found a new place. The idea of going through that hassle again made my stomach twist.

In the side mirror, I made eye contact with Tundra who sat behind me. "I'm sure I could find a new roommate, but I'm thinking I might be better off moving. Get away from the memories and start fresh."

Tundra reached up and gave my shoulder a squeeze. "I understood you being here when you could room with Simone, but - JU has a dental program."

If I had a dollar for every time I'd heard that. Simone's mom graduated from Jacksonville University, and she raved about how much she loved it.

I shot Tundra a small smile through the side mirror. "I know, but now I have a part-time gig with a cool pediatric dentist and I only have another two years to go."

The air in the cab felt stifling.

"Seems the prospect doesn't like that," Beast said.

"Not exactly. I didn't know JU had a program, that's all," Rafferty said.

Tundra chuckled. "Bet you're more motivated than Jackie for her to apply there."

Rafferty turned as though he were checking his blindspot. It struck me that he was probably hiding his disgruntled reaction to Tundra's razzing.

"It's not like the brothers will give him much free time. Or have you stopped running prospects ragged?"

Beast laughed. "You're right. He couldn't be so lucky."

Rafferty pulled into the parking lot for a large shopping center, and parked in front of McAllister's.

———

By the time I was half way through with my food, Beast crumpled up his sandwich wrapper. When I glanced his way, his concerned expression made me brace.

"When your roomie was working for the auto parts place, did she ever talk about someone giving her a hard time?" Beast asked.

I thought back, then frowned. "No. She talked about them being misogynistic, but that goes with that territory."

Tundra picked up a potato chip and pointed it at me. "Anybody ever corner her outside your gym? You two were workout buddies, right?"

I nodded. "We were, but she was far more committed to gym life than I was."

"What do you mean?" Rafferty asked.

"She'd go twice a day some weeks. It depended on which classes were on offer. So, if someone confronted her in the parking lot or something when she went alone, she never told me."

We lapsed into silence.

I caught Beast's attention. "Are you going to tell me what's going on? Should I be on the look-out for someone who was giving her a hard time?"

Beast sighed. "No. It happened when she first met Brantley."

"It's how they met, to hear him tell it," Tundra said.

Rafferty looked at Tundra. "You don't believe him?"

Tundra shrugged. "Like I told Alexandra, I don't trust anyone when drugs enter the picture."

"I don't think Brantley was lying about that. Ines said she met him outside the gym one night. I never really asked more than that because it was a while before I met him."

Beast sipped his drink and put it down. "It's good you're coming back home. You probably don't have anything to worry about, but giving this shit a week to die down doesn't hurt."

Tundra glanced at his watch. "We gotta get you back if you're gonna make it to your study group."

The following afternoon, I opened the door to my apartment, and saw Rafferty in the kitchen.

"Did your finals go well?" Rafferty asked.

"They're done. At this point that's all I care about. I'm starving," I said, while setting my backpack on the couch.

He grinned. "I thought you might be hungry when you got back, so I took the rest of the mochi out a few minutes ago."

I hurried into the kitchen. "You're the best!"

Rafferty held the plate out to me. I grabbed a mochi piece, popped it in my mouth, and gave a small moan.

Rafferty stared at me like I was cute. "You aren't going to like this idea."

I swallowed the ice cream. "If you know I'm not going to like this, why not come up with a different idea?"

"I think we should leave your car here."

I blinked. "That would leave me without a car in Jacksonville."

"Yeah... but you stay with me - I'll take you anywhere you want to go."

My eyebrow arched with the sardonic twist of my lips. "The brothers are going to put you back to work."

"Maybe, but you never know."

"Who are you trying to convince, me or yourself?"

He put the plate down and crossed his arms. "Seriously, Lex. There's no point in both of us driving back."

This was true, but I hated being so dependent on him to get around. "Fine. But it'll be harder to look into JU without wheels."

A 'don't-give-me-any-bullshit' grin spread on his face. "You can do that online. And really, someone will take you if you're serious."

"Okay, when are we leaving?" I asked.

"My bike's already loaded into the bed of my truck. How soon can you be ready?"

My brows drew together. "You want to go tonight?"

His eyes turned molten. "I want you in my bed at my house at my mercy. The sooner, the better, baby."

I felt myself get wet. "I thought you had an apartment."

His lips quirked. "I said I was renting. Didn't say what type of place." He dipped his chin. "You wanna stand here and talk real estate, or you want to get your shit together?"

<hr>

Two and a half hours later, Rafferty pulled his truck into a narrow, gleaming gray driveway. From the outside, the house seemed small, but it also looked brand-spanking new.

The house was located on the edge of Avondale, a few blocks off Highway 17, where the homes could be affordable, but *this* house looked pricey.

"How much is your rent, Raff?"

He pulled the keys from the ignition. "Half of what it should be."

My eyes widened and I turned my head toward him. "Half? How on earth—"

He chuckled. "Dad bought it, and it was in shambles according to him. I put in the roof with the help of a few buddies I used to work with in roofing. It took five days when it should have taken two. Roofing has to be one of the hardest fuckin' jobs I've ever had, but I saved Dad over ten grand doing it."

"Really?" I asked, impressed and proud of him.

He nodded. "Did most of the re-wiring. Helped re-plumb both bathrooms. The kitchen isn't done yet. Needs a new sink, new cabinets came in just before I went to Memphis, the appliances are dated, but they work."

I shot him a small closed-lip smile. "And your dad gave you half rent because of that?"

He shrugged a shoulder. "Got half rent because all the work I did saved Dad a minimum of thirty grand and since I did most of it, he knows I'm gonna take great fucking care of the place."

We hopped out of the truck and Rafferty grabbed my bags. "What about your stuff?"

He fiddled with the key ring until he had a single key between his fingers. "My clothes and shit are in the saddlebags. I'll grab them when I unload the bike. Let me give you a tour."

The inside of the house was even more impressive than the outside.

The hardwood floors were honey-colored and gleamed like they'd been waxed. The walls were freshly painted in a soft beige, and he had a wooden sunburst hanging over the couch. I knew it came from Relax, Aunt Lisa's furniture store, because I'd had my eye on it for over a year.

"I can see you have great taste." I tipped my head toward the wall. "If I'd had somewhere to put it, I was going to buy that piece."

A knowing gleam hit his eyes as he gave me a wide grin.

"What's that grin for?"

"Jazz told me that you wanted it."

My reactions warred within me. "Um... that seems creepy."

He shook his head. "No. I did it out of spite at the time. Luckily, it seems it worked out."

My head tilted. "Do you think we would have worked this out?"

He stalked closer to me. "I don't know. I know it's not worth thinkin' about that shit. It wastes energy."

I wandered into the kitchen and stopped short. "You think this room still needs work?"

A lopsided smile flitted across his face. "Not gonna do a job half-assed."

"But—"

"You should see the bathrooms first."

I followed him through the rest of the house. The guest bath had a large walk-in shower with dark metal fixtures and marble hexagon mosaic tiles on the walls and floors. The toilet looked different to me.

Rafferty leaned toward me. "It's a bidet."

"Okay."

He chuckled. "Don't knock it until you try it."

Everything from the floors to the bidet to the fixtures shone like a showroom, and it even smelled new.

He guided me to the nearby guest room, which served as a catch-all for tools and kitchen cabinets still in their boxes.

"No pressure, but you transfer to JU, this'll be your office to study or whatever."

Excitement and nervousness bubbled in my veins. "You're thinking ahead."

"Not wasting any more time."

"Right."

He grabbed my hand and led me to the other side of the house. We hurried through the roomy living room again. We hit his bedroom, and the thick bundle of flattened cardboard boxes waiting to be assembled stole my attention.

He really had intended to move.

I focused on his king-sized bed. The dark sheets were rumpled, the comforter hanging off to one side.

"I thought you made the bed now," I muttered without thinking.

He chuckled, the dark sound filling the room. "I make the bed when I'm a guest. I don't make it when I know I'm gonna get right back in it."

I glanced up at him. "I thought you'd turned over a new leaf."

He shot me a pointed look. "Does that shit really matter to you?"

"I guess not."

He leaned over and tugged off his motorcycle boots. "All right then. Let's have sex, shower, then we'll walk over to Okinawa."

I loved Okinawa. As hibachi restaurants went, it couldn't be beat, but I couldn't imagine trying to cross the busy streets between here and there. "We'll walk there?"

"It's five blocks, woman."

I nodded once. "Yeah, and those are five blocks we could ride on your Triumph."

He shook his head, a small smile playing on his lips. "We totally owe Blood."

I did a short eye roll. "Maybe we owe Dad. He's the one who left his phone behind on Sunday."

He put his hands on my hips, his fingers gliding along my belly to the button of my shorts. "No more talking about who we owe. It's time to get naked, baby."

I tugged his t-shirt free of his jeans while he undid my shorts. He shrugged off his cut, tossed it to a nearby rocking chair, and yanked his t-shirt off. I multi-tasked by taking off my shirt and toeing out of my sneakers simultaneously.

Rafferty undid his jeans. "I really thought you'd be a matching-underwear kind of girl."

I smirked and threw his words back at him. "Does that shit really matter to you?"

His brow ticked up and down. "No, but I like that any matching sets you have are gonna be the ones I buy for you."

The possessive thread in his voice sent a thrill through my whole body. I stepped closer to him and shoved his jeans down his thighs. He grazed his finger along my jaw to tip my face up and he kissed me. I went up on tiptoes to kiss him harder. His hands found the clasp of my bra and he unfastened it.

He broke the kiss to pull my bra off. His eyes raked over my chest. "Goddamn, you are so fuckin' gorgeous."

I felt heat gathering in my chest. "So are you, Raff."

He shook his head and carefully removed his underwear. "Not even close, woman. Take off your panties, or I'm liable to shred them."

I shimmied out of my panties, then I dropped to my knees and ran my tongue along Rafferty's thick cock.

"Shit," he hissed.

I reached toward him, but he grabbed my hand.

"Get up, babe. You need to be in my bed. Now."

He pulled me to my feet and stepped closer. So close, my nipples brushed against his smattering of chest hair. I stepped back and felt the edge of the bed behind me.

A devilish grin lit his face. "Lay down, Alexandra. I'm hungry."

I climbed into his bed and he followed me, crawling across the mattress toward me. His eyes gleamed with hunger and determination. I loved watching him move, all of his tattoos shifting and rippling as he moved.

He put his hands on my thighs and spread my legs. His eyes locked with mine, and he dragged a finger through my folds.

I inhaled through my nose, his touch lighting my blood on fire.

"You're so wet for me, Lex."

"Yeah," I whispered, shifting my hips - wanting more of his touch.

He smiled. "You like that?"

"Yes. Please, do it again."

"Never have to beg, baby," he murmured and slid two fingers through my wetness.

Then he moved those fingers inside me. I spread my legs wider.

"What do you want now?" he asked.

"More."

He chuckled. "Good. I can definitely give you more."

He lowered his body and withdrew his fingers. Then he licked at me, and sucked on my clit. My hips jerked and his hands went to my ass and held me still.

I moaned and pressed my head back into the pillow.

Then he went to work with his tongue and proved just how hungry he really was for me. I drove my fingers into his hair, trying not to pull it.

He made a noise against me, and inadvertently I pulled his hair anyway.

"Mmm," he hummed.

"Raff...I'm gonna..."

I trailed off because my orgasm hit faster and harder than I'd expected.

He surged up, then surged inside me.

I mewled and grabbed his ass to hold him to me.

He stilled his hips. "You good?"

I stared up into his brown eyes. "Better than good... way fucking better."

His eyes warmed and he kissed me.

Something about tasting myself on him turned me on and I threw a leg over his ass.

He broke the kiss. "Somebody's getting impatient."

I dragged my tongue across my upper lip. "I want you to fuck me... Now."

He pressed his lips together. Then sighed. "Shit. I need to get a condom."

I held him tighter with my hands and my leg. "Don't you fucking dare, Rafferty Rolland. You're right where you need to be. I'm on the pill. I want you. Just you. I love feeling your cock inside me. Let me have this, please."

He hung his head even as he slowly glided in and out. "Fuck. You're putting me to the test already, aren't you? Said you'd never have to beg."

I slid my hand along his cheek. "I love you."

He leaned into my hand. "Love you more, Lex. Are you ready?"

I nodded.

He kissed me, but it was short. "This might be fast, Lex. You feel so fuckin' good, so fuckin' right."

"I know. Now fuck me so we can both feel good."

He reached back and moved my leg. Then he pulled my other leg up and rested my calves on his shoulders. "Can you handle that?"

"Yeah," I breathed.

His hips moved and I realized this position changed the angle, and that was even better. Then he picked up the tempo and pounded into me. It became clear he'd lost control.

I felt another orgasm building with every powerful thrust. We were moving up the bed, and I reached back to the headboard. I pushed back and matched his rhythm.

"Fuck," he grunted.

The sound of skin slapping and our labored breathing filled the room.

"Yes, Raff," I whispered.

He began to grind into me, and the building orgasm crashed over me.

I'd never had such a long-lasting orgasm. I was so caught up in it, I had no idea how long it was before his thrusts stilled and I felt him come inside me.

What he said after my first time replayed in my mind. 'Honey, you'll probably like it better that way. I sure as hell will.'

Oh yeah, I definitely liked having him bare much better.

Ever so gently, he lowered my legs, then lowered his bulk onto me, tucking his face in the crook of my neck and shoulder. "I shouldn't have done that."

I wrapped my arms around him, enjoying having him this close. "What? Why?"

He lifted his head to look me in the eye. "I never, ever want to be the reason you're hurt."

I shot him a look. "Have you skipped condoms with anyone else?"

His eyes slid to the side. "No."

My eyes widened. "Then it's unlikely that you aren't clean."

He shot me some side-eye. "But the chances aren't zero."

I leaned up and nipped his jaw. "Stop. You're borrowing trouble. I should probably clean up before I leave a wet spot."

He gave me a lascivious grin. "Learn fast, Robertson: I don't care if you leave a wet spot. Just proves we fucked and fucked hard."

Chapter Sixteen

Put Me to the Test

Rafferty

"I KNEW WE SHOULD have ridden the bike over here, Rafferty. I'm way too full to walk all the way back."

We were holding hands and walking back to my place after stuffing ourselves silly at Okinawa.

I swung our hands up higher. "You'll be fine, woman. We only got two and a half blocks to go. Think of it this way, it gives your food time to digest."

She leaned her shoulder into mine. "Whatever. Maybe you can give me a piggy-back ride."

I laughed. "Don't be a wimp. You can hack it, Lex. Think about something else."

She glanced up at me with a half-pout. "Fine. Who else is prospecting with you?"

It struck me that with her being in Gainesville, there was quite a bit going on here that she didn't know about.

"There's five of us. I'm not sure one guy is going to make it, but Killian, Ryan—"

"Wait! Ry and Kill... from Biloxi?" she asked, excitement and confusion in her tone.

"Yeah," I asked, fighting against unfounded jealousy at her reaction.

"When did that happen?"

I glanced at her. "End of January. Mickayla moved out here for school."

"She did?"

"Yeah."

Her head tilted. "I feel like I've been out of it. Why wouldn't Jasmine or Gabby tell me this?"

I shook my head. "I'm not sure they know since they don't care about prospects until they earn their patches."

Her lips twisted and she nodded. "That makes sense now that you mention it. Nobody mentions word one about prospects until they're members."

"Very true."

"So there are three legacies, right now?"

We turned and walked up the flagstone path to the front porch. I let us into the house and locked the door behind us, tossing my keys in a bowl next to the door. "Four. Bobby just got his bike and started prospecting after Mother's Day."

She closed her eyes for a beat. "Bet that upset Aunt Jackie."

I shook my head. "Not from what he or Volt says about it. Then again, I think Volt's looking forward to giving his son the shit jobs prospects get."

Her teeth grazed her upper lip. "They're going to hold my crap against you, aren't they?"

I shrugged a shoulder. "It could go either way. Right now, I doubt it. But I don't care."

Her eyes went wide. "Might mean Kill or Ry patch in before you."

I bent and pulled off my boots, setting them beside the couch. "I don't care if the brothers patch them in before me."

Her mouth dropped open. "Really? Do you have a fever? You're almost as competitive as I am."

I shot her a half-grin. "Yes, really. An older brother has taken Kill and Ry under his wing and they're putting their all into a bar he just opened on the Westside near I-10 and State Route 23."

Her eyes locked with mine. "There's *nothing* around there right now."

I nodded. "That's true... for now. Lark chose a location in a small strip mall with a corner store at Halseema. There are people who live around there, and he seems to be in tune with what they want in a neighborhood bar."

Lark was a transfer to Jacksonville from the Memphis chapter. He had the air of a loner. None of the other brothers had that kind of demeanor, but they all accepted Lark with open arms. I figured he had a past and it wasn't any of my business.

An impressed expression crossed her face. "Oh. Well, I hope it does well."

I grinned and sat down on the couch. "We can go there Saturday night. They're soft launching tonight and tomorrow. I'm sure Mickayla would love to see you."

She smiled and settled in next to me. "What's the name of the bar?"

I huffed out a chuckle. "On a Lark."

She laughed. "That's... That's actually a kick-ass name even if it seems a little over the top."

My brows furrowed. "You don't like Lark much."

She took a deep breath. "I never said that. I've only been around him maybe three times. He just seems different. Like he has a past."

My brows shot up and I pulled her closer. "All the brothers do. Even you and I do — though we're just getting started."

From the far-away look in her eyes, I knew she was considering my words. She slid her hands up to my shoulders. "What was it like being with the Devil Lancers?"

I felt her body go stiff at the pointed look I gave her. "Not the same as Jacksonville... and not for me."

Her eyes narrowed a touch. "That's a bullshit answer."

"No, I'm being diplomatic."

"Why wasn't it for you?"

I ran a hand up and down her back. "They break the law... every day."

"Ah. So you're—"

My chin dipped so that an inch separated our noses. "Lex, I'll do anything to protect you and my brothers. Even if it means serving time. But I'd rather stay on the right side of the law when I can. The Lancers don't share that view - or they didn't when I was there with Steel."

She nodded and I saw her fight back a worried expression.

"Are you thinking about Simone?" I asked.

Ever so slowly she wobbled her head. "Yeah, I can't help it. Though Mom made it clear a long time ago that if I grew up to marry a biker, I had to trust the man in my life to make the right choices. Simone knew that too, and I've never seen a man more devoted to her."

"That's true. Steel would never put her in jeopardy."

"Right."

"Is that worry the reason you were so against the MC life?"

She twisted her lips to the side. "It's a lot of trust. Even if I know you or Dad is doing the wrong thing for the right reason, courts rarely see it that way."

I wrapped an arm around her waist. "You can trust me, Lex."

Her hazel gaze made me still. "Yeah. I know I can. Are you going to tell me what really happened with Brantley? Beast said I don't have anything to worry about, but I'm not buying that."

I shifted us so we were lying on the couch and she was on top of me. "You're determined to put me to the test."

She narrowed an eye at me. "What are you talking about?"

"Told you I'd share with you as long as it didn't incriminate you, and now you're putting me to the test."

She put her hand on my pec, then rested her chin on top of her hand with a shameless smile. "Well... I'm guessing he told you that someone gave

Ines a hard time outside the gym, but you three were there for an awful long time."

I gathered her hair in my free hand and watched it fall through my fingers. "Yeah. We were trying to get a grip on the whole crypto thing. She had an ATM card to convert the crypto to cash. Brantley claims he was looking for that on Monday, but couldn't find it where Ines said she'd leave it. We had him call her parents to find out if it was still in her wallet."

Her eyes went wide. "Are you kidding me? She just passed away."

"Yeah, but it wasn't like we could trust Brantley to let us know later. Plus, Beast is damned good at concocting a cover story."

"Really?"

"Yeah. Anyway, our guess is that Ines was stockpiling cash and hid it in your room."

She leaned up. "Ines wouldn't do that."

I stroked her back and waited out her anger. When she settled back on me, I said, "If she thought someone was on to her, there's no telling what she'd have done. It's pretty clear Brantley doesn't think fast on his feet. Tobias isn't much better since he has no problem spending the cash and doesn't think about high-ticket items raising questions."

With a heavy sigh, she laid her head on my chest.

We were quiet for a long while.

"I hate that this shit's going down," I muttered.

"You and me both," she murmured.

"Can I ask you something before we watch TV?"

"Sure."

"Are you determined to get your degree from UF?"

Her body went limp with her sigh. "Shoulda known you'd ask that."

"It can wait."

She leaned up. "I wouldn't say I'm determined to stay at UF. I'll check into transferring while I'm here, but I'm signed up for summer classes starting next week. Fall registration happens soon at UF. I'm guessing JU's registration is similar."

"It might be different."

"If I make the switch, I'll need to find a place close to campus since Mandarin traffic is horrible."

"Lex," I said, my voice laced with meaning.

"What?"

"Are you forgetting something?"

"What do you mean?"

I stared at her and let the silence build. "Me. You can stay with *me*."

"Then we'd be..."

"Living together," I supplied.

Her head bobbed up like a gentle wave of understanding hit her. "Doesn't that seem soon?"

I laughed out loud. "We wasted five years on high school bullshit. No, it isn't too fucking soon. We've loved each other for years. Why in the hell would we wait?"

"Um...," she drawled.

If I wasn't mistaken, she sounded afraid.

She rubbed at her chest. "You're sure you want to stay here?"

I sat up. "I'm sure you're the one. Do you have doubts?"

"You can't abandon me again." Her eyes went wide, then she whispered, "Why did I go and blurt that out?"

My instincts said she wanted to bolt, and I wrapped my arms around her. "Lex, I never abandoned you."

She pulled in my hold and I loosened it a touch. "You were gone for over a year - nobody said anything. Then you were back and hanging with the Devil Lancers."

I shook my head. "I never left town. I tried to figure out my life. See a way out of the MC world since that's what you wanted."

Her head reared back. "Like I knew anything at eighteen!"

"It's only four years ago. Do we know anything now?"

She chuckled ruefully. "Mom and Dad would say no, but I damn sure know more now than I did then."

I nodded. "Okay, then what's the issue here? Your jackass ex-boyfriend said I broke your heart. Had no idea what the hell he was talking about... I'm guessing this is tied to it."

She sighed and stood. "Yes. You just... the way our parents are friends and our worlds are so intertwined, you ghosting me... Hell, you didn't even ghost me. I had to be around you, but not be around you. That hurt... No, it killed."

Mid-way through what she said, she'd started pacing. I stood in front of her. "You're right. It killed because it fucking killed me too, Lex. Probably worse."

She scoffed. "As if."

I put my hands on her shoulders and stared into her eyes. "Between Cal and my own sister, I knew you'd had four guys over to meet your parents, but you'd dated at least twice that many. I hated hearing that shit. Seemed like there wasn't anywhere I could go to avoid it."

Her eyes shifted side to side like she was trying to read me. "But you're the one who shoved me aside. All because I stuck up for you to those high school jocks."

I tipped my head back and let her go. Righting my head, I drove my hands in my hair. "It was high school. No guy wants to be known as the one who had to have someone else stick up for him." I dropped my hands to my hips. "And you know me, you know my dad. I definitely don't want to rely on someone else taking care of shit for me."

"But there were five of them."

"Four."

"Five. Colton was coming out of the woods."

I didn't know if that was true or not, but Alexandra had a memory like a steel trap. "Fine, there were five. It was years ago, and I was immature, but I knew I didn't want you to get in trouble and those assholes would make sure we *both* got blamed for shit."

She stared down at her feet for a beat. "You're right."

I closed the distance between us and grabbed her hands. "I won't abandon you, Lex. We're older now, and if shit goes bad, we'll talk it out and deal with it. Like adults."

She lifted her hands and put them on my chest. "All right. I'm sorry I got a little weird."

I smiled. "Don't be. We gotta be open with each other. Right?"

"Right." Her eyes skated to the side. "Wait, is that...." She looked up at me with a disgusted expression. "Is that the couch from your parents' house?"

I nodded.

Her eyes widened. "The same one we..."

I grinned. "Where we had our first kiss. Yeah."

"Wow," she said with a grimace.

"It's a great couch, Lex."

She sat down like the couch might bite her. "You aren't exactly close to the clubhouse here."

I sat next to her. "No, but I'm not that far. Besides, it's more central to wherever the club might send me. Lisa's shop, Platinum's, your dad's business. The only time it's a problem is when I have to go to Hock's Pawn shop. But even then, I'm going against the flow of traffic."

"What do you want to do in the club?"

"Haven't decided. Figured I'd have to do whatever the Memphis brothers wanted. Now, it looks like I might be able to start my own general contracting business after all. Not sure I want the club investing in it, but their terms could be better than a bank. I'll have to take it one day at a time."

She yawned and her eyes watered. I caught sight of the microwave and saw it was quarter to eleven. "Let's go to bed, Lex. It's been a long-ass week."

She shot me a grin. "And it's only Thursday."

———

I parked my bike outside the clubhouse at six-thirty Friday morning. Prospects were expected to keep the common room clean at all times, but we had to do a deep clean before the start of the weekend.

I went inside through the back door, and grabbed the mop bucket from the utility closet near the back door.

I'd gone ten feet when Volt, Blood, and Razor stalked my way.

"He actually looks scared," Razor said.

Blood kept his eyes fixed on me. "I don't think so. He's definitely not scared enough."

At this stage, it was hard for me to know if this was all bluster to provoke me and then force me into more bullshit chores, or if they actually meant to be intimidating because Alexandra and I were involved.

"Take it easy on him, Beast says he took care of two threats to Alexandra," Volt said.

Blood shot him a dose of side-eye. "I only heard about one."

Razor stepped forward. "He should do that for any brother's daughter." He leaned toward me. "You hurt her, you're dead."

I fought off a heavy sigh.

"What? You're not going to tell him that if you hurt her, you'd deserve it? I thought those words were hollow."

I glowered at Blood. "No. They weren't hollow words. I'm not going to hurt her. Hell, if anything, she might hurt me."

Razor pointed at me. "Watch what you say about her, prospect."

Volt stepped forward. "All right, now that they've had their fun, where is Alexandra?"

"She's at my place."

Volt nodded. "Good. We're having church at ten. Our lawyer will be here for it. Anything else you need to know will come from me or Blood."

"Yes, sir."

"Do I detect attitude?" Blood asked.

"No."

"Beast said you plan to go back with her next week," Volt said.

I nodded. "Unless that's a problem."

Volt shook his head. "No, that's a good plan because Beast took a closer look at those rolls of bills. Someone definitely wanted to set her up...or maybe you, since you were around most of the week, but all the rubber bands around the cash had Riot MC written on them."

My body froze. "Seriously?"

"Yeah. Watch your back," Volt said, sauntering to his room.

Razor wandered down the hall to his room.

Blood shot me a look. "That floor better fuckin' sparkle."

Full of Murphy's Oil and hot water, I rolled the mop-bucket out from behind the bar when Killian and Ryan came in through the front door.

"It's about fuckin' time," Killian said.

"You can say that again, Kill. I thought he'd been sent back to Memphis, but no...he's finally pulled his head out of his ass," Ryan, Killian's triplet, said.

"Shut the fuck up, assholes," I muttered.

They both went behind the bar and got bottles of disinfectant and rags.

Killian raised the blinds over the windows behind the pool tables. "Did some asshole really try to get in the shower with you?"

I shoved the lever down to wring out the mop. "He thought I was Alexandra."

"That makes it worse, you know," Ryan said, wiping down the bar.

"Yeah, which is why I gave him a bloody nose."

"Naked. I knew you liked it rough," Killian said.

"Fuck off with that bullshit. If I'd been Alexandra, then what? He'd have finished what he tried with her the day before."

"He was there the day before?" Ryan asked.

I nodded and slung the mop back and forth faster than I should have. "Yeah, I interrupted him just as Lex hit him with a rolling pin."

Killian choked on laughter. "That's fucked up."

"Yeah, so I didn't care if I had to beat his ass while naked and wet."

Ryan moved to the high-top tables. "Yeah, that asshole deserves a lesson."

I kept moving across the common room, making sure the floor had a high shine. "How did the bar's soft opening go last night?"

"Not so soft," Ryan muttered.

"What's that mean?"

Ryan glanced at Killian, then at me. "Let's just say I almost became a twin instead of a triplet."

The air went tense.

"They were talkin' about Mick. You'd have done the same damn thing," Killian bit out.

Ryan took a deep breath. "Brother, you know how gorgeous our sister is. They aren't the first assholes to talk like that and won't be the last."

Killian stared at him for a long moment. "Well, she isn't dressing like that again. That's for damn sure. On a Lark isn't *Coyote Ugly* or some shit."

I looked between the two of them, then locked eyes with Killian. "Did you tell Mickayla that? And did she agree?"

Killian sneered at me. "Mop the damn floor, Raff."

I chuckled. "Right. Lex and I are gonna be there tomorrow night."

Ryan glowered at me. "Oh fuck no. If you're there, you're workin'."

Blood strolled into the common room. "Did I hear a prospect give another prospect an order?"

"Sounded that way to me," Beast said.

Blood scuffed his boot on the floor where I had already mopped. "You missed a spot, prospect."

One thing about being a prospect... it put me in close touch with my temper and forced me to control it.

"Over here, too," Beast said after he stomped his boot in an area I hadn't gotten to yet. He left behind a pile of dirt that looked like chocolate cake crumbs. "Did you even sweep first?"

Blood grinned, then pointed his finger at me. "Fuckin' sparkle."

"How many more months of this do we have?" Ryan asked in a low voice.

"Don't ask. They'll stretch it out," I said.

CHAPTER SEVENTEEN

MORE OVER THE TOP

ALEXANDRA

I OPENED THE DOOR to Aunt Jackie and Mom coming up the walk to Rafferty's house.

Aunt Jackie practically bounded up the steps. "This is so exciting! You might actually transfer to JU *and* I get to see Rafferty's handiwork on this house. I only saw it when it was... still a pit."

I gave her a light hug and a cheek kiss.

Mom came inside and I gave her a longer hug and she looked me in the eye when we were done. "Be sure to ask all the questions you can think of, sweetie. There are probably transfer fees, and make sure all your courses count for the same number of credits."

I shut the door. "I know, Mom. If there's a way for a university to make money, they'll find it."

"That's for sure," Aunt Jackie said, wandering to the kitchen. "Well... this isn't as spiffy as the outside."

I chuckled. "Rafferty has cabinets in the guest bedroom, and plans to put in new appliances. Apparently, the kitchen was the last thing he planned to renovate."

"Okay, well, show me the rest."

Mom stood in the middle of the living room. "I can't believe he has that piece you had your eye on for so long."

"Don't read too much into that, Mom. He did it out of spite."

Mom laughed. "What?"

"It's a long story."

I gave them a tour of the house.

We meandered back to the kitchen and Aunt Jackie leaned against the counter. "Okay, we can hit Carmine's for lunch, then drive to the campus and—"

I held up my hands. "Aunt Jackie, I already called the registration office and then the head of the dental program."

"Oh. What'd they say?"

I pressed my lips together. "Their deadline to apply for a transfer is in three days, but that's for a winter start." I looked at Mom. "I'll still have to be in Gainesville through the fall semester."

Mom's eyes turned sharp. "Would all of your credits carry over?"

"I'm waiting to hear from the dean of the dental department about that."

"Let's go to the living room. You two seem tense," Aunt Jackie suggested.

Mom sat on the sofa with Jackie and I perched on a nearby chair.

"Your father's told me a little of what's going on, but are you safe in Gainesville?"

"I should be."

That earned me a pointed look. "This isn't the time for 'should be' to enter the chat, as you say."

I fought off a cringe and an eye-roll. "Right. Rafferty is going back to Gainesville with me for a day or two to make sure everything's good."

"I'll just bet he is," Aunt Jackie said.

I turned wide eyes to her.

She grinned. "What? Now you know how I felt last year when you were being so snarky about Simone and Steel."

Mom sighed. "Have you put out feelers for a new roommate?"

I tilted my head. "No. Ines just passed this week, Mom."

She did a long blink and nodded once. "I know, but it'd be better if you stayed in that place if it's still safe. That way you don't have to put up another deposit or get tied to a nine- or twelve-month lease."

"I wouldn't agree to that anyway," I said.

Mom shrugged a shoulder. "The other thing is that it gives you time to save money for a place here, though given that we help with your rent already, I guess we'd be helping with that too."

I took a deep breath and debated saying nothing, but I knew better. "I won't have to worry about finding a place here."

Aunt Jackie smiled. "Of course not. By then, I'm sure Jasmine would be more than willing to room with you."

"No, Rafferty offered for me to stay here."

Mom's head reared back, and I swore she paled. "*Here*. You're going to move in with him?"

I hadn't realized how much tension I held in my shoulders until they drooped with disappointment. "Yeah, and there's no need to sound so judgey. We were best friends growing up until we weren't, and now... we're older and—"

"And not much wiser," Mom muttered.

I widened my eyes. "Not only is that not fair, you know it isn't true. Both of us recognize that we've matured, and for once the timing is right. I hate to break it to you, but until this accident, Raff planned to move to Memphis to get away from memories of me... no, of *us*. There's an entire stack of moving boxes just waiting to be folded into shape, but I know it's always been him, and as he put it, he's as much mine as I am his."

Aunt Jackie leaned forward and leveled a calm look at me. "I believe you, sweetie. However, that is *not* the tune you were singing just a few months ago. The two of you avoided one another, and you didn't want a biker in your life."

I shook my head. "You're right. To a degree. I didn't want to say this in front of Mom, but if I hadn't been wearing my seatbelt... Well, the doctor made it clear things could have been much worse. A near-death experience opens people's eyes. Rafferty said the same thing - hearing that I was in an accident woke him up. Life's too damned short to conform to what other people think I should do."

Aunt Jackie lifted a finger and opened her mouth to speak, but I kept talking.

"I know what I said before. I did a bang-up job of convincing myself that I wanted to be free of the MC world. But that was the only way to be free of Raff. I tried that, and I failed. Epically."

Mom's eyes were full of patience. The same patience she always showed me. "Honey, that's the thing, are you sure you're good with the club? I can't tell you the number of times I've asked questions and Cal tells me it's club business. I'd like to take that trite phrase and shatter it like a beer bottle, I'm so tired of hearing it."

I couldn't help but huff out a chuckle.

"What's that for?" Mom asked.

I hesitated because I didn't want to share too much. "Let's just say I've heard my fair share of that phrase in the past week. Especially from Beast and Tundra."

Mom nodded. "Okay..." She paused and bit her lip for a second. "Are you sure you can deal with that response from Rafferty in the months, and God willing, years to come?"

"Yes."

Mom's head twisted. "That was a little too fast, sweetheart."

I shook my head. "No, because Raff already shared club business with me... but I'd appreciate it if you'd keep that to yourself."

"My lips are sealed," Aunt Jackie said.

Mom nodded.

"He told me he'd always share with me unless it would incriminate me. He didn't have to share about the crap going on in Gainesville, but he did, so yeah, I can deal with him telling me it's club business. He's proven that he'll share later, and that works for me."

Aunt Jackie shot me a knowing stare. "Not all the brothers are the same... but they tend to have some similarities. Are you sure you can deal with the... What did you call it a few months ago? The overbearing protectiveness?"

I lowered my chin in a slow nod. "I think so. I mean, the way he's being right now is because this situation is extreme. But, I don't think he's going to be overbearing once things get back to normal."

Aunt Jackie smiled. "That's true. Until you get pregnant."

"Jackie!" Mom cried, giving her a playful shove.

Aunt Jackie laughed. "Hey, be happy Abby isn't here. She'd be all about her getting knocked up, the sooner the better."

I shook my head. "Are we going to lunch or what? I'm starving."

Mom stood and looked at Aunt Jackie. "These kids. You always gotta feed 'em."

Rather than take me back to Rafferty's after lunch, Mom took me back to her house on the other side of town. I caught a quick nap and woke up to my cell phone ringing.

Rafferty's name lit up the screen.

I smiled and took the call. "Hi."

"Hi, yourself. Where are you?" he asked.

"Oh, I'm at Mom's. I thought you'd be at the clubhouse all day."

"Yeah, but I get an hour break, and thought I'd have a late lunch with you at my place."

I pressed my lips together. "Sorry. Mom and Jackie took me out to eat, and then...it made sense to bring me back here."

He went silent for a beat. "How are you planning to get *back* here?"

"I hadn't thought that far ahead. Worst case scenario, I can catch an Uber. It almost sounds like you have plans for us tonight, but we never really discussed that, other than hitting the bar on Saturday."

He blew out a breath. "Yeah. I thought we'd hang at the clubhouse tonight."

My brows furrowed. "Prospects don't get to just hang at the clubhouse."

He chuckled. "You're right, but *you* can hang at the clubhouse."

"I see."

"No, there's more. My plan was for us to spend the night there because I know neither of our parents will be around tonight."

I tipped my head back for a slow nod. "Ah. I'll see if—"

"No, I'll call Jasmine. See if she can bring you over here. She works at One Night Taco Stand, and she's got a shift tonight."

"Oh, no. I'm such a bad friend. I should have called her about all the crap going on... She's going to be mad at me."

"No, she isn't," Rafferty said in a steely tone.

"You don't know that."

"Why do you think *I* want to call her?" he asked, his tone back to normal.

"Oh." A thought struck me. "As much as I appreciate that, it isn't cool to tell her she's not allowed to be mad at me because I didn't call or text when—"

"You had finals. You just lost your friend and roommate. And you also had me to deal with. No, your plate was full enough, she should cut you some slack."

My lips twisted to the side. "When you put it like that, I guess you have a point."

"You guess?"

"She should be able to—"

"No, I care about both of you and she'd feel like shit if she lays into you and then finds out everything you were dealing with - this way I'm protecting you both."

Maybe I'd been wrong when I'd said I'd be cool with the overzealous protectiveness.

"You're quiet, Lex."

I smiled. "Let's just say, I'm seeing the ways you're just like Dad... but even more over the top."

He laughed, deep and long. "This is far from being over the top, baby."

I liked hearing him call me 'baby' over the phone, but I wouldn't let him charm me right now. "Agree to disagree... baby."

He growled. "This is why you should be here. Need to kiss you, and I can't."

"I'm sorry. There'll be plenty of time for that later."

"You're right. Gonna grab some grub. I love you."

I loved hearing him say that. "I love you, too, Raff."

Half an hour later, Jasmine strutted into Mom and Dad's living room carrying a drawstring knapsack. "My brother explained a lot of things, but I still want the scoop. You can tell me while we go swimming."

I shook my head. "I don't have my swimsuit."

She opened her knapsack. "Don't give me that. You've worn one of your mom's before, or you can wear one of mine."

I had a decent figure and adequate curves. Jasmine's figure was down-right voluptuous and she had to have at least an extra cup size on me.

"Jazz, there's no way I'll fit into one of your swimsuits."

She arched a brow. "It's a string bikini, you can just tie it tighter."

"I don't think it works that way."

She tossed two scraps of hot pink material onto the couch and shrugged. "Well, I don't care if I see your side-boob or whatever. We're swimming."

"Do you have time for that?"

Her eyes widened. "I don't have to report in until six. We got a good two hours we can spend in the water."

"Friday traffic."

She waved a hand at me. "Will you stop it and get a swimsuit on? Don't make me push you in the pool with your clothes on. That's your other option."

"When did you get so pushy?" I asked, picking up the bikini.

"When I found out my brother woke the fuck up."

"Jasmine," I murmured.

A devious smile curled her lips, her brown eyes twinkling. "And that you woke the fuck up, too."

I laughed. "Okay. Enough gloating, let's go swimming."

"You're gonna wear my suit?"

I glanced over my shoulder at her. "Probably not, but I'm curious to see how it fits."

As I expected, my girls were not up to the task of filling Jasmine's bikini top. No matter how tight I tied it. Instead, I wore one of Mom's old suits.

"Chicken," Jasmine said when I came out of the bathroom.

I handed her a beach towel and led her out to the back patio. "Whatever. I'm sorry I didn't call you this week. A lot's been going on."

She tossed her towel on a lounger. "That's all right since now we're gonna be sisters!"

Somehow, I hadn't thought of that. It thrilled me and scared me. "Not for a while though."

She shot me a saucy grin. "Soon enough, Lex." She took off running and shouted, "Cannonball!"

I waited for her to come up to the surface before I dove in after her - just a normal dive, no cannonballs for me.

When I came up for air, Jasmine was hanging on the edge of the pool watching me.

"The only thing that sucks about this is that we can't talk about our sex lives."

I chuckled. "Like we did that anyway."

Her hand landed squarely on her chest. "I did. You always held back."

"I was a virgin," I blurted.

Her eyes went wide and she dropped her hand into the water. "What? You're joking."

I shook my head. "No, I'm not. I don't know how it never came up, but after a while I figured it was worth keeping to myself. Then, with Rafferty and what he said to me, I really couldn't talk to *you* about it for obvious reasons."

"Yeah," she drawled, her lips stretching out into a grimace.

"Anyway... we should—"

"Was it worth it? The waiting?"

I shrugged. "That's hard to say, don't you think? I know being called a tease and all the other shit from my prior boyfriends wasn't any fun. And I always felt like I should have given it up sooner."

Jasmine nodded. "Yeah, but you've always done your own thing. I admire that about you."

My head reared back and I shot her some side-eye. "You are the same way...Miss Coleslaw Wrestling Queen."

She wheezed out a laugh. "That's a great example. That isn't *me*. That's me following in my mom's footsteps."

I wagged a finger at her. "Nah. You've got a flair for it that comes naturally to you. I mean, you garnered a *lot* of attention your first time out - even when you didn't win."

She splashed water at me. "I couldn't win that time... I lied on my application about being eighteen, and that lady I wrestled probably knew it. Killed me to let her pin me. And that attention wasn't exactly the good kind, you know."

I flicked water back at her. "I do know, but you still went back again. That's doing your own thing, no matter what you say."

She leaned into the water to float on her back. "You're right. I just wish I knew what I wanted to do. Waiting tables is all right, but that's not a career."

"I can't help you with that."

"You always knew you wanted to be a dentist?"

I stared out across the backyard toward the dock. One of my earliest memories was going to the dentist and how much I'd loved it. I shifted my gaze to Jasmine. "Yeah. From like first grade or so, every time I had to go to the dentist, I knew I wanted to work there. Not at Mom or Dad's dentist, but *my* dentist, and help other kids not get cavities."

"Who did you know who had cavities? It wasn't like me, Raff, or Simone had cavities."

"There was a girl in my school who talked about it in second grade. Plus, the hygienist and dentist both emphasized how important brushing and flossing was... so I don't know. That stuck with me."

Jasmine shifted to an upright position. "Guess I'm not that ambitious."

I shoved my hand through the surface of the water, sending a plume of water at her. "Don't be like that. It'll all work out for you, honey."

"Alexandra! You're gonna pay for that."

"As if! I'm going inside or you're gonna be late."

Rush-hour traffic wasn't that bad for a Friday evening, and Jasmine decided to follow me into the clubhouse to shoot the shit with some of the brothers.

Rage and Yak were shooting pool to my left. Beast, Liar, and Vamp were sitting at the bar having a drink. I turned to the right and caught sight of Rafferty, or rather his back.

A set of female hands were linked behind his neck and a slim blonde woman stood in front of him.

Jasmine leaned so close to me her bicep touched mine. "That's Bianca, she's Laura's daughter."

I'd heard bits and pieces of stories about Laura, one of the few club bunnies who hung around longer than the others.

Rafferty's hands hung by his side, then Bianca lowered her hands to grab his and put them on her waist.

"You aren't going to stop this bitch?" Jasmine asked.

"Not yet," I whispered.

"Maybe I should go over there."

"Don't you dare," I said.

Suddenly Bianca pushed up against Rafferty and managed to turn him around so she could push him onto one of the nearby couches. He'd pulled his hands from her hips, but had a surprised expression when he found himself seated.

His eyes darted past her and locked with mine. A remorseful expression stole over his face. He started to shake his head, but I waved a finger at him.

I didn't think I was the jealous type. Not only was that no longer true, but also I intended to teach this girl a lesson.

Her blonde hair was in a high ponytail, and she wore a crop top with skin-tight denim shorts. She settled herself on his lap, oblivious to anyone else in the room. Just as she lowered her face to kiss his jaw, I wandered up behind her.

"Don't do this," Rafferty said.

I didn't know if he was talking to me or Bianca.

She still hadn't sensed my presence. "Why not?" she said against his jaw.

I fisted her ponytail and yanked her head back.

She gasped and her eyes were wide as saucers.

Once she focused on me, I spoke. "Why not? Because he's taken. Now, get off my man."

I let go of her hair, but kept my angry gaze on her.

She stood and sneered at me. "There's no need to be such a bitch. You could have just told me."

Rafferty knifed off the couch and towered over her. "Apologize. Now."

Bianca's lip curled. "What? She needs to apologize to me. That hurt."

Rafferty leaned forward. "She isn't a bitch. Now apologize."

Defiance lit her expression. "No. You can't do anything to me if I don't. You're just a prospect."

The air around us felt electric with Raff's anger. "She's the daughter of a club officer, and you think you can disrespect her? Fuck, no. I may be a prospect, but I'll be sure the officers get the memo, and you'll be barred from the clubhouse."

"Permanently," a gruff voice said.

I turned to see Rage standing behind us, his arms crossed, feet shoulder-width apart, and nearly as much anger on his face as Rafferty's.

Oh, dear.

I swung my gaze back to Bianca, but she was staring at Rage.

"What are you waiting for? The prospect told you what to do," Rage said.

Slowly, she faced me. "Sorry."

"Tell her what you're sorry for," Rage said.

Her eyes darted toward Rage, then Rafferty, then to me. "Sorry for calling you a bitch."

"And..." Rage prompted.

I turned to him, a little confused. This seemed like overkill... though the lesson would surely sink in for her.

Bianca gave a short head-shake. "I'm sorry I hit on him. He's a whole meal, and I thought he was down to fuck."

She barely kept eye contact with me, and immediately turned back to Rage.

He sighed, and gave the barest of chin lifts to indicate she was done.

"Get a clue! They're the definition of OTP," Jasmine said.

"These damned acronyms! What does OTP mean, again?" Yak asked.

Jasmine shot Yak a grin. "One true pair, or pairing."

Bianca slunk out of the room and after a minute, I heard the back door close.

Rafferty faced me, and I pressed my lips together trying to get a read on his silence.

I twisted my hands up. "I'd say I'm sorry for causing a scene, but I'm learning that I might be a wee-bit jealous."

He roared with laughter while wrapping an arm around my shoulders to pull me to his solid bulk. I wrapped my arms around his waist and looked up at him.

After a moment he tipped his chin down to catch my gaze. "That is not a problem, Lex."

"You said, 'Don't do this.'"

He smiled. "Yeah. I said that to *her*. I know better than to tell you not to do something. It only ensures you'll do it any damned way."

I widened my eyes, but I couldn't argue with him.

"Okay, you two. Don't make out in front of me. I can't go to work feeling nauseous," Jasmine said, sidling up to us.

Rafferty shifted so that we stood side by side in front of her. "Speaking of work, shouldn't you be leaving?"

"Ha-ha. I can manage my schedule."

Rafferty frowned. "But you can't manage the traffic lights, and you don't need to lose another job."

Jasmine's brown eyes narrowed. "Way to spill my tea."

I reached out and gave her hand a squeeze. "I don't judge."

Jasmine looked at me. "Yeah." She tipped her head at Rafferty. "Unlike him. Thanks for swimming with me this afternoon. Call me Sunday. I don't have to work."

"She's busy," Raffery said.

Jasmine shot him a look. "You're being so extra. You can't take up all of her time."

Rafferty arched his brows. "That sounds like a challenge."

"I'll call you, Jazz," I said before they continued bickering.

CHAPTER EIGHTEEN

HIS BUSINESS

RAFFERTY

JASMINE TURNED TO ME when she unlocked the doors to her car. "I'm pretty sure I'm safe in the forecourt, Raff. You didn't have to walk me out."

I shoved my hands in my pockets. "Yeah, I did because if something happens to you, I'd hate for the last thing I said to you was some snarky bullshit after spilling your tea."

She rolled her eyes. "OMG, if being with Alexandra has turned you into a complete pot of mush, I'll have to find a way to stay away from you."

I shook my head. "Shut up, squirt. Life is short, and I give a damn about you, okay?"

With wide eyes, she nodded. "Yeah. That sounds more like the brother I know. Get back in there to your woman. I'm not sure Bianca really left, even if I heard the door close."

I gave her a quick hug. "Fine. Try not to piss off your boss."

"That's no fun. Love you!"

Back in the clubhouse, it took a moment for my eyes to adjust from being outside. I saw Alexandra drinking a beer at the bar and sitting next to Beast.

Killian focused on me and raised his brows, as though asking what I wanted. I tipped my head toward Alexandra's glass and he grinned.

She and Beast caught the by-play and twisted to look over their shoulders.

"Good. I won't have to repeat myself now," Beast muttered.

I leaned into an elbow on the bar, to the right of Alexandra so I could look at Beast while he spoke to her.

Killian pushed a pint glass toward me and moved to the other end of the bar.

"The club lawyer sat in on church today. Our instincts were right. If we took everything to the cops, we'd have a helluva time convincing them you - or Rafferty - didn't have something to do with the drugs."

Lex and I kept quiet.

Beast drained his beer bottle and set it down. "The money is a different matter."

"It is?" Alexandra asked.

"It's dirty," I surmised.

Ever so slowly, Beast dipped his chin. "Obviously, our lawyer can't tell us how to get around that. In theory, we could launder it through Platinum's or one of the club's other businesses."

"Then why don't you?" Alexandra asked.

Beast threw out a hand as though considering her words. "That draws attention, believe it or not. Final decision was that we're stashing half of it in safe-keeping. The other seven thousand five hundred is being split. Thirty-six hundred or so is going to find its way to your bank account, sweetheart."

"What?" Alexandra demanded. I couldn't see her expression, but her tone was doused in outrage.

Beast put a hand on her shoulder. "Don't worry. It's being routed through your parents' bank account, so it won't raise suspicions."

"Which means you're using Dad's company to launder it," Alexandra said.

A steely glint hit Beast's eyes. "I didn't say that. It's just going to come from their account. Beyond that, you don't need to worry about it."

Alexandra held both her hands up in front of her torso for a moment. "You don't know this about me, Beast, but I don't know how to not worry about something."

I pulled her hair to one side, and put my lips close to her ear. "Don't worry about it, babe."

Beast leveled stern eyes on Alexandra. "I didn't say it would hit in one sum. Your parents have been putting money in your account every month to the tune of roughly two grand each month. This isn't even double that amount."

"Not every month," Alexandra said.

Beast shot her a pointed look. "They'd be likely to front you more cash while you look for a new roommate."

After a beat, she said, "Well, that's definitely true."

"Exactly what Cal said."

"What about the other half?" I asked.

Beast stared at me for a long moment. "We're taking a risk and routing that through a club business, and you'll be paid."

"Me or him?" Alexandra asked, tipping her head back toward me.

"Him. If you need help to pay rent, he can write you a check for his half."

"But he doesn't live with me," Alexandra said.

Beast arched a brow. "He has been the past week. You're staying with him tonight and for however long you're here."

"That's different," Alexandra argued.

A humorous light hit his eyes. "You nearly started a catfight and I definitely heard you call him your man. The two of you are together no matter what you say, and his name doesn't have to be on the lease to pay his half of the rent."

"Thanks, I guess," Alexandra said.

Beast shook his head. "You're not getting it. No matter who tried to set you up, cops would have taken that cash and you'd be out at least that amount in legal fees and shit. Don't feel guilty. Whoever came up with this half-baked idea didn't consider you finding the cash. You did, so you might as well reap some benefits from it."

Alexandra nodded.

Beast stood. "I need to get home. If you go back earlier than planned, tell me. Either me or Tundra will follow you back just in case screwy shit hits the fan while you're away."

"That's ridiculous," Alexandra said.

Beast gave her a pointed look. "Two weeks ago, did you think you'd have found that much cash hidden in your furniture or that you'd find out your friend was selling drugs?"

"No," she said in a small voice.

"Right. It isn't ridiculous. Catch you two later," Beast said, and sauntered out of the common room.

We were in my room at the clubhouse on Saturday morning, and we'd woken up not long ago. My knees were bent and Alexandra was kneeling between my legs. She had my cock in her mouth and over the past ten minutes she'd proven that she could give head like a champ.

"Oh, shit," I breathed when she dragged her fingernails up my inner thigh to my groin and then lightly traced around my balls.

"You like that," she whispered, then ran her tongue up my shaft and around the head of my dick.

"Love everything you're doing, baby," I whispered.

She hummed and took me deep inside her mouth. I loved seeing her lips wrapped around my cock. Loved it even more when she bobbed and sucked in earnest.

I ran a hand through her hair, gathering it at her neck. My breathing had become erratic as she kept at me. "Fuck, Lex. You keep this up, I'm gonna come in your mouth. You sure you want that?"

She didn't answer me, but I saw her other hand delve down to her center.

I reached under her arms and hauled her off me.

"Rafferty," she whined.

"Save it, Lex. Not gonna watch you touch yourself when I'd much rather come inside your sweet, tight pussy. Bonus, you're gonna ride me, and I get to watch you."

A moment before I eased her down onto my cock, I thought better of it. Instead, I shifted my hands to her waist, eased my body further down the bed, and pulled her up to my face.

"What are you doing Rafferty?" she asked, putting her hands on the metal headboard.

"Feasting," I said, and brought her pussy to my lips.

She looked down her body at me. "This is..."

I ran my hands along her thighs, feeling the tension as she kept her weight on her knees.

After a quick drag of my tongue through her salty, sweetness, I said, "Sit on my face, Lex. I won't tell you twice."

It took a beat, but she relaxed and gently dropped down.

I licked and laved at her. She moaned. I reached up and kneaded one of her breasts.

"Raff," she breathed.

Her hips jerked when I sucked on her clit. I increased my suction, which got me a keening cry. The sound of her nearly made me smile, but I stayed focused. Eating her out was the best, better than with anyone else.

Her hips were moving and she was riding my face outright. I grabbed her hips again and moved her down my body.

"Hey! Things were just getting good," she complained.

I grinned up at her. "Yeah, and they're gonna get much fucking better."

She smirked at me. "I don't know, that could have been the most epic orgasm."

I lined my cock up with her pussy, she sank down while I raised my hips to thrust. She gasped, but the heated look in her hazel eyes told me she liked what we were doing.

"Ride me," I breathed. "Hard."

She leaned forward to grab hold of my shoulders, then did as told. I reveled in watching the show that was Alexandra. Her long dark hair fell over her shoulders, but didn't obscure her breasts. I held on to her hips to help her maintain her rhythm.

"You're so fuckin' gorgeous," I whispered.

She shot me a look, and through her labored breathing, she said, "Not really."

That went through me like a jolt.

With all my might, I twisted like a corkscrew so she was on her back in the bed. I halted on an inward thrust. "What did you say?"

"I'm not gorgeous."

I grabbed her hands, putting them at the sides of her head, then leaned my weight into them. Her eyes locked with mine. "You fuckin' are. Nothing more beautiful than watching you ride me, baby. Don't know how you can think that, but I'm gonna fuck it out of you if it's the last thing I do."

She raised her legs, and I withdrew only to slam back into her.

"Oh God," she whispered.

I repeated the motion over and over. My balls grew tight. Time was of the essence. I let go of one of her hands, reached down, rubbed her clit, and only when I felt the spasm of her pussy, did I let myself come, too.

It took effort to keep from collapsing on top of her. I grabbed her hips and rolled us to our sides without losing contact with her, though that would happen soon enough.

"You good?" I asked.

"Yeah," she sighed.

"I mean, I didn't hurt you, right?"

"No. That was intense, but that's a great way to start a Saturday morning."

I chuckled. "Yeah. I could start every Saturday that way."

She drew circles on my chest. "I have to go clean up."

I gently withdrew from her. "We both do. Let's go."

We settled back in bed when we came out of the bathroom. Alexandra drew the sheet up over her body.

"Lex, I was serious. You're gorgeous - naked, dressed, it doesn't matter."

"Rafferty," she said, pulling away from my hold.

"Nope. I mean it. Doesn't matter if you're fucking me, or fighting with me, you're gorgeous no matter what you're doing."

"Okay," she said, exasperation lacing her tone.

"I'll let it go, but I know your dad told you all the time, so—"

"He's always going to say that, all right."

I widened my eyes. "Maybe, but legit, baby, you are pure fire."

She pressed her lips together. "Okay, I believe you, and I'll work on it. Now, what are we doing about breakfast? We could go to First Watch if it's not too late."

I grinned. "Or I could make you breakfast. I have prospect shit I have to do pretty soon."

She almost pouted. "Okay, but let's eat outside. I'm feeling a little stir crazy. Probably because your room has no windows."

"This is the most bizarre set-up," Alexandra said, as her gaze wandered about the bar area of On a Lark.

"What do you mean?" I asked, using my hand at the small of her back to guide her to the far end of the bar.

I liked that corner of the barroom because I could keep an eye on the people near the stage, and also watch as people entered from the vestibule-slash-small room where merch was sold and cover charges were collected.

Alexandra settled on a stool and shot me a semi-incredulous look. "What I mean is that the small entry area reminds me of a tourist restaurant - when this area is anything *but* touristy - and it strikes me as being presumptuous, because this isn't what I expected after going through all that."

With my elbow on the bar, I rested my head on my upturned fist. "Going through what, Lex?"

She shook her head. "Maybe it's living in a college town, but most bars and clubs, the bouncer is at the door, checks IDs, collects the cover, and you go inside. Ryan out there behind a counter is... pretentious."

"What are you drinkin'?" Killian asked, standing behind the bar in front of us.

I looked at Lex. She appeared to be mulling it over.

I leaned toward her. "If you want a cocktail, you only get one. I can't get you home safe if you're sloshed on the back of the bike."

She turned her head to me. "I thought we were gonna be here a while. Why can't I have two drinks?"

I dipped my chin. "Shit can change. If we were in the truck, I'd be down with that. Order what you want, babe."

Killian shook his head and sighed. "You're takin' too long. I'm making you a Lark's Lemonade, and you're gonna like it."

"What's that?" Alexandra asked.

Killian grinned and his blue eyes twinkled. "A Long Island Iced Tea without any tea."

"Kill," I muttered, irritation lacing my tone.

He shrugged. "You heard her. You're gonna be here a while."

A couple minutes later, Killian put a Blue Moon in front of me and a curvy cocktail glass in front of Alexandra. "Enjoy. I'll be back. It's time for me to check in on Ryan up front."

Alexandra leaned to the side a touch. From her vantage point, she could see more through the open doorway to the entryway. "There's nobody out there. I'm sure he's got it handled."

Killian glanced that way and chuckled. "Still gonna check in with him. Drink up."

I didn't have a decent angle to see that area of the bar. "Scoot down a seat or two, Lex."

We shifted and from the new position I saw a very petite, very curvy woman walk inside, stop short and stare at Ryan. Then awkward discomfort took over her expression.

A woman staring at him was not unusual. Ryan was the more laid-back triplet, and much more chill than Killian could ever hope to be. He worked that to his favor with all the women. Yet, from his profile, I could see he had his jaw clenched while he scrutinized the woman standing at the counter.

Killian joined them and the woman's eyes widened, her mouth opened, and her head turned ever so slightly.

It looked like she whispered something, and Killian stepped closer to Ryan.

She glanced toward the doorway and threw out a hand in the same direction before saying something.

I didn't realize their sister, Mickayla, was in the building until the office door opened and she scurried out to the front.

"What do you make of that?" Alexandra asked.

"Nothing good."

She sipped her drink and glanced at me. "Why do you say that?"

I shrugged a shoulder. "I don't know. The way Killian insisted on checking on Ryan, and then watching Mick run out there, too. They downplay it, now, but in the past they've joked about having that mental communication between twins and triplets. I got a feeling Kill and Mick knew something had tweaked Ryan. Seeing as how Ryan is the calmest one of the three, that can't be good."

Alexandra shook her head. "I don't get it. She's really cute. What sort of problem could Ryan have with her coming in here?"

I leveled my eyes on her. "Ryan would have to tell us, but take a good look around, Lex. This may be a soft launch, but this is already a biker bar - even if Lark didn't want it to become that. A woman like her isn't likely to do well here."

Alexandra was unimpressed, from the expression on her face. "You might be right, but she should be the one to determine that, don't you think?"

"The problem with that is if she figures it out too late that she was wrong. Makes it risky for everyone all around."

I glanced back to the doorway. Ryan and Mickayla were headed our way.

Mickayla beelined to Alexandra, opening her arms for a hug. "It is so good to see you, Lex!"

I watched them embrace, glanced toward Ryan, but he stormed past us.

"Where's he going?" I asked.

"To move some kegs around. Said he's edgy," Mickayla said, letting go of Alexandra.

Alexandra perched on her barstool again. "Does that woman have something to do with it?"

"Seems that way. How long are you in town?" Mickayla asked.

I tuned out their small talk and finished my beer.

Ryan went behind the bar and came to me. "Another?"

"Sure."

Mickayla watched him pull a bottle of beer from a cooler. "Are you over your snit?"

Ryan put my beer down in front of me. "Not a snit. Like I said, I don't trust her."

"How come?" Alexandra asked.

Ryan rested both hands on the bar at an angle and leaned forward. "Instinct. She's my age, maybe a little younger. A woman like her shouldn't be strolling in here, asking about Lark."

"Why not?" Alexandra asked.

"Lex," I warned.

Alexandra turned to me. "It's a valid question. Why can't anyone come in here and ask to talk to Lark?"

"Why couldn't she tell me what she wanted with him?" Ryan asked.

Alexandra turned her hands up. "I'm just saying, it's a daunting task to go anywhere looking for someone. It's even worse when it's a biker bar and you *aren't* part of our culture. I didn't hear what she said, but from the way she held herself - I don't think she's ever met a biker."

Ryan leaned back and crossed his arms on his chest. "That might be true, but even if this were a mom-and-pop shop, and someone asked *why* she was looking for someone, saying it's private isn't going to cut it."

Mickayla shook her head. "I don't know about that, but where is Lark? Did you tell him about this?"

Ryan shook his head. "No. I went to the keg room to cool off. I don't know why that woman made me mad, but she did. You can let Lark know that a woman who's probably thirty years younger than him is looking for him."

Mickayla narrowed her eyes at Ryan. "She's not thirty years younger than him. She looks like she's twenty-one, maybe twenty-two, and Lark is early forties, tops."

Ryan wiped down the bar to the left of us, then locked eyes with his sister. "Nope, Lark will be forty-nine next week. That puts twenty-eight years between them."

Mickayla stepped closer to the bar. "Okay, but why do you sound angrier?"

Ryan dipped his chin. "What he does in his free time is his business, but he loves attention from younger women. She said the reason she wanted to see him was 'private'. What else am I supposed to make of that?"

I shook my head. "That seems like a stretch, Ry."

Mickayla spoke before he could respond. "He doesn't act on any attention he gets from younger women, Ryan. But you said it yourself, it's 'his business,' so maybe you shouldn't jump to conclusions here."

He took a deep breath, then leaned toward his sister. "I'll do that. But like you said to her, if she comes back she's still gotta tell one of us what she wants before she'll get to Lark."

"Why are you three his keeper?" Alexandra asked.

Mickayla hustled behind the bar before she said, "Part of proving ourselves to him."

Ryan shot me a dry look. "I thought it was bullshit until now."

"Maybe she was a plant," Alexandra suggested.

Mickayla laughed. "Honey, Lark doesn't have the time to plan something like that."

Ryan stared into space for a beat. "No, but I could see another brother doing that to fuck with us."

Mickayla shrugged. "Whatever. Time will tell. If she even comes back."

Alexandra's head bobbed in a couple of short nods, then she looked at Ryan. "Yeah, and maybe you won't be here when she does."

"Fat chance. We get no days off here if we want part ownership," Ryan said.

"Really?" Alexandra asked.

"As Lark pointed out, small business owners don't get vacations in their first year," Mickayla said.

Alexandra tilted her head. "But not even *one* day off?"

"His terms," Ryan said, looking between the two of us. "I'll see you when you leave. Have a good time."

Alexandra and I sat at the bar, and between serving customers Mickayla gabbed with Alexandra about the things going on in Gainesville. We stayed through the first set of live music. During the break, the crowd had grown and it felt like they were going to get rowdy... or rowdier.

"You look like you're ready to roll out of here," Lark said, from behind the bar, strolling toward us.

He had his steel-wool colored hair pulled back into a low pony-tail and his octagonal shaped glasses perched on his nose, magnifying his sharp, blue eyes; a shade of blue that bordered on being violet, depending on the lighting.

I reached out to shake his hand. "You're right. The crowd's changing."

"Nothing wrong with that," he muttered.

"No, there isn't, but I've got to be at the clubhouse early in the morning."

He looked at Alexandra, who stared at him with an expression I hadn't seen before. A blend of respect and reluctance in her eyes.

"Are you going to the clubhouse with him?" he asked Lex.

She shrugged. "I'm not sure. I doubt it. He was pretty busy while I was there today."

He nodded. "You should find a way to get back here in the morning. Brunch is being served, but only to brothers and their families. I want honest feedback about whether the food's good enough, and then I'll look at whether it'll make sense to offer that on Sundays to the after-church crowds."

"All right," Alexandra said.

Lark pointed at me. "I'm pretty sure his sister's comin', maybe catch a ride with her."

"I'll see what I can do," Alexandra said.

Lark nodded. "Y'all better go. The crew in the corner are wild cards, and the loudest assholes I've had to deal with in this town."

"Are they from a rival MC?" I asked.

Lark blew out air through his nose. "No. Not sure they'd cut it with an MC. Hell, maybe that's the problem. They need to prospect and have their asses kicked for a few weeks...or months. Take the piss and vinegar out of them."

"Thanks for the heads up, man. I'll see you at the clubhouse."

"I need to use the bathroom," Alexandra said.

I eyed the group of men. They were at a table near the hallway to the bathroom. "Be careful of those assholes."

She grinned at me. "Always."

CHAPTER NINETEEN

WE DON'T DO DRAMA

ALEXANDRA

RAFFERTY AND I HAD a great time at On a Lark Bar and Grille, but after we got home, every so often I'd catch a whiff of the smoke in my hair from being in the bar, so a shower was a must. Rafferty was at one with my plan, and made the most of demonstrating how much fun shower sex could be.

Afterward, we got dressed for bed - pajamas for me, boxer briefs for Raff.

Rafferty stood watching me pull on my sleep shorts. "Is there a reason Lark makes you uncomfortable?"

I let my head tilt side to side ever so slowly. "I don't know if I'd put it like that—"

"Lex."

"I guess for the same reasons Ryan got so mad about that woman. He didn't say it outright, but he must think she's been involved with Lark."

Rafferty narrowed an eye at me. "You don't know that."

"You're right. I suppose it's how he doesn't mind so much attention from young women... *Much* younger women."

He dragged his fingers down the sides of his mustache and down his chin. "Mickayla said he doesn't act on it, though. That doesn't reassure you?"

I shrugged. "Not sure that matters. It isn't my business, is it?"

"True."

"But it doesn't mean I can't be a little weirded-out."

He came closer to me. "Fine. I take it you aren't going to brunch, then."

I shook my head. "I knew I forgot to tell you something. I ran into Mickayla in the bathroom before we left. She asked about brunch. Seems Mom and Dad are going, so she already texted them, and they're my ride."

He didn't quite frown, but he stayed very quiet.

"You seem annoyed."

He shook his head. "No. Not annoyed. Just realizing some things about my dad."

I shot him some side-eye. "Care to elaborate?"

A patient grin spread on his face. "I used to think he was too accommodating of Mom and her crazy ways."

I turned my face to the side at the word 'accommodating.'

He continued. "Now I'm seeing you and the other women are a separate force to be reckoned with."

I arched a brow at him. "That sounds *almost* complimentary."

"I'm not being critical of you... I'm recognizing I was too hard on Dad. I expected you to be around here tomorrow, but Mickayla found a way to get you out there. I see I'm gonna have to adjust to that sort of thing."

"Okay. Or, more likely, you and I will get more in tune with one another, and I'll know you'd prefer me to be here."

He shook his head. "No, it isn't that. I can see that Lark makes you uncomfortable. Figured that would keep you home, but I'm guessing your Mom will make for a great buffer."

I nodded and smiled. "Yeah. Is it wrong that I really want that girl to show up during brunch?"

His hands went to my hips and he pulled me to him. "We don't do drama in this house, babe."

I grinned. "Wouldn't be *me* doing the drama, Raff."

"Let's hit the hay. It's been a long-ass day."

I put my hand on my forehead. "Oh, that reminds me! I know I agreed to stay here until the semester started again, but something slipped my mind."

"What would that be?"

I pressed my lips together. "Text books. One of them can't be ordered online. So, I need to get to the campus bookstore on Friday or Saturday because they're only open until noon on Saturday and closed on Sunday."

One of his hands on my back drew a spiral pattern. "Can't you get by without it the first day?"

A rueful chuckle bubbled out of me. "You'd think that, but this professor hits the ground running no matter what. People a year ahead of me told me that having the book and the companion workbook are a must on day one. No mercy for anybody."

His lips twisted to the side, his body stilled, and he was so silent, I wondered if he was angry.

"If you can't take me, I'll have Mom—"

He gave me a quick squeeze. "No, I'll let Blood know what's up. My luck, I'll have to hang back and Beast or Tundra will take you back instead."

I fought against a frown. "I hope not. The ride back is much better with you."

He lowered his head and kissed me. His tongue teased mine enough to get his point across, but not enough to start anything. "That's good to know, baby. Let's get to bed."

At nine-thirty, I opened Rafferty's front door to Mom coming up the walk with Auntie Natasha. Mom wore a pair of jeans with a fitted, aqua t-shirt sporting the logo for one of her favorite bands. Auntie Natasha looked like she was going to a brunch downtown, not at a neighborhood bar and grille slash biker bar. She wore black dress pants with a caramel brown short-sleeved blouse that brought out the flecks of gold in her deep brown eyes, but also accentuated her umber skin. Her dark wavy hair was pulled back with a headband in a stylish 'do.

While they proceeded toward the house, it struck me strange that Dad was missing.

On auto-pilot I asked, "Where's Dad?"

Auntie Natasha aimed a supremely disgusted face at Mom. A matching attitude laced her tone, but it was so over the top, I knew she didn't mean anything with the attitude. "Do you *hear* this daughter of yours? 'Where's Dad?' I haven't seen her since the holidays, and she asks where Cal is. Are you sure you raised her right?"

Auntie Natasha was my godmother, and I grew up going to her house when Mom and I weren't at the Riot MC clubhouse, since Natasha's family lived about three miles away. Her sons, Nate and Derek, were like my big brothers since they were seven and five years older than me, respectively.

I padded out onto the front porch in my socks and lounge wear. "I'm sorry, Auntie Tasha. It surprised me Dad isn't leading you two up the walk."

I gave Natasha a hug.

From beside us, Mom said, "Your dad had to go to the clubhouse. He's meeting us at brunch."

I nodded. "Come on in. I can give you the tour, Auntie Tasha - Mom already saw the place yesterday."

She waved a hand at me. "Nope. No need. This isn't exactly *your* home yet. You move here permanently and put your mark on it, then I'll get a tour. Go get dressed. I've got a mimosa calling my name and some waffles to judge."

"You're judging the waffles?" I asked.

Auntie Natasha aimed a stern look at me. "Girl, he wants honest opinions about his food. When it comes to food, I'm nothing but honest. I'm just hoping I don't have to be scathing." Her eyes traveled quickly up and down my frame. "Get dressed, girlie."

I beamed at her. "In case I don't mention it, I've missed you! You aren't going to be scathing today."

Less than fifteen minutes later, I set the alarm and locked up Rafferty's house. We loaded into Mom's Toyota.

Once we were moving toward I-10, I realized something was off. "Did Dad ride to the clubhouse or did you drop him off?" I asked.

Mom caught my gaze in the rear view mirror. "I dropped him at the clubhouse, then picked up Natasha. Why do you ask?"

I shrugged a shoulder. "I don't know. How's he getting to On a Lark if he doesn't have his bike?"

From the passenger seat, Natasha looked over her shoulder at me. "Derek's picking him up and having brunch, too. Then Derek can take me home."

"Really? Derek's gonna be there? I haven't seen him since—"

"Since the holidays when you came over for New Year's Eve. You gotta stop being so scarce, Alexandra."

"You're right. And who knows, by next January, I might be finishing my degree at JU."

Natasha twisted in her seat. "What? Did your mother's head explode? You aren't going to get your degree from UF? No orange and blue?" She stared at Mom for a beat. "Stop the car, I gotta check the skies for flying pigs or bovines."

Mom gave a quiet growl and shook her head. "Cows aren't gonna fly - and neither are pigs."

I laughed. It was hard to say who had a greater flair for the dramatic, Mom or Auntie Natasha.

"What brought this on?" Auntie Natasha asked.

I caught Mom's gaze in the rearview mirror.

She shook her head. "It's yours to tell, Alexandra."

After a deep breath, I told Natasha about everything that had happened since last Sunday.

As I went on, Natasha's eyes went wider and wider.

When I finished, she said, "All that happened in a *week*?"

I glanced out the window. "Yeah. I guess so. Seems like it's been longer than that."

Natasha pointed her finger at me. "Girlie, we're gonna get this handled."

"What are you talking about? You can't—"

"Nate works as a police officer now."

Mom glanced at Natasha. "You should hold off on that. At least let me tell Cal what you want to do."

Natasha aimed a skeptical look at Mom. "Those brothers of his gonna handle it? Don't seem like it's very well-handled so far."

"I'm just saying, Nate may be assigned to something else," Mom said.

"That might be true but he can put in a word or something."

I leaned forward. "I appreciate that, but Beast, Tundra, and Rafferty have it handled."

That got me a full dose of side-eye. "You keep saying that, but you got a good head on your shoulders. The idea your roommate was pulling an illegal side hustle and you completely missed it? No, I do not see you missing those signs."

I sighed, looked out the car window, and watched the trees going by as Mom drove along US 90. "To be fair, I swore Ines was set up, but from everything the brothers tell me, I really did miss the signs."

Mom made a tsk sound. "From what your father says, Ines was good at leaving *no* signs, so don't beat yourself up."

"Easier said than done."

Natasha shook her head. "But to find money in your bedposts? That's crazy. I bet it was that boy Brantley. If you were still with Porter, I'd have suspected him from the jump."

"I didn't know you didn't like him," I said.

Natasha looked over her shoulder at me. "I didn't *trust* him. Whether I like him is irrelevant because whether you like him matters most. Him being suspicious is a different story."

"Why didn't you tell me that?" Mom asked.

Natasha chuckled. "You'd have told her. Or worse, you'd have tried *not* to tell her, which would make it seem like *you* didn't like him."

In the rearview mirror, I saw Mom bite her lower lip. "I love and hate it when you make round-about sense like that."

"It's a gift. Are we there yet or are we headed to Baldwin?" Natasha asked.

Mom turned on her blinker. "The turn off is right here."

***

Five tables had been pulled together to make one big seating area for all fourteen of us. At the farthest end of the table were Punc and his woman; Yak and his woman Nora; Rage, and Lisa. Seated in the middle of the table were Mickayla, Ryan, and Killian. I sat at the corner next to Dad, Mom sat on his other side. Across from me was Auntie Natasha and Derek.

To start everyone off while we looked at the menu, Lark brought out baskets loaded with biscuits, sweet cornbread, and bacon-jalepeno-ched-dar cornbread. I was a sucker for cornbread, and had one of each, but then Mom said I *had* to try the biscuits because they were divine. She wasn't wrong, but I had every intention of stealing Lark's recipe for the jalepeño cornbread. And I normally didn't like jalapeños.

I couldn't decide between the glazed French toast and the BEG bowl, a bowl of grits topped with bacon and eggs, but Lark decided for me.

"You're having a bowl because it comes with avocado bread on the side."

"You mean avocado toast," Derek said.

Lark slowly shook his head once. "Nope. It's avocado bread. Mick can explain."

With that, he turned and stalked back to the kitchen.

I turned curious eyes to Mickayla who smiled. "You're gonna love it. It's bread with avocado baked in."

"That sounds whacked," Derek said.

Mickayla shook her head. "There's a baker with a bunch of YouTube shorts."

"The one who does the vintage recipes?" I asked.

She nodded. "Yeah, and Lark made one of those recipes. It's way better than I expected it to be. It goes perfectly with the BEG bowl."

I picked up my ice water. "I hope you're right."

Natasha made eye contact with Dad. "I'm telling Nate about her problems."

"Not sure what he's gonna do—"

Natasha frowned. "Nate's a police officer."

"Oh," Dad muttered. "Where is he working? Is he even in Gainesville?"

"He's with the county."

"That's kind of you, but—," I started.

"But, nothing," Natasha said.

"Mom, Nate could make things worse," Derek said.

Natasha turned to him. "Since when are you on their side?"

Derek tipped his head at me. "I'm on *her* side. If she needs the police, she knows who to call."

Natasha aimed her stern gaze at me. "You better be careful, you hear? Especially if Porter didn't get the message."

I smiled. "Trust me, I'm redefining careful, I'm being so vigilant."

Natasha's gaze cut to Mom. "Reminds me of you during your troubles."

Our food was delivered, and conversation trailed off as we all began to eat. In no time, I leaned back and put my hand on my belly.

"Are you gonna make it?" Dad asked me.

"Yes. That was a lot of food."

Mom leaned forward and made eye contact with me. "That's an understatement. My portions could have been cut in half and I still would have had a lot of food."

———————

Later Sunday night, Rafferty turned off his bedside lamp, twisted in bed toward me, and pulled my back to his front. "Did you get a show at brunch?"

I chuckled. "No. It slipped my mind. I'd meant to ask if either of the triplets told Lark about the woman showing up."

"Not your business," Rafferty said with a sigh that gave away how tired he was.

"You're right."

"What are your plans for tomorrow?"

I ran my hand along his arm at my waist. "I'm calling Jacksonville University in the morning to see if they received my transcripts and verify how many credits will transfer with me. After I know that, I'll have to get in touch with my adviser in Gainesville."

"Would it be better to be on campus to do that?"

I shook my head. "I doubt it. What about you? Are the brothers sending you to the pawn shop or did they assign you some other crappy job?"

"Didn't say yet. Supposed to get a text at six, letting me know where to be."

The alarm clock on his nightstand read eleven-forty-five.

I snuggled into his hold. "We should get some sleep, then. Good night, Raff."

He groaned. "Do you know what you do to me when you wiggle like that? We both just came pretty damned hard. Don't tempt me, Lex."

I fought against a grin. "Sorry about that. I'm just getting comfy."

He nipped my shoulder. "Sure you are. Love you."

"I love you, too."

Five days later, on Friday morning, my eyes flew open and I leaned up to check the time. It was a quarter to nine. I darted my arm out to Rafferty's sleeping bulk.

He groaned sleepily.

"Raff, you're late. The brothers are gonna—"

"Not late. I'm off for today through Wednesday," he said, his voice husky with sleep.

"Oh."

I settled back under the covers. Rafferty flung them off both of us.

"Hey! I was gonna go back to sleep."

He rolled on top of me. "Maybe when I'm through with you."

I spread my legs and rubbed my hands up and down the ridges of his muscular back. "What are you going to do to me?"

His lips caressed my neck. "Make love to you, shower with you, and after that, take a cat nap with you."

"Just a cat nap?"

He raised his head and caught my gaze. "Yeah. We're riding back to your place after lunch today so you can get your books."

"You aren't loading your bike into your truck?" I asked.

He shook his head. "Not if I don't have to, and I'm pretty fuckin' sure you'll like the ride much better on my bike than in my truck."

I brought my hands up to his cheeks and gave him a quick kiss. "Yeah. I definitely like the sound of that plan."

CHAPTER TWENTY

STOP RIGHT THERE

RAFFERTY

HEAVY KNOCKS SOUNDED AT the door. My gut said those were cop-knocks, but plenty of people wielded heavy-handed knocks.

We'd hit the college bookstore first when we got back to town since Alexandra said they closed at five. When we got back to her place, it had been three-thirty. I estimated we'd been here an hour since we came back from campus.

Alexandra pulled up the doorbell camera and her brows furrowed. "Why are there cops at the door?"

The brothers were convinced that someone was setting Alexandra up and if so, sending the cops around would make sense.

I held out my hand, palm up. "Gimme your phone and answer the door."

She arched a brow. "Do I have to?"

I nodded once. "Better to get this shit out of the way, but give me your phone first."

By the time she opened the door, I had her phone tucked into my back pocket. I debated grabbing my cut from where I'd hung it in her closet, but decided against it.

The officer at the door showed Alexandra a search warrant. We were instructed to step out of the apartment while they conducted their search.

I joined Alexandra out on the breezeway and sent a text to Blood, Beast, Tundra, Cal, and Volt.

Cops are at Lex's place with a search warrant. We're outside - guessing the club doesn't have a lawyer who can help with this.

Lex leaned against the iron railing. "This sucks. The clean-up after the break-in was bad enough. Standing outside while the cops trash my place feels like adding insult to injury."

I slung my arm around her shoulders. "It'll be fine, Lex. We'll get it taken care of again."

She twisted out of my hold to look out over the parking lot. "You can't be serious."

I turned to peer in the same direction. A couple had gotten out of a car and were walking toward the stairs. "Are they Ines's parents?"

"Yeah. What am I supposed to say to them?"

"The truth, honey. That's all you can say."

Mr. and Mrs. Tallow came upstairs, bewildered looks on their faces. Alexandra opened her arms to Mrs. Tallow and gave her a quick hug. Mr. Tallow hugged Lex, but cut their contact short.

I stuck close while Alexandra awkwardly explained the search warrant situation.

Mr. Tallow cornered an officer coming out of the apartment. I thought little of it until I heard him say, "This young woman is from a biker family. She's the person—"

"Stop right there," I warned.

Tallow glared at me. "Or what? You aren't wearing any leather, but you're one of them, too."

I shook my head. "You have no proof of that."

Tallow's brows rose. "I saw you at the hospital. You wore your leather then." He glanced at the officer. "Search this man, I'm sure he's hidden whatever you're looking for."

The officer directed his brown-eyed gaze at Mr. Tallow. "Sir, do not make false accusations against someone."

The officer moved past us and went downstairs.

Mr. Tallow glowered at me, turned, and guided his wife to the opposite end of the breezeway.

An hour and forty-five minutes later, an officer came out of the apartment and looked at Lex. "We're done. You're free to go back inside."

Lex nodded somberly. "Thank you."

What the hell she was thanking him for, I'd never know.

Alexandra headed inside and Mrs. Tallow followed. She abruptly turned around, glancing past me. "You're leaving this huge mess behind?"

"We're police officers, not housekeepers," the last officer said, closing the door behind him.

Alexandra shot Mr. Tallow a pointed look. "We'll be in my room while you gather Ines's things."

"I didn't mean to say—"

Alexandra cut him off. "I'm sorry, but you *did* mean to say it. Ines was brilliant and quick on the uptake. She told me we had that in common, so I know you meant it. I'll leave you to it."

I admired her so much. My temper boiled and there was no way I'd have stayed half as calm as she had. It took a special kind of grit to stand up to a close friend's father, and she did it with cool patience.

It took us the better part of an hour to get her room back to normal after the search. Mr. and Mrs. Tallow wandered in and out of the apartment, first taking boxes, and then taking four large trash bags of items out to their car. Every time they passed by, tears slid down Alexandra's face. She tried to hide it from me, but I was hyper-focused on her.

I moved to close the door. She rushed to my side, grabbed my wrist, and silently shook her head.

That didn't make sense to me, but she pulled me back to the bed and we sat down.

"It's strange, but I'd rather know when they're done. If you close the door, I'm not going to know," she whispered.

I nodded, and realized it would be better if I kept count of how many trips they made. The cops didn't specify that we couldn't remove anything from the apartment, but the Tallows taking so many items right after an official search could be misconstrued.

Mrs. Tallow came to Alexandra's door. "We're finished."

Alexandra hurried to the door. "Are you sure?"

Mrs. Tallow nodded.

Lex grabbed her hand. "I mean, if you need anything else, I'm more than happy to get it to you."

With a very wan smile, Mrs. Tallow shook her head. "No, but thank you. We took all her clothing and the items from her desk and nightstand." She paused for a deep breath that hitched.

Alexandra's breathing stuttered, and I fought against pulling her into my arms.

Mrs. Tallow squared her shoulders. "We're waiting on a mover to call us back, but tomorrow or the next day, there will be someone coming for the furniture. The landlord knows, so if you aren't here, he'll let them in. I hated the idea of blindsiding you."

Alexandra pulled in a deep breath through her nose, blinked, and two large tears traced a path down her cheeks.

"Thanks for the heads-up," I said, edging in close to Alexandra's back.

Mrs. Tallow nodded at me, then looked at Lex. "I... there's no easy way to say this, but we decided against any sort of services. I wish the circumstances were different, Alexandra."

I hadn't realized she still held Mrs. Tallow's hand until Lex squeezed it again. "Thank you for letting me know. I'm incredibly sorry for your loss."

Tears filmed over Mrs. Tallow's eyes, but didn't fall over. She gave Lex's hand a squeeze, nodded, and left.

I hustled us both to Alexandra's bed, shifted her around to face me, and settled in the bed so she was on top of me. "Let it out, baby."

She cried, but she seemed to cut it short like last week.

I stroked her back. "We all process shit differently, but are you holding back on me?"

She lifted her head, her brows furrowed. "No. Not really. We should probably lock the door."

"I'll handle that," I said, rolling us both gently to the side.

Saturday morning, Lex and I were doctoring our coffee. Her stomach growled and her eyes filled with embarrassment. "Sorry, I'm getting hungry. Not sure if I have any food worth eating in the fridge. We can go somewhere and grab breakfast. I'm glad we hit the bookstore yesterday instead of the supermarket."

"Why?"

Her lips quirked with skepticism. "After yesterday, I have a feeling I'll need a free schedule today."

I sipped my coffee and swallowed. "It's all good, Lex. We'll hit the store today."

The moment I set down my coffee cup, there was a knock at the door.

Alexandra's eyes rolled to the top of her head. "Who could that be this early?"

I prowled to the front door and through the peephole I saw Beast and Tundra.

"Well?" Alexandra whispered from behind me.

"Beast and Tun are here," I whispered and opened the door.

The moment they caught sight of Alexandra and our heavy mood, they both scowled.

"What the hell? You hurt her already?" Tundra asked.

I crossed my arms on my chest. "No. Her roommate's parents got here not long after I sent the text about the search warrant. Before they left, they said movers will be here today or tomorrow. It's sooner than Lex expected."

Alexandra plopped down on the couch and took in a deep breath. "Sorry, I'm such a wuss."

Beast sat next to her and slung his arm around her shoulders. "Stop it, Alexandra. You're not a wuss. Nobody expects to lose their child at any age, and you never expected to lose your roommate. All of it is blindsiding. Though, sending the movers so soon is probably a good thing, gives everyone - including you - closure."

I settled in an arm chair. "What brings you by?"

Beast sat forward. "The club lawyer has some connections in town and they did some digging. Gainesville PD got a tip about money and drugs being here."

"That seems obvious after the search," Alexandra said.

Beast continued. "Right. The tip came from an anonymous source."

"Also not surprising," Alexandra muttered.

Beast smiled. "Our lawyer says a judge can't sign off on a warrant unless the informant is reliable and there is a credible basis of knowledge."

Tundra propped a hip on the arm of the couch near Alexandra. "Bernstein also said the tip has to be information a police investigation can independently corroborate. Plus, there's more to getting a warrant with just a phone call. It's highly likely the police were already watching your apartment for drug activity."

She nodded. "Okay, why the legal lesson?"

Beast shot her a patient grin. "Unless your roomie had more than one boyfriend, my guess is that it's either Brantley or Tobias who called in the tip."

"Or Porter," I said.

Alexandra shot me a sideways glare. "I'm not thrilled with Porter, either. But seriously, Raff. That's going too far, don't you think?"

Tundra nodded. "Yeah, don't get distracted by her ex-boyfriend."

I shook my head, fighting against my rising temper. "Not distracted. He was at Brantley's when I confronted him about the drugs." I looked at Lex. "And we found some money and drugs in your roommate's bed, but most of that money was in *your* room."

Beast pressed his lips together and stared at me. "One more thing, not sure if you told Alexandra, but I didn't notice this when we found the cash. The rubber bands on each roll had Riot MC written on them - somebody knew enough to throw her - or possibly you - under the bus."

I heard a key slide into the lock, but the door didn't go.

Alexandra's eyes widened and she rose. "I forgot to give the Tallows the new key."

Beast, Tundra, and I stood to block her path.

A man's muffled voice from behind the door said, "One minute, that's the wrong key."

"That's our landlord," Alexandra said, and shot past us.

She opened the door and greeted the landlord. The Tallows came in, followed by two movers.

Alexandra wandered back toward the couch.

Mr. Tallow stopped on his way back to the bedroom. "The couch belongs to my sister. We're moving it, too."

The air grew heavy.

Beast didn't help matters when he spoke. "Could have told her that yesterday."

Tallow's eyes sliced to Beast. "With the death of my daughter, it slipped my mind."

On the one hand, that was undeniably true, but on the other hand, this man was going out of his way to be an asshole.

"We're sorry to hear about your girl, but there's no need to be a jerk right now," Tundra said.

Mr. Tallow went into a stare-down with him.

I sauntered up behind Alexandra and gently put my hands on her shoulders. "Does the lock on your bedroom door work?"

She nodded.

"Good. We're gonna go to your room, put on our shoes, lock your door and head out."

She twisted her head and whispered. "I don't have a key."

"It's a knob lock, honey. I can pick it," I whispered.

She turned back to Mr. Tallow. "I'll just gather the afghan and throw pillows since those are mine, and we'll get out of your way."

While she gathered those things, I sidled up to Beast and shared the plan with him in a low voice.

Beast nodded. "Be *damn* sure that door locks when you close it."

CHAPTER TWENTY-ONE

THOSE FIVE WORDS

ALEXANDRA

WHEN CLASS LET OUT on Monday, I squinted at the late-afternoon sunlight as I hurried out of the main corridor.

I paused on the sidewalk to get myself together and fight off the instant headache. Other students filed past me, and I trudged forward.

Before I made it twenty paces, a black man approached me. He had a huge smile that almost distracted me from the thick gold chains around his neck, and the slouch of his jeans. Something about him said he wasn't a student, but even as alarm crept up my spine, I had the bizarre sensation that I knew him.

As he drew closer, it hit me. "Nate? What are you doing here?"

I hadn't seen Nate since New Year's Eve. He looked rougher around the edges, almost sinister.

In an expert move of fluidity, he had me in what felt like (and probably looked like) an affectionate hold and hustled me into his car at the curb. My instincts said something about this was wrong. By the time I had my fingers wrapped around the door handle to get out, Nate slid into the driver's seat and locked the doors.

"The Sixers want to talk," he bit out.

My world imploded on those five words.

He started the car and sped toward downtown.

I shook my head. "How do you know that? And why are you taking me to them?"

Nate's features were hard-set and he kept his gaze on the road. "When we roll up we *don't* know each other."

My eyes slid to him three seconds before I turned my head his way. I recalled that he'd majored in criminal justice, then went to grad school to master in the field.

"You're undercover," I said.

"You know nothing."

My eyes widened. "We aren't there yet. I'm not going to blow your cover."

"You *think* you won't. Hell, everyone thinks that."

"Fine, but why me?"

He glanced at me for a beat. "They didn't tell me. I just got in with them two months ago. The only reason I volunteered for this was because I knew you lived in that building and I guessed that was your apartment number."

"Raff's going to be pissed." Then I added, "So is Beast."

"Yeah. Hard to say if that biker's the reason you're still breathing or if he made shit worse. I'm thinking it's worse because of them wading into this situation."

"You would," I muttered.

The entire Russell family was cool with Mom being with Dad. Nate and Derek hadn't given it a second thought when they were younger. Once he hit college though, Nate had a chip on his shoulder about the Riot.

He had once asked Dad, "Why are you with them?"

"We're not criminals," Dad had answered.

"You're runnin' a strip club. Nothing but crime around those places."

"Not ours," Dad clipped out.

Nate doubled down. "So that woman who got beaten in the parking lot. Did she just take a bad stumble and land herself in ICU?"

"We didn't beat her," Dad said, his voice steel.

Leon, his dad, had waded into the conversation. "Son, let it go. Running a gentleman's club is legal."

"What I want to know is, how did you end up in this shit?" Nate asked, pulling me from my thoughts.

"Believe me, I've been asking myself that for the last couple weeks, and if Ines were still around, I'd have gotten to the bottom of it by now."

"What do you mean, 'were still around'? We heard she'd been in a car wreck, but..."

I took a deep breath. "She didn't make it."

"Fuck," he hissed.

He stopped the car at a red light, and I glanced at his profile. "Why do you sound torn up about it?"

"This changes things."

I nodded once. "I know why it changes things for me, but why do you say that?"

"Can't tell you exactly. The Sixers wanted to use you as leverage against Ines. With her out of the picture... not sure what good you'll do them."

"Are you saying this gang had contact with Ines?"

Nate shook his head. "Not that I'm aware of. They knew she moved the product Tobias and Brantley *think* they stole."

I took a moment to turn his words over in my mind. "Why would they let Tobias and Brantley steal their cocaine?"

"They haven't told me. There are theories, but I'm not sharing those."

We turned right on University Avenue, and even though we were motoring away from campus, the traffic still moved at a crawl.

As I watched the crowds walking along the sidewalk, part of me thought about getting out of the car at the next traffic light. But I knew Nate wouldn't let me get away like that.

"Since Ines is dead, do you really have to take me to them?"

As though he knew my thoughts, Nate said, "Don't give me a hard time, Alexandra. If my cover gets blown, we both pay the price."

My lips twisted to the side. "Do they think I know anything?"

He speared me with a hard look. "This isn't the time to try lying your way out of things. They got word about Gainesville Police having a search warrant for your address. *I* told them it didn't turn out well. My guess, they think you or the bikers have their product *and* their money."

Even though he was right, I asked, 'Why would they think that?"

Nate used his thumb and forefinger to stroke down his mustache. "Someone called in an anonymous tip about your apartment."

"Right."

"The caller spoke to an officer the Sixers have on payroll. He was able to trace the phone number back to a punk named Parker. No, that's wrong—"

"Porter?" I asked reflexively.

"Yes. How'd you guess that name?"

"It's my ex-boyfriend's name."

Nate sighed. "He called into GPD and told them to search your place."

I gave my head a quick shake. "Then why did you need to tell the gang how the search went?"

Nate glanced at me and back to the road. "Because that cop works the desk. It took time for the judge to sign off on the warrant. This officer wasn't around for the aftermath."

I sighed.

"I want to know why you have an ex who would set you up for a search warrant."

Probably to set up Rafferty, but that seemed so far-fetched, I couldn't believe it myself. I shrugged a shoulder. "Things didn't end well."

Nate shook his head. "Tell me something I don't know. No man with any sense would let you get away. But sending cops to your door is extreme."

Dad had taught me to keep my cards close to my chest, but seeing as Nate kept me from being picked up by some other member of the Sixers, I felt like I owed him something.

"My guess is that Porter wanted to set up Rafferty. The two of them got into it after Porter tried to attack me."

The air grew heavy and Nate whipped the car onto a side street and parked.

He put his right hand on the headrest and his left hand on the center console near my knee. "Porter attacked you? And you didn't report that shit?"

I gave him a dry look. "He'd have turned it around on me, Nate. Besides, I hit him with a rolling pin. Then Rafferty pulled Porter off me and taught him a lesson."

"Taught him a lesson," Nate muttered under his breath. Then he asked, "So, he witnessed it?"

I opened my mouth and closed it.

"You should have reported it, Alexandra."

"Shoulda, coulda, woulda," I murmured.

He put the car in gear. "Stay away from Porter."

"That's the plan. Hell, I thought he'd be well on his way to Missouri by now."

We were waiting to turn back onto University. He glanced at me and back to the on-coming traffic. "What's in Missouri?"

"His family's business."

"What's his last name?"

I gave it to him, and he leaned forward, grabbed a burner phone from under his seat and tossed it to me. "Press and hold the three button. The moment it connects, put it on speaker."

The phone rang twice before a male voice said, "Yeah?"

Nate told this man to look into Porter and his family, then ended the call.

"This is nuts. Porter doesn't have—"

Nate spoke in a firm tone. "He fucked with you. That deserves something, and my gut says you aren't the first, but you'll damn sure be the *last* woman he jacks around like that."

And that *was what he had in common with Dad and the Riot brothers.* "Thanks, Nate."

He chuckled. "Don't thank me. Thank Derek. He'd kick my ass if he found out something happened to you and I didn't handle it."

I nodded. "Still, I appreciate it."

"Yeah. We're almost there. You need to look scared out of your mind."

With two men on either side of me, each one holding an arm, I didn't have to act scared, because I was terrified. My fear rolled off me as though every pump of my heart created a new wave. Nate might have gotten me here in one piece, but I had *no* idea how I was going to get out of here. And that scared the hell out of me.

They shoved me into a small bedroom that appeared to be converted into an office. A stocky black man sat in a leather swivel chair. He had tightly braided dreads peeking out from the edge of his satiny-looking black doo-rag. His brown eyes turned sharp and he eyed me up and down. Then he focused on a point behind me.

"She didn't give you a hard time? Why didn't you rough her up?"

"Cornered her on campus, K.C. If I roughed her up, it would cause a scene. That wouldn't help us," Nate said from behind me.

K.C. - or whoever this person was - stared at Nate for a long moment, then nodded. "Yeah. Ain't got no time for cops today." His eyes locked on me. "You know why you're here?"

My eyes widened, my lungs expanded with my deep breath, and I focused on K.C. Even though I was scared, when I got nervous, I didn't talk faster. No, my words dragged out like they could buy me more time. "Um, no... Sir."

He tipped his head back and bellowed with laughter. "No, sir! I don't think any white girl's ever said 'No, sir' to me." He locked eyes with someone behind me, and I guessed Nate still stood there. "Eightball, without even roughing her up, you scared the hell out of her."

I almost flinched at the use of a street name for Nate, but growing up around the Riot brothers, I recognized the name for what it was.

"Where's Ines?" K.C. asked.

Again, I took a deep breath. "She passed away on Tuesday."

"What the hell?" K.C. muttered.

"She says there was a car accident, and that other bitch didn't make it," Nate said.

I clenched my teeth and closed my eyes. It took a lot not to argue that Ines wasn't a bitch.

K.C. chuckled at me. "I can't tell if you're just that stupid or if your loyalty to Ines means you were in on it with her. Those white boys say you weren't, but I don't trust them."

I opened my eyes and stared at him, unsure how to respond. Part of me still wanted to believe she'd been set up, but I didn't have anything to support it.

"I wasn't in on it," I said, my voice quiet and controlled.

He leaned back in his office chair. "Not like you'd admit it if you were. Got any idea where the money is? Heard the cops tore your place apart, but didn't find nothin'."

I shook my head. "Ines didn't have any money. I had to constantly remind her to pay her half of the rent every month."

"Did her boyfriend take the money?"

My eyes widened as I reared back my head. "I have no idea. After the accident, I spent the night at my parents' house. So for all I know, he could have."

I left out the part about finding him at my place because I didn't want to mention Rafferty or the Riot MC - though I suspected K.C. knew about my ties to them.

"You ain't much use to me," K.C. said.

"I can use her," a man to my left muttered.

Other men must have filed in behind us since I heard two others make 'mm-hmm' sounds of agreement.

My unease turned to fear.

"Could kill her and set up those white boys," the man on my left added.

Outrage filled K.C.'s expression. "Do you know how much work it takes to move a body? Or anything, Jamal?"

"Those idiots would rat out their mommas. We'd face more heat," Nate said.

K.C. scrutinized Nate. "You think an awful lot like a cop. But the cops aren't that smart."

The tone of Nate's voice shifted to a deadpan. "Neither are the two men who took your coke."

"Yeah," K.C. said after a long moment. He focused on me again. "You been with Toby?"

My brows furrowed while my mind whirled for a moment before realization hit me. "You mean Tobias? No."

"Hmph," K.C. muttered with disappointment. "Asshole said he'd been with you."

"He wishes," I muttered, then I clamped my mouth shut.

K.C. laughed and the others joined in.

I thought about pressing my luck to ask if I could go home.

K.C. said, "Put her in LaTrease's room."

Nate grabbed my hand.

"Not you, Eightball. Let Digit do it."

Nate let me go, and a man came around from behind me.

He waggled his long, thick fingers at me. "Time for some fun."

Before he could turn me around, a woman's voice hollered, "Kevin Calvin, there's two white boys here!"

As much as I wanted to hope Beast and Tundra were here, every instinct told me that wasn't the case. Otherwise, she'd have said two bikers because neither Beast nor Tundra qualified as boys. For that matter, neither did Rafferty. No, the more I thought about it, the more my stomach felt like a dead weight had taken root inside me.

I expected Tobias and Brantley to come through the doorway.

Instead, it was Brantley and *Porter*.

KC's gaze hardened on Brantley, then cut to Porter. "Who the hell's this?"

"A friend of mine," Brantley said.

"That don't answer my question," KC said.

"I'm her ex-boyfriend and I can help you get the men helping her," Porter said.

KC stared at Porter for a very long moment. The way he shifted his stare to Brantley, he'd dismissed Porter outright. "My beef's with Ines. She had my product and I've heard she sold two kilos with *your* help. Now you got this boy with you. Wasting my fuckin' time."

Brantley shook his head. "Three Riot MC members came to my place last week. One had a name patch that read, Beast. He said he had the drugs and knew Suarez."

KC made a skeptical noise, not quite a tsk, but close. "Like Suarez knows any bikers. They lied."

Brantley opened his mouth to argue, but stayed silent.

KC turned to me. "Did you find the drugs?"

I shook my head. "No. Someone broke into my place - twice if you count Brantley picking the locks last Monday. He wanted to get Ines's ATM card for her crypto account. If anyone could get your money, it's him."

"The money was hidden in her bed," Porter blurted.

"How would you know that?" Nate asked.

"I ask the questions, Eightball," KC said.

Another man entered the room.

Next to me, I heard Digit whisper, "Suarez."

"I don't care *who* asks the questions, I want an answer," Suarez said, glaring at Porter.

The power dynamic in the room shifted when Suarez stood in front of KC's desk. As clear as it was that Suarez was the mastermind, it still felt like a pissing contest - a contest I hated being around.

Silence lingered for a moment.

"Answer me!" Suarez thundered at Porter.

He and Brantley stepped back a pace. Their faces were pale and their eyes wide with fear.

"Uh... I called in the tip," Porter stammered.

Suarez leaned forward. "Did you call in the tip or hide my fuckin' money, *pendejo*?"

"Both," Brantley said.

Porter shot an enraged look at Brantley.

"Why?" Suarez asked.

"To get the biker out of the way." He paused, and added, "I didn't know there were two more in town."

"Did you put him up to that?" KC asked Brantley.

"No. He came to me this morning about it. Wanted to know if I'd heard anything about the money being found. I decided to bring him to you."

Suarez made eye contact with the guy standing next to me, then he tipped his head at me and then Porter. "Take those two to a room. I want to talk to Brantley alone."

My body went rigid. "No," I almost yelled. I exhaled and lowered my voice. "He tried to attack me the last time I saw him. Please, don't put me in a room with him."

"You were my girlfriend."

"*Ex*-girlfriend."

"He tried to rape you?" Suarez asked, a trace of gentleness in his tone.

I dipped my chin.

"No, I didn't. We couldn't have sex in the car."

I inhaled and willed myself to keep calm. "You tried again when you shoved inside my apartment."

"Digit, take him to the garage," Suarez said.

Relief rolled over me like a gentle wave.

Suarez continued, "Eightball, go to LaTrease's room with her until I call you in."

Digit had wrapped a hand around Porter's bicep.

Porter glared at me. "Lying bitch."

Nate took me to a room with a twin bed and Bluey decorations.

"He has a kid?" I asked.

Nate stared at me for a moment. "LaTrease does," he whispered.

This room wasn't far from the one we'd just left. The murmur of voices rose.

"Tobias broke in, not me!" Brantley yelled.

"That doesn't sound good," I muttered.

"No," Nate whispered.

His phone vibrated with a notification. He glanced at the screen. "Shit. All right, I gotta get back in that room, but I have to tie your hands."

My eyes slid to the side even as I held my wrists together. "Can you not, and just say you did?"

"Hey, look at me."

I met his brown-eyed gaze.

"Not gonna tie them tight. You pull on the end, it'll come undone. Just try not to do that in front of anyone."

He told no lies, and wound a rope around my wrists, not too tight and did it in what I considered to be record time. Then he was gone.

I debated whether to sit on the bed, one of the kid-sized chairs, a beanbag, or just plant my ass on the floor. Part of me wanted to lay down on the bed, but I hated the idea of a little kid finding me in their bed. Like a messed-up version of Goldilocks.

The beanbag looked inviting, but would be a bitch to get out of in a hurry if someone stormed in here - or worse, if Porter found his way in here.

There was a small window near the bed. I moved the blinds to see what was outside. The window was covered by security bars. On closer inspection, even if I opened the window quietly, I wouldn't be able to get past the bars without someone hearing me.

I went to the door, and tried the knob. It was locked. With another look at the handle, I saw it had been turned around, and I'd been locked in from the outside.

Who did that to a kid?

I settled on the floor next to the beanbag. The house was quiet. Deceptively so.

My phone was in my backpack... in Nate's car.

I didn't know what time it was, but Rafferty expected me to be back by two.

My eyes closed and I exhaled. I hated that he was probably freaking out right now.

There was carpet on the floor, but it was threadbare. My butt began to ache in no time. I decided to shift over to the beanbag. Even if it was hard to get out of it, I figured it was better than being a sitting duck on the bed. As I sat there, willing my mind not to race, I somehow fell asleep.

Chapter Twenty-Two

Last Thing I Want to Do

Rafferty

"Where the fuck is she?" I hissed to myself.

This had to be what paranoia felt like. I hadn't taken a college class before, maybe the first session ran late.

Deep down, I knew that was bullshit.

I glanced at my phone again. It was three-thirty. I'd texted her forty-five minutes ago.

No response.

Even if she were running late, normally she'd respond.

Something was wrong. I grabbed my phone and hit Beast's number.

"Yo, Raff."

"Hey, Lex should have come home by now. It's been two hours since her class let out."

"Are you sure she didn't have somewhere else to be? A shift with that dentist she mentioned?"

I clenched a fist to stay calm. "She didn't mention it and she hasn't responded to my texts."

"I'm guessing you don't know where Porter lives."

My brows drew together. That was a possibility I hadn't considered. Didn't *want* to consider. "No. My gut says the Twenty-sixers have her."

"Raff…" Beast drawled, and lapsed into silence. Then he said, "That's a stretch."

"Is it? We got drugs, money, and a roommate who's dead."

"You can't assume it's them. Besides, how would they know where to find her? There's a shitload of buildings on that campus with classrooms and labs in almost every building."

That argument held merit, but it worked both ways. "How would Porter know where to find her?"

Beast's chuckle held no humor. "He knows where she lives. Could have followed her to campus and waited. Hell, you don't know she made it *to* class. Call the cops."

My stomach lurched at those words.

"That's the last thing I want to do."

"Hang on, I'm at the clubhouse and Cal just walked in. Let me tell him what's going down."

Scratchy sounds came over the line as though the phone had shifted hands.

"Let me call you back," Cal said. "Natasha mentioned sharing Alexandra's problems with her son Nate. He's supposedly working at the Alachua County Sheriff's Office."

"All right, but what is he going to be able to do for us?"

Cal made a strange humming sound. "I'm not sure, but it's a start."

While I waited for Cal to call me back, I went to Alexandra's bedroom. She had a spare set of keys to her car in one of her dresser drawers. I only knew about the keys because it had taken us so long to straighten her room after the police left on Friday.

Beast's suspicion of Porter nagged at me. Not knowing his address irritated me, too. The most fucked-up idea struck me, and I needed to see if she had a GPS system in her car. If she did, maybe she'd programmed

Porter's address into the system. It was one helluva long shot, but at this point, I'd do anything to figure out where she was.

I grabbed her keys and went downstairs. Her older-model Honda was parked near the stairwell. I hit the key fob and the lights flashed. A gust of heat wafted out when I opened the door, and I crammed my frame into the car. At a glance, there wasn't a GPS system and the car was old enough there wasn't a navigation screen on the console either.

"Dammit," I whispered.

No sooner had I unfolded from the car, than my phone rang. I hit the locks for the car and closed the door, putting the phone to my ear.

"Yeah, Cal."

"Natasha talked to Nate last Tuesday. He asked when her classes started again, and said he'd check in with Lex on Monday. Which is today."

I stopped short. "How was he planning to do that? Call her? I'm guessing he didn't have some way of locating her on campus."

Cal blew out a sigh. "That's the thing. I called Mallory, and Nate spoke to her on Friday afternoon, and asked her what Alexandra's schedule was for the summer."

I blinked and pulled in a deep breath. "Let me guess. She gave him her schedule and exactly where her classes were."

"Yeah."

"You don't sound as concerned as I am," I clipped out.

"Don't put words in my mouth. Nate wouldn't hurt her, but it doesn't make sense that she hasn't gotten in touch."

"Do you have any way of contacting him?" I asked, climbing the stairs to Alexandra's apartment.

A dark chuckle came over the line. "Asked Mallory to get me his number. I should have it very soon."

I'd only met Nate once when Alexandra and I were still on speaking terms. At the time he'd been on the verge of getting his criminal justice degree.

It struck me that if Alexandra was in danger, I didn't want to be on the right side of the law. I wanted her back, and I didn't care what I had to do to get her back.

"Is Beast still there? I'd like to talk to him, if he is."

Cal hesitated. "He's here, but what do you want to talk to him about?"

I went inside her apartment, closed the door, and locked it. "I wanted to ask him a question."

"About the Twenty-sixers?" Cal asked.

I sighed. "I'd like to know where they are, and I got the impression that Beast knew that... at least from things he said to Brantley and Tobias."

"I'll put him on, but you can't put that together on your own?" Cal asked.

I rolled my eyes. "They could be anywhere along State Road 26."

Cal chuckled. "Yeah, but that road has another name besides Twenty-six."

My grip on my patience slipped. "Cal, no disrespect, but I don't want to play your games right now. Not when Lex might be in danger."

"Yeah. Twenty-six is also University Boulevard in Gainesville. I'll put Beast on, but you *don't* go in there half-cocked. It could get you both killed."

I heard the sound of the phone switching hands again.

"Raff. It'd be better you waited for someone else to have your back," Beast said.

"Agreed, but she's almost two hours late. Hell, you pointed out she might not have even made it to class, so time is in short supply."

"Yeah, which is why I'm gonna tell you how to get to the Sixers, but tread lightly with them," Beast said.

I listened to his directions and nodded. "If I pass where the road forks, I've gone too far."

"Yeah, and it'll be a bitch to turn around because it's a two-lane road, but *don't* turn around at the work camp. You'll get the wrong kind of attention being on your bike, so don't miss it."

I had Alexandra's car keys in my pocket. "Thinking I'll take her car. It hasn't been driven in a while, and it'll be quieter."

"You got keys to her car?" Beast asked.

"I do."

"Go find Alexandra. If you get a bad vibe, do not hesitate to call the cops."

"Will do. Later."

———

I turned right a block before the street Beast mentioned. The surrounding area had four side streets off State Road 26, and I wanted to check for any cross roads connecting the neighborhood. Two avenues ran perpendicular to the side streets, and allowed me to approach the house without being noticed.

I parked her Honda Accord three houses down and walked toward the house. Voices carried from the driveway of the house. I hunched behind some bushes and saw two men push Brantley into the backseat of a black BMW sedan. All four windows were rolled down, and I could see Brantley was the only person in the back.

Shit.

I found it strange that he'd been shoved into a car. No, it wasn't strange, it forced me to realize something about Brantley. He was a follower, not a leader. Ines handled the drug money, not him. Porter planned to ride along to the concert, Brantley just let him hang at his apartment. Tobias hadn't said outright, but my guess was that Tobias did most of the sales or found people willing to buy.

The BMW peeled out of the drive and sped toward State Road 26. After a rolling stop, it took a left, heading back toward campus.

One man went back into the house while two others milled about in the drive.

My odds were better one-on-one, but I could probably handle two-on-one.

I crept out from behind the bushes, walked toward the house, and up the drive. One of the two men was shorter and wore an Atlanta Hawks t-shirt. The other was leaner and stood at six feet tall. He wore baggy pants, and a loose FAMU t-shirt.

The Hawks fan noticed me first. "Who the fuck are you?"

"I'm here to pick up Alexandra."

"We don't know who you're talking about," the man wearing the FAMU shirt said.

I locked eyes with him. It might have been five years since I'd seen him, but I knew it was Nate, and I knew not to give away that I'd recognized him.

"You heard him. Now, get out of here," the Hawks fan said.

"I'm just here to get my woman," I said.

Nate stared at me, completely dead-eyed.

The Hawks fan swaggered up to me. "Ain't any woman here, asshole."

I debated my next move.

The garage door went up, and another black man came out. He was stocky up top, but not through his legs. A shiny black doo-rag sat on his head with dreads sticking out. He glared at me, but I ignored it. My gaze slid past him into the garage. I saw Porter laying on the floor.

"Eightball, who's this?" the stocky man asked.

"Nobody. We told him to leave, KC," Nate said.

"Then why's he still here?" KC asked.

Movement behind KC caught my attention.

Nate's head twisted in that direction, too. "You didn't tie him up?"

KC turned, but it was too late. Porter had closed in on him.

Nate ran to them, but stopped half-way there. "Put that down. You don't know what you're doin' with that piece."

KC faced Porter fully, and I saw Porter holding a gun. The way KC reached to his back, Porter must have snagged it from KC's waistband.

My gun was at my hip. I reached for the butt and stopped.

"Don't move or I'll shoot," Porter yelled. He had the gun trained on me.

From the crazed gleam in his eyes, he was going to shoot no matter what I did.

"Drop the piece," Nate ordered.

"Not so tough now, are you, Rafferty?" Porter sneered.

"He's leaving. Put the gun down," Nate said.

"I'm not leaving without Alexandra," I said.

"She ain't here," Nate said.

Porter's attention shifted to Nate, though the gun was still aimed at me. "Where is she?"

"She left with Brantley," Nate said.

Earlier, I had a clear view of the inside of the Beamer. Lex wasn't there. Nate lied to Porter, and I could imagine why.

Porter glared at me for a beat, then a slow, maniacal smile spread on his face. "Good. She won't hear him yell in pain."

"Don't," Nate yelled.

The gun went off.

I intended to drop to the ground and roll away.

All I felt was my body violently jerking backward, then warmth mingled with pain blooming in my chest.

Chapter Twenty-Three

Taken Away

Alexandra

The door to the room opened and I woke with a start, despising that I fell asleep. With effort, I forced myself to sit up from the beanbag, but I'd been right earlier: getting out of the thing was a trick.

Suarez entered the room and shut the door. My instincts were on high alert, though some part of me believed I had nothing to fear from him.

Even with my hands tied, I managed to unfold from the beanbag and stand.

"I don't like men who rape women."

Very slowly, I raised my chin and lowered it, fighting against my reflexive response that most people didn't. Even if he wasn't going to hurt me, he probably didn't like smart-asses.

"Brantley has been taken away."

"Okay," I drawled. "Is that a euphemism?"

He stared at me in thought. "No. He's been driven away from here."

I turned my face a fraction of an inch. That statement oozed with feigned ignorance... And yet it would probably work during a police investigation.

"Why are you telling me that?" I asked.

"Do you want Porter taken away, too?"

"Like you care," I blurted, inadvertently. "Sorry. I don't mean any disrespect, that slipped."

His lips tipped up and humor lit his eyes. "You're funny. Did he hurt you?"

My lips pursed. "No. I was able to stop him both times."

"Both?" he asked, one eyebrow arched.

We both jolted at the sound of the garage door opening. Suarez looked genuinely surprised by the sound. I jerked because I'd never heard such a screechy garage door.

After a deep breath, I turned back to Suarez. His eyes weren't on me, they were aimed in the direction where the sound had originated.

He held up a finger. "Hold that thought."

I nodded, but he'd turned and left the room.

The door didn't quite catch, so I wasn't locked in any more.

A bang sounded, and I realized it was a gunshot. A second shot rang out, then a third.

I pulled at the rope Nate had put around my wrists. It came free, and I whipped the door open.

I heard men yelling outside, and the rumble of footsteps coming toward me. A small bathroom was next to the room. I closed the bedroom door behind me, and quickly ducked into the small bathroom.

Once the sound of people running through the house subsided, I left the bathroom and headed toward a sliding glass door. It led out to a concrete slab that served as a patio. My plan to sneak around the backside of the house changed when I heard the men shouting about calling 911.

"Eightball, put your gun down!" someone yelled.

I edged toward the garage.

"Put pressure on his chest," Nate shouted.

Peering around the corner of the house, I saw Digit standing close to Nate. There was someone on the ground between them.

"Why?" Digit asked.

"Because the cops are gonna assume we did this shit. Take your damned shirt off and put pressure on his chest," Nate yelled.

I leaned forward to try and see who had been shot. Movement caught my eye, and I saw Porter rocking back and forth, holding his leg.

KC stood near him with a gun aimed at him. I couldn't rush out from my hiding spot since I didn't trust KC not to shoot me.

My mind raced. If Brantley had been taken somewhere, and Porter was shot...who was on the ground?

Porter kept rocking almost as if he was trying to scoot away. KC moved to the other side of Porter. Now that KC had his back to me, I hurried toward Nate's car parked in the drive.

Multiple sirens wailed in the air.

Nate held his gun in one hand and his cell to his ear. He shifted as Suarez joined him, and I saw who lay on the ground.

The full beard, his well-trimmed brown hair, and the shock of colorful ink on his outstretched arm.

Rafferty.

No.

No!

A guttural sound burst from my lips, and I charged forward, yelling. No, screaming, but I didn't sound anything like myself.

In the same moment, a police cruiser swung into the drive at an angle, lights flashing.

I felt stinging pain in my knees after I hit the ground at his side. My vision blurred with tears as I put my hands on top of Digit's. His hands felt warm, abnormally so. Then I noticed the stickiness from the blood.

"Don't you go anywhere, Tee. I'm not gonna lose you. No way," I said.

A man crouched down next to Digit. When Digit tried to move, I held tight to his fingers.

Another man squatted next to me. He spoke in a low, firm voice. "Let go. We're going to get him to the hospital."

In some corner of my mind, I realized he was a firefighter/EMT. More tears rushed down my cheeks and I stood.

Someone pulled me back.

I resisted, then lips came to my ear. "It's me. I'll get you to him," Nate whispered.

His words calmed me by the most minuscule degree. That degree made a world of difference, though. It brought me back from the brink of my darkest thoughts.

Looking around, I saw two more EMTs were tending to Porter. Half a dozen police officers were on the scene, and had Suarez, Digit, and two other men I hadn't met in handcuffs.

Before Nate could take his arm from around my shoulders, I turned an insistent look at him. "Can I go with him? Please."

Nate blinked for a second. "I wish I could say yes, but I had to shoot Porter. Now that dumbass has to go to the hospital, and they're gonna take them both in the same ambulance." He shifted me so I faced him. "I will get you to the hospital. I promise."

***

The last forty-five minutes, I had sat in the ER waiting room, feeling forlorn, angry, and useless.

Nate had told me to grab my backpack from his car, then he had a patrol officer drop me off at the hospital. On the ride over, I'd called Blood to let him know what happened. I wanted to call Trixie, but I didn't trust myself to keep it together while talking to her. And, I figured Blood would call Roll, who could handle Trixie far better.

My triple threat of feelings were a result of not being Rafferty's next of kin. I hadn't played my cards very well when I asked about his condition. If I'd been smarter, I'd have claimed to be his sister, cousin, anyone who was family. But I hadn't been thinking straight, and I blurted out the truth. We were dating.

The nurse behind the desk suddenly went all stringent and strict. Now she wouldn't tell me anything about Rafferty's condition.

I hung my head and said a silent prayer.

He had to be okay.

He had to *be*.

I couldn't begin to fathom a world without him in it.

I stared out the window at the gathering dark clouds. It had to be almost five-thirty, which was when the summer thunderstorms rolled in this time of year.

"Alexandra!" Jasmine nearly yelled.

I turned and saw Rafferty's sister rushing to me. By the time she reached me, I stood and hugged her. Over her shoulder, I saw Trixie and Roll go to the nurse's desk.

"Oh my God, do you know anything?" Jasmine asked.

I shook my head and fought off tears. "No. They won't tell me. I'm not…"

"You're not what?"

"Family."

Anger filled Jasmine's expression and she turned her gaze to the desk.

"How did you get here so fast?" I asked.

Her brows furrowed. "It's nearly six-thirty, Lex. It took us two hours to get here."

I turned my phone over in my hand, and saw she was right.

"Come on, Mom's waving us over," Jasmine said.

The moment I drew even with Trixie, she pointed at me, but her eyes were on the nurse. "You see her? She's my son's woman. If she needs to know something about him, you tell her."

"It doesn't work like that—"

Trixie leaned forward. "She's family. They're gettin' married. Is there any update on when he's gettin' out of surgery?"

The comment about us getting married took me aback. Then Rafferty's voice played in my mind. *'This accident opened my eyes.'*

Him getting shot didn't just open my eyes, it flung the doors open on my heart and mind like a horse breaking free from a barn.

"There should be an update any minute now. I'll keep you posted," the nurse said.

We trudged back to the bank of chairs where I'd been sitting.

Before I could sit down, Roll slung his arm along my shoulders. "Take a walk with me."

"Oh, no. Whatever you're gonna talk about I want to hear it," Trixie said.

"No," Roll said in an extremely firm tone.

I glanced up at him. "It's okay—"

He shook his head, his shoulder-length hair swaying. "His mother doesn't need to hear this."

I shrugged. "There isn't much to hear since I don't know exactly what happened. I was in a room that was locked from the outside."

"Excuse me," Trixie said.

Roll's lips pressed into a thin line before he blew out a defeated sigh. "That's what I didn't want them to hear."

I quickly ran down the afternoon, and what I knew.

"Nate knows what happened, but he wasn't able to leave the scene. My guess is that Porter shot Rafferty. Nate said he had to shoot Porter."

'Did Porter make it?" Trixie asked.

I shrugged. "Nate shot him in the leg. I think he's okay, but I don't give a damn about him."

Jasmine patted the chair between her and Trixie. "Sit down."

I settled in the seat. Jasmine rested her head on my shoulder and grabbed my hand.

Within half an hour, Beast, Tundra, Mom, Dad, Volt, and Aunt Jackie had arrived. Even though their presence should have given me comfort, I forced myself to ignore the many people who were there. It only reminded me that one gunshot wound to the chest posed a tough challenge to overcome. Two gunshot wounds made that challenge almost insurmountable.

I couldn't think that way. It didn't serve any purpose.

I stared out a nearby window.

Warm hands hit my knees and I faced forward.

Razor squatted in front of me. "I told him not to hurt you, you know."

I shot him a stern look. "*He* didn't do this to me. Someone else - very likely Porter - shot him, so really Porter's the one who hurt me."

Razor gave my knees a squeeze. "Yeah. You're right. And logical, like your mom."

I swallowed hard and gave a short head-shake.

He returned my stern look. "Don't deny it. You're just as strong and resilient as your mom. You keep the faith. I'm telling you, he's gonna be all right. What's happening with this punk named Porter?"

"He got shot in the leg, and they brought him here, too."

A twinkle hit Razor's eyes. "If you want me to take care of him, say the word, sweetie."

I almost smiled, but Razor reminded me of how Rafferty insisted that I was ruthless. Looking back, spending time with Razor, Tennille, and Sally Mae, Razor's daughter from his first marriage - that influenced me to be ruthless, too.

"Where's Tennille?" I asked.

He stood. "Working. She's sending you both positive energy. My offer stands. Don't forget it."

I watched him walk away, and taking in the whole waiting room, I saw the number of people here for Rafferty had doubled. Blood, Abby, Vamp, Rainey, Gabriella, Yak, Nora, Punc, and Liar were milling about on the far edge of the room.

"Rolland," a doctor in green scrubs called out from the mouth of the hallway.

"That's us," Roll said, moving toward the doctor.

Trixie grabbed my hand, stood, which forced me to stand, and took me with her across the room.

"We've removed the bullet from his lung. It didn't fragment when it entered his body," the doctor said.

I squeezed Trixie's hand, and inhaled deep.

"He's very lucky that the bullet missed his ribs and any major arteries. It will take time for his lung to heal. His condition is serious, but stable. He will be closely monitored over the next twenty-four to forty-eight hours," the doctor continued.

"But he'll live?" Roll asked.

The doctor's head swiveled in an almost-circular nod. "Barring any complications or infections, he should recover."

"Wait. Wasn't there a second bullet?" I asked.

"Based on the flesh wound along the lateral side of his torso, the second bullet grazed him. We've stitched up the resulting wound. He was also given a blood transfusion because of the blood loss."

When I inhaled, my breath hitched with a slight sob. Trixie squeezed my hand and bumped her shoulder into mine.

"When can we see him?" Trixie asked.

"He's in recovery. We're moving him to ICU due to his serious condition. I'll send a nurse out when you can see him. One at a time."

I turned around. All of the Riot MC brothers were huddled close by. Beyond them, I saw the sliding glass doors open, and Nate strode over to us.

I skirted around the group to him. "Are you okay? Did...the others figure out who you are?"

Nate grabbed my hands. "I'm fine. They know who I am now because they committed enough crimes right in front of me that I could arrest them. How's Rafferty?"

"In recovery. Then he'll be in ICU."

"I'm glad to hear it."

I tilted my head. "Did you come here just to check on me?"

"Not exactly, though Mom would never let me hear the end of it if I didn't come see you."

"Thanks. Out of curiosity, did Porter shoot Rafferty twice?"

Nate's lips stretched out in a grimace. "Yeah. I'm pissed that he got the jump on KC. That shit's fucked up, and I should have double checked that Porter had really been knocked out. That could have turned into a far worse situation."

I nodded. "Where's Suarez?"

"In custody."

"I kind of feel bad."

"Why? He didn't care about you."

"That wasn't the impression I got from him. He seemed to care that Porter had hurt me."

Nate did a slow nod. "Yeah, but he'd have thrown you to the wolves just like KC wanted to do."

"Sorry if I blew your cover."

He gave me a slight grin. "You didn't. Put it out of your head. I have to go talk to the ER staff, make sure they know Porter's being taken into custody." He took two steps and turned around. "You need to give a statement about what happened. Call me, and I'll let the detective know you're coming."

Dad wandered up to me. "What did the doctor say, sweetheart?"

"They're moving him to ICU, but they got the bullet out, and no broken ribs or nicked arteries."

He pulled me into a hug. "That sounds promising."

I tipped my head back. "Trixie told the nurse, he and I are getting married."

His lips quirked and his eyes twinkled. "She'll say whatever it takes to get her way. That goes triple when it's one of her kids in trouble."

I lowered my chin and hugged Dad. "Yeah."

Trixie sidled up to us. "The nurse told Roll he could go back to visit him. I'm goin' when he's done, then you can be with him."

I nodded. "Thank you."

She went down the corridor.

Dad let me go. "You should head that way so you don't waste any time."

———

Woodenly, I dropped into the chair next to Rafferty's bed. The dim lighting of his room couldn't hide the pallor of his skin. The contrast of his skin against the bright colors of his tattoos only made it worse.

I wrapped my fingers around his hand. "You better fight, Tee."

The heart monitor beeped rhythmically.

"Your mom told the nurse we're getting married. I'd ask if you can believe that - but I'm pretty sure you can. She's crazy that way. You know I'm nothing like that."

The monitor beeped a little faster.

"Yeah, you are," he rasped.

My eyes widened and I looked around foolishly -for someone to tell, a pitcher of water - but there was nobody and nothing I could give him.

"Shit! Are you supposed to be awake?"

The smallest smile curled his lips. He'd never looked more handsome. "Dunno. But you're just like Mom - in your own way."

I wheezed out a laugh and shoved his words out of my mind. "I love you. Let me get a nurse."

His hand beneath mine twisted up and gave a weak squeeze. "No. I love you, too. I'm tired."

I held onto his hand and watched him close his eyes.

A nurse approached, I waved her into his room, and told her he'd been awake.

She nodded. "That's great news. Your time is almost up. It would be good to let him rest."

I didn't leave immediately. For some reason, I was determined to take all of the time they'd give me with him. I leaned over, cupped his cheeks, and kissed his forehead.

In the waiting room, Jasmine stood near the doors to the ICU with her arms wrapped around her waist.

I hurried to her and gave her a hug. "Your turn. He was awake while I was in there and he fell back asleep."

With a teary-eyed smile, she nodded and went to see her brother.

Roll lumbered toward me. "You goin' home now?"

I frowned, realizing I didn't have any way to get home. "I don't know. I'm not ready to leave."

He put a hand on my shoulder. "You do him no good if you're spent from lack of sleep."

"I know, but—"

"No buts. They gave me his bag of personal items. I got your car keys."

"Why did he have my car keys?" I interrupted.

Something stirred in Roll's eyes. It might have been admiration or regret. "He didn't want to draw attention going into that neighborhood on his bike. He told Beast and Cal he was gonna drive your car instead. I gave your keys to Cal, and he went to get your car. I'm taking you home so you can get back here fresh in the morning."

"All right, but where are you staying? There's an empty bedroom at my place and Jazz can stay—"

Roll dropped his hand from my shoulder. "We got a hotel room already. He's gonna be here for a while. Jasmine comes back out, we'll go."

Chapter Twenty-Four

Trixie's Idea

Rafferty

"I think that's all I need," Detective Jones said. He stood and glanced out the open door to my hospital room.

"Will I need to come back to testify?" I asked.

The detective looked down at me and shook his head. "Not likely. Mr. Ogden provided enough information that you shouldn't be needed in court. Take care of yourself, Mr. Rolland."

Alexandra must have been milling about in the hallway because she immediately came into the room as Detective Jones left.

She sat down in the chair next to my bed and grabbed my hand. "Who's Mr. Ogden?"

"Brantley."

"Oh, that's right."

"Did you hear the whole conversation?" I asked.

She shook her head. "No. My ears perked up when you asked if you'd have to testify."

I dipped my chin. "I'm guessing you gave a statement last week while I was in ICU."

She nodded. "I did. The club's lawyer went with me. I can't believe they killed Tobias."

I shook my head. "You don't mean that. He and Brantley took their product. Drug dealers don't let that shit slide. I'm just surprised Brantley didn't get killed, too."

She leaned closer. "Nate talked to me. He was able to notify another undercover officer about Brantley being taken from the house and they intercepted at the apartment complex where Tobias lived. It's also how they found out Tobias was dead. Otherwise, who knows when his body would have been found."

I'd been in and out of it on pain meds for the last few days. The detective took my statement about the shooting, but he didn't share any information about Porter. As much as I hated to bring him up to Alexandra, I hated not knowing what was going on with him.

"Do you know if Porter had his arraignment?" I asked

A humorless, closed-lip smile twisted her lips. "Yeah. The judge denied him bail because he's a flight risk, seeing as his family came down from Missouri to post it."

"Really?"

She nodded. "I don't care what this says about me, but it makes me feel better knowing he isn't roaming around Gainesville."

Clouds outside my room shifted and the sun brightened the room.

I squeezed Alexandra's hand. "Don't you have class today?"

She grinned. "It's Tuesday, so no classes today. Only Mondays and Wednesdays."

"Slacker," I muttered.

"Whatever. Aren't they going to discharge you today?"

I looked toward the door. "I sure as hell hope so. It's too fuckin' noisy around here and the food sucks."

She shot me a half-hearted glare. "I bring you food every time I visit and so does your mom and sister."

I widened my eyes. "Yeah, because the food here sucks."

A metal bang came from the doorway right before a nurse pushed a wheelchair into the room. "Mr. Rolland, if you're dressed, I've got your discharge papers and can wheel you down to the parking lot."

Alexandra's eyes lit up and she beamed at me. "Excellent! I don't know about you, but after this, I don't want to see another hospital for a long, long time."

———

Two weeks later, on a Thursday afternoon, Alexandra stood in my drive-way with her arms crossed under her tits.

She glared at me like she could singe my soul. "You aren't cleared for this kind of activity, Rafferty."

I twirled my keys on my index finger, then mirrored her pose. "Woman, I didn't check the discharge papers, but I'm pretty sure I'm good to do this. Regardless, I don't give a damn about medical clearance. We're goin' to the clubhouse, and I'll be damned if we don't get there on my Triumph."

Her arms unfolded, she put her hands on her hips and stepped into my space. "Almost four weeks ago, you were shot and I held someone else's hands to your chest to keep you from dying. For almost three hours, the idea that you could die was a *very* real possibility and I'll never forget that feeling. I'll be damned if we get on that bike since it might put us *both* in danger."

I exhaled and wrapped my arms around her, pulling her to me tight. Even though I was the one who got shot, it had taken a heavy toll on her, too. A toll she never let anyone see, not even me.

That was my woman, though. Stubborn, strong, and opinionated.

"I'm sorry, Lex."

She gazed up at me, her eyes shiny. "It's not your fault, but we can take your truck...or even better, my car."

I rested my forehead on hers. "Baby, I'm strong. I'm off the heavy-duty pain meds because I'm not in pain. That bike is an extension of me, you know that. And I'd never - not ever - put you in danger. We'll be fine."

She glowered up at me, and hell if it wasn't cute. "You're not going to listen to me, are you?"

"I heard you, baby. You're worrying for nothing. It's five-point-five miles from here, door-to-door."

Her eyes widened. "Yeah, most of it on Blanding Boulevard, are you nuts?"

I laughed...and for once it didn't hurt. There hadn't been too damned much to laugh at in the hospital.

She pulled her head back. "This isn't funny."

I smiled. "It is funny, but we can take Roosevelt instead."

Her mouth dropped open, then closed. "That might actually be worse, it's three lanes of crazy bob-and-weaving drivers speeding down the road." She narrowed her eyes. "And you'd have to take that short stretch of Interstate to get over to Blanding... You just want to ride fast. I'm onto you, Raff."

"Honey, I just want to ride. Period. Are you gonna get on my bike with me, or what?"

I loved watching her war with herself. The moment her expression softened, I knew she'd come around.

"Fine."

That made me laugh again because Dad, Cal, and nearly all the brothers had told me, when a woman said 'Fine,' things were rarely anything but fine. I loved Alexandra so much, I'd enjoy every second of convincing her things weren't just fine, but fuckin' great.

Twenty minutes later, I parked my Triumph at the far end of a long line of bikes. I noticed Cynic and Gamble's bikes in the middle of the row, which meant the Biloxi brothers were here.

"Is there a party tonight?" Alexandra asked.

I slung my arm along her shoulders. "Not sure."

We entered through the back door and strolled past the kitchen. Abby and Fiona were at the counter chopping vegetables. Blood and Cynic were at the small two-seater table cutting four whole chickens into pieces.

Abby glanced at us and locked eyes with Alexandra. "Tell me you drove."

Alexandra tipped her head toward Blood. "Would *he* let you drive when he's convinced he's good to ride his bike?"

Abby gave her a wry look. "Honey, he doesn't *let* me do anything. I thought we taught you better."

Blood winked at us. "That's not true, Abs. I just *let* you think that."

Cynic glanced at us over his shoulder. "Glad you're here, Raff."

His words took me aback, and an unexpected surge of emotion clogged my throat. I swallowed it down. "Thanks, man."

He nodded. "Go grab yourself a beer, and bring one back for me and Blood."

Fiona arched a brow at Cynic. "Are you sharing one beer with Blood? You two are so close now."

"Smart-ass, stop being a wordsmith," Cynic muttered.

We wandered into the common room and went to the bar.

"It's about fuckin' time you showed up," Beast said from behind the bar.

He was pulling a draft beer. Roman stood a foot away from Beast, holding a cocktail shaker in the air. Tundra and Cal were uncorking bottles of wine at the other end of the bar. It surprised me there weren't any prospects around because all of this was shit we normally handled.

"Listen, Cynic and Blood want a beer. I'll take those to them and get back behind the bar so you four can—"

Tundra shook his head. "Open your eyes, Raff. We're having church in ten minutes."

"Okay," I drawled.

Beast put a pint glass full of dark beer on the bar. "Don't tell him, asshole. Volt's not even here, yet, is he?"

Cal chuckled. "He got here half an hour ago. Bobby's with him around the side, setting up for tonight."

Tundra's eyes slid to the other end of the bar in a pointed way.

"Oh," Alexandra said.

I followed his gaze and saw two brown paper wrapped packages.

I nodded. "Cool. Killian and Ryan deserve their patches, man."

Beast's expression went flat. "You're shitting me, right?" He glanced at Tundra. "Do you think he might be trying to... *Bluff*?"

The way he emphasized the word bluff made my stomach sink, but in a good way.

Alexandra nudged my bicep with her shoulder. I looked at her and seeing that huge smile felt like a gut punch. "This is great, Raff! You're getting your patch. No wonder they're getting ready for a party."

Roman put the cocktail shaker down, and leaned an elbow on the bar. "Nobody said *he* was getting patched in tonight, *cher*."

Alexandra gave him a 'Don't bullshit me' look and Roman chuckled.

The front door opened and an ear-splitting whistle filled the air. I turned and saw Volt and Bobby had come inside. The common room quickly filled with the rest of the brothers and other members from the Biloxi chapter.

Once he had everyone's attention, Volt said, "I don't think we need to be so formal with this one. We voted Monday. It was unanimous, and yesterday I got word from the mother chapter. There's one less prospect in the Jacksonville chapter because he earned his patch."

He nodded and Beast opened one of the packages then unfolded a new leather cut, holding it in the air.

The name patch read 'Bluff.'

The emotion I felt earlier from Cynic's words was nothing compared to the onslaught I felt now. I willed myself not to cry as Alexandra slipped my prospect cut off, and I took the leather from Beast.

I shrugged on my official cut and lost count of the back slaps I received as brothers crowded around to congratulate me.

Once they cleared away, Beast shot a devious smile my way. "Do you know what the best part about your road name is?"

"The fact you came up with it?" I guessed.

He chuckled. "No, that was Tundra."

"Yeah! You were there, I'd think you'd remember that, numbnuts," Tundra said.

I rolled my eyes. "Fine. What's the best part?"

Beast wheezed out a chuckle. "You won't be able to bluff anybody again. Everyone's gonna know you're a bullshitter."

I shrugged a shoulder. "Could refer to a type of landscape."

Beast's eyes went dramatically wide. "Right…'cause you're a geography buff. Pedal that shit somewhere else. Bluff!"

Dad lumbered up to me, and I wondered how he wasn't one of the first people to congratulate me.

"Wanted to wait, son," he said, reading my face. "Really fuckin' proud of you. It's an honor to call you my son *and* my brother."

My throat clogged again.

He wrapped an arm around my shoulders and slapped my back harder than anyone else had. "Love you."

"Love you too, Dad."

He backed away.

I spied the other package on the bar. "Who else is getting their patch tonight?"

A strange look stole over Dad's face and he sighed. "I want Cal to tell you about that." Before I could respond, he tipped his head back and bellowed, "Callous!"

"I'm standing right here, Dad," I muttered.

He smirked at me. "It's hard to get anyone's attention on a night like this."

Cal sauntered our way with a gleam in his eye I'd never seen before. It was part resignation, part knowing, and part… disgust, if I wasn't mistaken.

Suddenly, my hands went clammy and I felt nervous around Cal for the first time.

He glanced at Dad. "You tell him?"

Dad shook his head. "No, I want you to do it."

Cal gave Dad some side-eye and ran his hand over his mouth. "This is not the way things are normally done... Bluff."

Dad nodded once. "It was your mother's idea."

"And Abby's," Cal muttered.

Dad glanced past me for a moment as he weighed his words. "Your mother can be...resourceful."

Cal barked out a laugh. "You ever tell Trixie that to her face?"

A devious smile crossed Dad's face. "Yeah, when she's sucking my cock."

"I'm standing right *here*, Dad," I said.

He smiled at me. "Yeah, but you're one of the brothers, so get used to it."

Shit. This had also been an upside to joining the Memphis chapter...far less likely to overhear Dad share about his sex life.

Cal chuckled. "He's right, Bluff. This isn't how we normally do things."

"What do you mean?" I asked.

Cal put his hand on the package. "Each brother decides when he's ready to put his patch on his woman."

My heartbeat picked up and I forced myself to concentrate on his words.

"Your mom told people at the hospital that you and Alexandra were getting married. She ranted last week about how whenever you earned your patch, they should save time and money by just ordering your woman's cut at the same time."

"Nobody approved that, because it's supposed to be your call," Dad said.

Cal nodded once. "When Abby put in the order for your cut, she recalled Trixie's rant, and ordered one for your woman."

I felt Dad's gaze on me and turned my eyes to him as he said, "I still say we return it. If I were in Cal's shoes, and this were for Jasmine, I'd have raised holy hell."

Cal shook his head and leveled a serious look at me. "No. There isn't a better man for Alexandra than you, Bluff. This might have been Trixie's idea, but she's right. You have my blessing." He paused and held up a finger. "But I don't want to be here when you put this on her."

I gave him a chin-lift. "Is that why Aunt Mallory isn't here?"

"No. It's quarter-end, she's working late." He clapped my shoulder. "Have a great night, brother. I'll catch you later."

EPILOGUE

GIZMO

Alexandra

Two years later...

"ALEXANDRA ROBERTSON-ROLLAND," A DEEP voice announced.

I strode across the stage, my black gown billowing with every step, and beaming with a huge smile on my face. Most of my concentration focused on not tripping, I reached out and shook hands with the university president, a man I'd never seen before and likely wouldn't ever see again.

It was all one big blur, except the high-pitched whistles that came from the back left corner of the arena. Rafferty, Mom, Dad, Trixie, and Roll were here, and the five of them were loud with their excitement.

Following all the pictures and fanfare outside the arena, we went to Mom and Dad's house for a graduation party. I'd expected something small, but this party threatened to be a party for all time. It rivaled our wedding reception last summer, there were so many people at Mom and Dad's.

All of the Riot MC was there, and a few of the brothers from Biloxi. Mom's parents were sitting on the patio with Natasha and her husband. Across the yard, I spied Nate and Derek talking to Rafferty and Jasmine.

Barrel grills had been brought in to cook a variety of meat. There were tables dotted around the back yard, all loaded with food. Someone had draped a huge banner on the back of the house that read, "Congratulations Alexandra!"

"He won't listen to me, but your dad ought to switch professions. Takes a lot of planning to pull off a shindig this big, and he sure as shit didn't give me much notice on the amount of meat he wanted to serve," muttered Tiny, a brother from Biloxi who ran his own, wildly successful, butcher shop.

I smiled up at him. "I'm sure Mom and a few other people had a hand in this."

Tiny leaned toward me. "*He* would tell you that, but it's a cover. Congratulations on your degree, sweetheart." His cheek bulged as he moved his tongue around in his mouth. "Can you take a look at my back molar, I think something's wrong."

I smacked his forearm playfully. "You're lying. Uncle Vamp put you up to that, didn't he?"

He chuckled. "I'll never tell, but you should consider doing work for the club. The dancers at Platinum's need nice pearly whites to keep the money flowing, am I right?"

My response fled me when I heard the wayward sound of... a puppy barking?

I widened my eyes at Tiny. "Was that a puppy?"

He grinned. "I don't know. Go ask your man, he helped with this party, too. I'm serious, those two should start a company."

I looked toward the area where Rafferty had been talking to Derek and Nate. He wasn't there any longer.

"You lookin' for me?" Rafferty asked from behind me.

I turned around, and froze.

My man was sexy as all hell, but standing in front of me holding a brown and white Shih Tzu puppy...

Damn.

"Jesus, Lex. I don't know if that look is for me, the dog, or both."

"If you have to wonder, you need to go back to school. Who's puppy is this?" I asked, petting the puppy's soft fur.

"Yours. He's your graduation gift from me."

My eyes went wide. "You got me a puppy!"

"Yeah. I know how much you loved Zippy when you were growing up. Pretty sure we can handle this guy."

"He doesn't have a name?"

Rafferty handed the pooch over to me. "No. Mom told me to name him, but I think you deserve that honor. Besides, I couldn't decide between Colgate and Bicuspid."

I made a face at the wriggly puppy. "We are *not* naming you after toothpaste or teeth."

Rafferty chuckled. "It's better than Scaler because he was definitely trying to scale the baby gate back at the house."

This dog was a lot like me, he was drawn to Rafferty if the way he stretched and craned himself back toward my man was any indicator.

"I can imagine. He's very strong and determined to get back to you."

Rafferty took him from me, gave him a quick nuzzle and set him on the grass. The pup ran a few feet away and came back to us, doing that see-saw style run like puppies do.

"I think Scaler might be the right name for him."

"Nah," Rafferty said, picking up the puppy. "You know he was born in late April, just like us. He'll probably be just as stubborn."

"It's not like we can name him Bull or Taurus."

Rafferty shrugged. "We could, but I don't like those names either. Dad said he looks like a Gremlin, but I never saw that movie."

"He's right. We should name him Gizmo."

Rafferty stared down at the puppy. "For right now, that works. I reserve the right to change it if something better hits us later."

Across the yard, I heard Aunt Trixie calling out Dad's name. "Did you hear Cal? We're gonna be grandparents!"

I wheezed with laughter, then pointed at Rafferty. "That's not something your mom gets to 'make happen' like she did with you putting a cut on me."

"No shit, wife. We're a team and I'm with you on that. No kids until we're both ready."

Mom approached us and reached out for the puppy. "I love this little furball. He's such a good boy! We left him here all afternoon, and he used his potty training pad. It's like he's almost house-trained."

"That isn't true. I cleaned up his mess before you saw it, sweet cheeks," Dad grumbled, sidling up to mom.

Trixie and Roll joined us.

She opened her arms and gave me a long hug. "We're all so proud of you, girlie."

"Thanks, Trixie," I said.

"When do you start your job?" she asked.

I grinned. "To be fair, I've been working with a pediatric dentist the last three months, but now that I've got my degree and passed my boards, I'm going to be at their Orange Park office in two weeks."

She grabbed my hands. "I can't tell you how excited I am for you."

I leaned toward her, grinned, and whispered, "I think you just did."

She laughed. "All right. You gotta go mingle. You're the guest of honor. Now hand over my grand-pup, Mallory."

Rafferty wrapped his arm around my waist and led me toward the patio. "Think you should see your grandparents first, babe. Not sure they're gonna stay out here all night with the rest of us."

I leaned my cheek against his shoulder. "You're right."

Rafferty and I chatted with Mom's parents and Natasha and Leon. One of the brothers called Rafferty away and my grandparents went upstairs.

Natasha put her glass of wine on the small patio table, and aimed a look at me. "I never did hear this part, but why is that boy called 'Bluff.' He seems like such a straight shooter, is this another one of those tongue-in-cheek names?"

A wave of nostalgia came over me and I smiled. "When all my problems were going on, to figure out who was behind everything, Rafferty bluffed with Brantley and Porter. Tundra thought it would be a decent road name for him, and since they patched him in rather soon after his hospital stay, I guess that name stuck."

Natasha nodded. "All right, good. Your daddy's talking about a poker game in an hour, and I gotta know what I'm working with."

"Tasha, you don't play cards and tonight isn't the time to start," Leon said.

Natasha winked at me and turned to her husband. "Maybe I'm playin' so I can make sure this girl gets a leg up on the chip count."

Leon closed his eyes and shook his head. "All right, baby. You want another drink?"

"Sure, but bring our girl back something too, please."

"If we're not careful, your mom is gonna take Gizmo away from us," Rafferty said, pulling off his motorcycle boots.

"Seeing as we've known each other our whole lives, you'd think I'd remember this, but have you ever had a puppy?" I asked, toeing off my sneakers.

He yanked his shirt over his head. I never got tired of admiring his many tattoos - especially the Riot patch on his back. He unbuttoned his jeans. "No, we adopted adult dogs from the Humane Society. Mom told me when I was older that Dad had no patience for the puppy phase. That's why I asked *your* parents to keep the puppy during the graduation ceremony."

I stalked to him and traced a finger over the capital letter a on his chest. "Are you working tomorrow?"

With two fingers to my chin, he tipped my face up toward his. "That's the beauty of being a business owner. I set the schedule, baby. I'm not scheduled to be anywhere for eight days."

My head reared back. "That's over a week."

He grinned. "Yeah, partly because I'm between reno jobs, but mainly because I'm taking you on a vacation."

Not long after Rafferty earned his patch, he'd approached the club about investing in his business. He put together a full business plan that he'd have taken to a bank on the off-chance the brothers shot him down, and offered the club a percentage of his profit. After a few rounds of tweaks, they struck an agreement, and Rafferty had been running R & R General Contracting for the past year and a half.

"You're taking me on a vacation?"

"Yep. We're gettin' on my bike, and we're riding to Key West."

"Awesome," I breathed.

"Damn right. Me, you, and all your skimpy bikinis. I can't fuckin' wait."

I brushed his lips with mine. "That sounds like heaven."

"As long as we're together, Lex, everyday will be just like heaven."

If you want more of Rafferty and Alexandra, use your cell phone to scan the QR code to sign up for the Karen Renee newsletter and get their bonus epilogue!

The series will continue with *Break Inside,* Ryan and Ivy's story, coming in April 2026.

ACKNOWLEDGEMENTS

All my gratitude to you, the reader. As always, if it weren't for you, I wouldn't be able to do what I do, so thank you so much for spending your time reading my work! I appreciate it more than you'll ever know...though hopefully this helps!

Thank you to Barbara J. Bailey for editing my work, and reigning in my abundant use of the ellipse. It's my favorite, and I'll try to tone it down next time.

Thanks to Abigail Sharpe and Alyssa Day for the first page critique last year.

Thank you to Golden Czermak and Alex Michael Turner for yet another great image.

Thanks to Bee at Bitter Sage for the fantastic cover.

Special thanks to my reader group. It's getting more and more difficult for things to be seen in real time, but I appreciate the feedback I get from you when the algorithm finally shows you my posts!

Thank you to Enticing Journey and the many bloggers and influencers who help make every launch a success.

Last, but never least, thank you to my family and friends for all of your support. It means the world to me.

Beta Test

The O-Town Series
Relentless Habit
Wild Forces
Abrupt Changes
Holiday Fixation (An O-Town short story) – found in Romancing the
Holidays, Vol. Two
O-Town Series Complete Box Set

Riot MC Biloxi Chapter Series
Harm's Way
Brute's Strength
Roman's War
Cynic's Stance
Gamble's Risk
Block's Road
Tiny Problem
Finn's Fury
Mensa's Match

The Riot MC Next Generation
Break Out
Break Away
Break Inside

About Karen Renee

KAREN RENEE IS THE award-winning author of the Riot MC, Riot MC Biloxi, Beta, and O-Town series of books. She once crunched Nielsen ratings data but these days she brings her imagination to life by writing books. She has wanted to be a writer since she was very young, but it's taken the time for her to amass enough courage and overall life experience to bring that dream to life. Some of those life experiences came from the wonderful world of advertising, banking, and local television media research. She is a proud wife and mother, and a Jacksonville native. When she's not out and about with her family, you can find her at her local library, the grocery store, in her car jamming out to some tunes, or hibernating while she writes and/or reads books.

www.ingramcontent.com/pod-product-compliance
Lightning Source LLC
Chambersburg PA
CBHW060658190726
48289CB00002B/469